# SAND
# QUEEN

## HELEN BENEDICT

To my children and the children of Iraq,
may you live to see peace.

And for my father, Burton Benedict, 1923-2010.

Published by
Soho Press, Inc.
853 Broadway
New York, NY 10003

Library of Congress Cataloging-in-Publication Data

Benedict, Helen.
Sand queen / Helen Benedict.
p. cm.
HC ISBN 978-1-56947-966-7
PB 978-1-61695-184-9
eISBN 978-1-56947-967-4
1. Women soldiers—Fiction. 2. Americans—Iraq—Fiction.
3. Iraq War, 2003—Fiction. I. Title.
PS3552.E5397S26 2011
813'.54—dc22
2011013334

Printed in the United States of America

10  9  8  7  6  5  4  3  2  1

*For sweetest things turn sourest by their deeds;*
*Lilies that fester smell far worse than weeds.*

—SHAKESPEARE, SONNET 94

[ PART ONE ]

# CHECKPOINT

Perhaps if she curls up very small, she won't hurt anyone ever again.

[ KATE ]

IT'S THE BIGGEST frigging spider I've ever seen in my
life. From one hairy leg to the other, the whole thing's as long
as my forearm. So I make sure it's dead first. Nudge it with
the butt of my rifle till it flips over, limp and sandy. Then I
pick it up by a leg, haul it into the tent like a shopping bag
and nail it to the pole beside the head of my cot, right under
my crucifix. That should keep Macktruck quiet, at least for
the time being. He's terrified of spiders. Asshole.

The whistling is loud outside the tent today; a creepy,
skin-prickling sound I can never get used to. The desert
whistles all day and night out here. The hissing whistle of
the wind cutting past your helmet. The moaning whistle of
it winnowing through the razor wire. I stand under the hot
canvas a moment, just listening. And then it hits me again,
that deep-down ache that makes me want to curl up and cry.

"What the fuck are you doing, Brady?" It's Will Rickman, this bony young specialist in my squad with zitty skin
and an Adam's apple twice the size of his brain.

I wipe my hands on my pants. "Nothing."

Rickman steps closer and squints at my spider. "Look at
that thing. It's disgusting. It's fuckin' bleeding black ooze."

"Don't talk like that about Fuzzy."

Rickman raises his eyebrows. But all he says is, "Let's go, they're waiting."

I pick up my rifle and follow him, sunglasses over my eyes, scarf over my mouth. Ducking against the wind, the sand whipping my cheeks, I run to the Humvee and cram into the back behind the other guy in my team, DJ, and our squad leader, Staff Sergeant Kormick.

"We got better things to do than wait while you powder your nose, Brady," Kormick shouts to me over the wind, shoving the Humvee into gear with a grinding wrench. "Don't keep us waiting again. Got it?"

"Got it, Sar'nt."

While we drive along the dirt road to the checkpoint, the guys shooting their usual bull, I gaze out the slit of a back window into the early morning light. Dirty gray sand stretches as far as I can see, blending so exactly with the dust-filled sky it obliterates the horizon. On either side of the road are rows of rectangular olive-drab tents, their roofs droopy and covered in dust. The ones on the left are for us, the ones on the right behind the loops of razor wire are for the prisoners. But other than that, there's nothing out there but an endless gray blur. And a tree.

I like that tree, standing outside the wire all by itself in the middle of the desert. I call it Marvin. I spend so many hours staring at Marvin that I know every twist of his wiry little branches, every pinpoint of his needle leaves. I talk to him sometimes, compare notes on how we're doing.

We rattle along for twenty minutes or so, while I sit in a daze, too tired to line up my thoughts in any kind of an order. We work twelve-to-fifteen-hour shifts, and even so

I can never sleep. It's too damn hot and I'm sharing a tent with thirty-three snoring, farting members of the male sex, not to mention the prisoners only a few meters away, chanting and screaming all night long.

As we near the checkpoint, the deep-down ache starts up again. I hate this.

Sure enough, there they are. Fifty or so civilians waiting outside the wire, baggy clothes flapping in the wind. They've been coming every day for weeks now, arriving at dawn to stand in the sun for hours without moving, like shrubs. Most of them are women. Mothers and sisters, wives and daughters looking for their men.

Kormick pulls the Humvee up to the checkpoint and we climb out. Hitching my rifle strap over my shoulder, I head for the wire with my team, sand blowing up my nose and down my throat, making me cough. God, what I would give for a breath of clear air, one that isn't filled with dust and the stink of burning shit and diesel. Air like the air at home: clean, cool, mountain air.

"Brady!" Kormick yells after me, beckoning me back with a jerk of his head. "When you get over there tell the hajjis we'll mail them a list soon. Then make 'em fuck off."

"Yes, Sar'nt."

"And Brady? Get a move on this time."

I'm not any slower than anybody else, but I do what he says. What list he's talking about, though, I have no idea. There isn't any list. And even if we did have one, how in Christ's name am I supposed to tell these people, "We'll mail you a list of the prisoners" when we just bombed all their houses and mailboxes, too—if they even have mailboxes in Iraq?

When we drove through Basra on the way here from Kuwait in March, right after Shock and Awe started the war, it was flattened. Nothing but smoldering rubble. People living in lean-tos made of cardboard and scrap. Garbage piled so high you couldn't see over it, making the worst goddamn stink I've ever smelled in my life. Corpses lying in the streets, smashed and gory, like those run-down deer on the highways at home, only with human faces. But Kormick always gives me the job of talking to these people. He's got the idea that the sight of a female soldier will win hearts and minds. We've just pulverized their towns, locked up their men and killed their kids, and one GI Jane with sand up her ass is supposed to make it okay?

The minute I step in front of the checkpoint wire, the same old havoc begins: civilians shouldering each other to get near me, waving photographs and screeching. A checkpoint is supposed to be secure, but ours is nothing but a plywood shack no bigger than a garden shed, a rickety wooden tower, a razor-wire fence and a handful of badly trained reservists with guns. And sand, of course. Lots and lots of sand.

"Imagine being on an empty beach looking out at the ocean," I wrote to Tyler once. "Now take away the ocean and replace it with sand all the way to the end of the frigging world. That's where I am."

I miss Tyler so bad. The soapy smell of his hair, the warmth of his big body up against mine. And his eyes—he has the prettiest eyes you ever saw. Cinnamon eyes. We've been dating since eleventh grade, which is funny 'cause when I first met him I didn't like him at all. I was into class clowns those days, show-offy bad boys, not quiet, nerdy types like Tyler McAllister, who mumbled and blushed whenever we talked. But then he invited me to see him play guitar and sing at a place called The Orange Dog, and I was so surprised that a geek like him even played guitar I said yes.

The Orange Dog's in Catskill and the closest thing to a music club we have in our corner of upstate New York, although it doesn't serve alcohol, which is the only reason my parents allowed me to go there at seventeen. I asked my best friend Robin to come with me because we made a good boy-hunting team: Robin tall and dark, with creamy skin and big brown eyes; me small and freckled, with frizzy red hair and eyes so light they're almost no color at all. She picked me up in her rusty, third-hand Saturn and drove us the forty minutes south it takes to get to Catskill from Willowglen, our hometown. That was a big-deal expedition for us back then.

Soon as we walked into the club, I felt happy. It smelled of wood and beer (it had once been a bar), just like a music club should. On one side was a counter, where you could buy hippie things like carrot cake and iced mocha. Scattered around were ratty old couches and chairs that the owners probably rescued from the town dump. Colored lampshades hung low from the ceiling, making pools of soft light over the mismatched coffee tables—the place looked like a living room after it's been trashed at a party, which I thought was perfect. Robin bought us each a root beer, and we sank into a couple of stained red armchairs and stretched out our legs to admire our tight jeans and high-heel boots.

The club filled up pretty quick. Farm boys and local teenagers on the lookout for girls. A few boozy old men who'd probably stumbled in by mistake. Me and Robin smirked at each other. We were much more sophisticated than any of those folks. They were hicks. We, of course, weren't.

I had no idea what to expect from Tyler that night, if this was a date or if he was just collecting an audience. I didn't know a lot about boys yet, since I've got no brothers and I'd never had a regular boyfriend. Every boy I'd tried dating had turned out to be either a two-timing dipshit or stunningly dumb.

So we sat there, Robin tall and graceful, me short and gingery, until they finally turned off the music and lights and shone a wobbly spotlight on a single high stool on the stage. Then Tyler walked on, looking way cooler than I ever imagined he could, with an acoustic guitar slung over his shoulder, a tight black T-shirt and long hair swinging into his eyes. He perched on the stool, like a million other singers have, I guess, his guitar on one knee, and I don't know why, but suddenly I was ridiculously nervous. I felt like I'd known him for years. Like the two of us had been waiting for this performance all our lives, working for it, building up to it. Like this was going to make him or break him and I really cared.

Later that night I found out that Tyler wasn't a geek at all. He was just in love with me.

That was two years ago, and a whole lot of shit's happened since then. Tyler's in college now, back at home, studying music and playing gigs. And I'm stuck in the middle of this frigging desert, like I've been for almost three months, surrounded by jabbering civilians and wondering what the fuck I'm doing here.

Soon this old couple pushes through the crowd and hustles up to me, the woman clutching her husband's arm. They both look unbelievably ancient and withered. The woman is draped from head to toe in black, her cheeks lined with a million tiny cracks, her dark eyes watering under her wrinkly brow. The man is white-haired and knotty, with a tiny brown face like a walnut. Holding each other tight, they hobble up close, and that's when they realize I'm a female. The usual snort of surprise, like I'm some clown the U.S. military shipped out for their entertainment. Then they try to press the advantage.

"Lady, look," the old man says in a garble that sounds vaguely like English, and his wife pushes a photo at me with a trembling hand. "My son. He here? Does he live?"

I look at it, not because I'm interested but because that's my job. A wide-eyed Arab with a Saddam mustache, same as a million others. I nod like I know him and the old couple gets real excited. The woman even smiles, five teeth missing. Her whole wrinkly face is so full of hope that I have to turn away. We have seven thousand prisoners in this place and more coming in every day. How the hell am I supposed to know anything from some crappy old snapshot?

"If he's here, I'm sure he's safe," I say.

"Thank you, thank you lady soldier!" the old man answers, his voice quavering. That makes me feel bad.

"Go home now," I tell him and the crowd. "When we have a list of the detainees we'll let you know. But you gotta go now." I wave my arms in a shooing motion.

Nothing changes. The civilians just keep pressing around me, hollering and shoving their goddamn photos into my face. I shouldn't even be here by myself in the middle of a bunch of locals like this—one of them could shoot my head off any second. I glance over my shoulder. Where the hell is zit-face Rickman? He's supposed to be my battle buddy, out here with me, watching my back. But no, he's over behind the wire, nice and safe, chewing the fat with PFC Bonaparte, popularly known as Boner. I'm alone. As usual.

"GIRL, WHY YOU balled-up in the bedclothes there? Come on out now, or I'll pull you out myself, like I did yesterday. You didn't like that, did you?"

Yesterday? The soldier can't remember yesterday.

A wave of cold as the nurse pulls off the sheet. Wet gown bunched and piss-stinky. Back throbbing.

"Oh, honey. You had a rough night, huh? Come on, up you get and we'll wash you nice and clean."

The nurse wraps her big arms around the soldier and drags her out of the hospital bed, wet and reeking.

The nurse and the soldier dancing the waltz of shame.

## [ N A E M A ]

IT HAPPENED LAST night, while we were squeezed around my grandmother's table eating supper. Only a week had passed since we had fled the war and our home in Baghdad to take shelter in Granny's village house near Umm Qasr, so we were still shaken and disoriented, and trying to work out how to make sense of our days.

"I want you two to keep up your studies while we're here," Papa was saying to me and my little brother. "And no excuses."

"But I left all my books behind, so I can't study," Zaki replied, gripping the edge of the table while he teetered on the back legs of his chair. "I'll help you protect the house instead, Papa."

My father smiled, the lamplight glancing off his thick glasses, and reached out to tousle my brother's hair. "Don't be silly, my boy, you'll study five hours a day. Then you can help me. And sit up before you break Granny's chair."

Zaki ducked away from Papa's hand, but he obeyed. "Musicians don't need school," he muttered, smoothing his hair carefully back into place over his brow. "We are artists."

I laughed. Poor Zaki. Only thirteen and he thinks he has the talent to be a rock star. I can hear little evidence of it when he thumps away at his guitar. All he has are dreams. But we indulge him anyhow, for what is a child without dreams?

"Naema will tutor you," Mama said firmly. She was bent over the table, her long back curved, serving her mother lentil soup. Granny Maryam is so old that most of her teeth are missing and her hands shake, so she has difficulty eating without spilling. "She can keep you up on your English and science," Mama continued. I am the English speaker in the family, my big talent, although Papa, too, can speak it quite well. We used to practice together by listening to the BBC.

"But Naema's a rotten teacher! She's always blowing up at me."

"Don't talk that way about your sister," Granny scolded in her creaky voice. "We must all—"

Furious voices outside. A pounding at the door, so violent it seemed about to knock down the house. "What's that?" Granny said, her eyes wide with fear.

"Soldiers!" I whispered. "Americans!"

"All of you in the back room now!" Papa ordered.

"Open up!" the soldiers bellowed, kicking the door so hard it strained on its hinges.

Before anyone could stop me, I ran and unbolted it. If I speak English to these Americans, I thought in my innocence, they will not hurt us.

"Naema, get back!" Papa shouted.

If only he had not! Perhaps then we would have remained calm and these terrible things would never have happened. But who can know? No, I cannot blame Papa.

The soldiers tore in, first one, then another, then a third. Hideous in their bulky uniforms, their faces obscured by goggles and helmets, their huge guns thrusting, voices roaring fury and insults. They pushed me aside as if I were nothing but air and rushed at my father. With a blow to his head, they knocked him to the ground.

"Papa!" Zaki shrieked. We all know how frail Papa is, how his legs were broken again and again by Saddam's torturers. How his heart almost burst with the pain.

One of the soldiers turned on Zaki then, little Zaki, not even tall enough to reach my chin and as thin as a reed, and kicked him in the stomach. He doubled over with a cry. They threw him facedown on the ground next to Papa.

"Stop, please!" I begged in English. "He is only a child!" But they did not hear me. I had no voice to them, no existence.

My mother clutched Granny, who was wailing, all her memories of Saddam's brutes flooding back, I am sure, those men who had stormed into her house just like this and dragged her husband to his death.

Two soldiers stamped their filthy boots down on the necks of Papa and Zaki, pushing their poor faces into the floor. Then they bound their hands behind their backs and pulled those horrible pointed hoods over their heads. I could hear Papa choking and Zaki whimpering in terror.

"Stop!" I cried again. "This is a child, my father is sick. They will suffocate! Please!"

"Shut up!" a soldier barked at me, and he pushed me so hard into Mama and Granny we fell against the wall. All I could see of his face was a twisted grimace of hatred and fear.

They pulled Papa and Zaki to their feet by their bound wrists, as if they were sacks of grain, not human beings, and jabbed their guns into their backs, pushing and kicking them out of the door. I ran after them just in time to see two soldiers pick them up and throw them into the back of a truck, surely breaking their bones or tearing their flesh. I heard Zaki cry out in pain. But my father was silent.

"Don't hurt them!" I pleaded. "Please don't hurt them!"

"Why have they done this?" Mama cried, clutching her head as they drove away. "Why?"

And that is when I felt the anger grow over me like a skin. That is when I became merciless and numb.

So this morning, as I walk the four kilometers from Granny's village to the American prison, I am determined to do whatever it takes to find out what has happened to our men—both my own and those of my companions. Poor Umm Ibrahim, her face drooping and mournful, whose husband was arrested and killed by Saddam—she tells me her three sons have been swallowed by this prison now, leaving her with nobody. Little Abu Rayya and his wife, who have already lost two children to the Iran war—they were forced to watch their remaining boy and only comfort being beaten and snatched in the night, just like Papa and Zaki. And Granny's friend, old widow Fatima, who has been making this walk every day for three weeks already—her brother and sole support is also incarcerated there.

"Do they tell you anything at the prison?" I ask this widow on the way. "Is your brother all right?"

"I do not know, little daughter," she replies, shaking her old head. "They tell us nothing. All we can do is wait."

When we reach the prison at last—and the walk is long and frightening, with soldiers roaring down the road in their tanks and trucks—we see that many other families are already there, standing in a crowd beside the coils of wire that block the prison entrance. So we go to stand with them, burning under the sun and buffeted by the wind, ready to endure the same wait as any who have been beaten into passivity by war and history.

While we stand hour after hour, most of us silent, some of us murmuring thin assurances to one another, I look through the pitiless wire to the prison beyond. The British and Americans are in such a hurry to incarcerate us that they have not even taken the time to build a real prison. It is nothing but tents. Row upon row of them pegged to the sand, their olive sides already bleaching in the sun, the air between them thick with dust, the coiled wire around them bristling with a million sharpened blades. And as I look, it occurs to me that, to the soldiers, this is not a prison but a protection. They have barricaded themselves in here, safe and blind behind their wire and checkpoints, while the rest of us, sisters and daughters, parents and grandparents, are out here in the real world, suffering the real world's suffering.

We stand, my sad companions and I, until the sun has crept from the horizon almost to the top of the sky, and finally I see a tiny soldier plod up to the fence where we are waiting. He looks as though he can hardly walk under all he carries, with his helmet like an upside-down soup bowl and his sunglasses absurdly large on his little face. He looks like a child in his father's clothes. But of course he is no child. He is a killer and an occupier.

I watch him approach, shouting and waving his silly little arms, and I feel such hatred bloom in my heart I do not know myself. Then I notice there is something odd about him, something wrong. I look again.

It is a girl.

I would laugh out loud if there were any laughter left in me. How desperate the Americans must be to send their girls to war.

As soon as the people around me also see this soldier is only a girl, and out here all alone with us, they grow bold. "You have killed our sons!" they shout, closing in around her. "You're lying to us, bitch!"

I step forward to curse her, too, but then I stop. This behavior is futile. Better to wait for the chance to offer my English to this creature of destruction, for perhaps, God willing, in return she will tell us what she and her kind have done with our men.

## [ KATE ]

**I'M GETTING FREAKED.** No matter how much I yell
and try to shoo away the wrinkly old couple and the rest
of these damn locals, they won't budge. They just keep on
crowding around me, yelling in Arabic and pushing their
fucking photos into my chest. I'm just about to poke one of
them with my rifle, hard, when a female voice calls out from
the crowd, "I speak English—do you need help?"

Startled, I look around. An Iraqi girl about my own age
separates herself from the mob, walks right up to me and
stares into my face with no fear at all.

"You really speak English?" I ask, amazed.

She studies me without answering. She's wearing a long,
coffee-colored sack of a dress and a sky-blue headscarf
wrapped tight around her neck and forehead. Her face
is narrow, pale brown and pretty, except for her mouth,
which is clamped into a thin, schoolmarmy line. And her
eyes, which are huge and greenish-gold, look suspicious
as hell.

"Yes," she finally says in a low voice. "I am able to translate, if you would like."

"You would? Cool. Okay then, tell your friends here that

we're putting together a list of the prisoners and we'll give it to them soon. But right now they gotta go."

"I will. But first, please, I need to ask a question. We want to know, these people and I, when our men will be released."

"I don't know," I say, eyeing her warily. "But tell them not to worry, we treat the prisoners well. Now get them to leave."

The girl studies me again. She's half a head taller than me, but that's not saying much, since I'm only five-three. "This is the truth, you swear?" she says. "Because my father and brother, you have locked them up in here and they are innocent."

*Yeah, right. So's everybody in this whole friggin' sandbox, according to you people.* But out loud I only say, "Of course it's true. Now, tell these folks about the list and make them go. 'Cause this situation is getting dangerous for all of us. You included."

She gazes at me a second longer, then turns to the crowd and calls out something in Arabic. But instead of making the people leave, it only makes them more excited than ever, talking and shouting all at once. Fuck. I look around again for my squad. Sergeant Kormick and Boner are inside the shack, where they can't see anything. Rickman's over there, too, standing in the sand like a cactus, probably dreaming about his first grope or something, he's such a kid. Jimmy Donnell's up in the guard tower with his M-60. And DJ's out on the road, searching cars. Nobody's near me, nobody's paying attention, which is against all the goddamn rules. Double fuck.

The girl turns back to me. "They say they will go, but not until they know when you will have this list of our men."

"Soon. Now tell them to scat!" I lift my rifle to my chest, barrel up.

She sweeps her eyes over my face, her expression cold. "And what are you doing with the children? The little boys you arrested? My brother you took, he is only thirteen."

"We keep the boys safe in a separate compound. Now leave!"

"You mean he is not with my father?" She looks upset a moment, her cold manner gone. But then she clamps her mouth back into its schoolmarm seam. "My brother, his name is Zaki," she goes on. "Look," and she hands me a photo, just like the old couple did.

The last thing I need to do right now is admire some Iraqi chick's family snapshots, but I do it to keep her cooperating. The photo shows a skinny boy sitting on a rug, grinning up at the camera with just the kind of goofy expression my friends use on MySpace. His black hair flops into his eyes, which are the same green-gold as his sister's, and he's got one of those long, bony faces that'll probably look good once he grows into it but right now seems all wrong, like the head of a grownup stuck onto a kid's body. Next to him, leaning forward in a chair with his hand on the boy's shoulder, is a clean-shaven, middle-aged man with short gray hair, thick glasses and the same long face, but a real sad smile.

It's always so strange to look at photos of people before bad things happen to them. When they don't know yet. When they're so unsuspecting.

"That is my father," the girl says. "He is fifty-four. His heart is weak—he has had two heart attacks already. This is why I am so worried about him. He is not well enough to live in this place with hundreds of other men, he has not the strength. My father was put in prison by Saddam, tortured by him! My brother, he is a child! And you Americans arrest them? You understand nothing!"

I don't need to hear this crap, shouldn't even be listening to it, but I might as well be polite. "Listen," I say, "I'm sorry about your situation, but we've got thousands of prisoners in here. Thanks for your help, though. Really." I hold out my hand. "My name's Kate. Kate Brady. *As-salaam aleikum.*" Three months in Iraq have at least taught me how to say that. Kind of.

She glances down at my hand without touching it. "I am Naema Jassim. Keep the photograph. It will help you recognize them." She pauses and looks at me intently, like she's trying to see into my brain. "Miss Brady . . . Kate, I have a suggestion. If you will promise to look for my brother and father, I will come back every morning and translate for you, yes? These people here, they are angry. You need me to help keep control, I think." She leans forward and points at the photograph. "My father here, his name is Halim Mohanammad al-Jubur. And my little brother sitting there on the floor, he is Zaki Jassim. You will look for them, please?"

I'll never remember those weird Arab names. In one ear, out the other. "Tell me that again?"

"I will write them down, if you like."

"Okay, but hurry." I take out a pen from my utility vest and she scribbles the names on the back of the photo.

"You will look for them if I translate?" she asks again.

"Yeah, sure, I'll do my best." I tuck the photo and pen into one of my pockets. I'm not about to tell her that I never see the prisoners, except when they're driven in on the backs of trucks, and then they're all zip-cuffed and hooded anyway, so all I ever see is bodies with a sack on top. I'm not going to tell her this because she's right. I do need her.

Just then some woman squeezes between us and shoves a baby into my chest. It's limp and gray, and skinny as a chicken. I think it's a girl but I can't really tell. Pus-filled sores ooze all over its face and arms. I back away, disgusted, but she won't stop pressing the horrible thing right up against me—these people never do stuff like this to the male soldiers. I'm afraid it'll fall if I don't take it, though, so I grab it and hold it as far away from me as I can. It stinks. A sickly-sweet stink, like a dead rat trapped in a basement.

I glance down at it. The baby isn't even moving. It just lies there in its little dress, draped over my arms like a rag, while its mother stares at me with desperate eyes. I know what she wants. She wants a doctor and medicine. She wants me to take her baby to a hospital. But we don't have a doctor. We don't have medicine. And we sure don't have a fucking hospital.

I push the baby back into her arms and try to make her understand that I can't do anything for her. "Go home!" I keep telling her. "Go!" She won't move. I look around for Naema, hoping she can help me out here like she promised. But Naema's gone.

By the time I finally get the mother to take her baby and leave, along with all the other civilians, it's eleven in the morning and the sun's burning a hole in the sky. When my unit first arrived back in March, the heat wasn't this bad yet—we froze our asses at night, in fact. But now it's June, and the last time I saw a cloud I was so amazed that I took a picture of it. It must be a hundred and thirty degrees out here today, I'm not kidding. Imagine putting your oven on that high to heat up a pizza, then climb in, shut the door and lock it so you can never get out. That's what it feels like.

I drain my bottle of water—piss-temperature, plastic-tasting—but it isn't enough. My head already feels like somebody's stabbing it with a knitting needle, the inside of my mouth's like a dustball and I've got nine more hours to go on my shift. I need more water, which means I have to walk over to the shack, where we keep the bottles in a cooler. But Sergeant Kormick's still in the shack and even though he doesn't give a fuck whether or not Rickman does his job right, his rules are different for me. If he sees me leave my post, I'll never hear the end of it.

I pull a tube of hand sanitizer out of my vest pocket and rub it on, hoping to wash away the pus from that sad-ass baby. I use the stuff so often the skin on my palms is peeling like sunburn, but it doesn't seem to help much. I've dropped twelve pounds since I arrived in this sandpit and my period has stopped. My fingernails have turned weird, too, all weak and flabby. They keep lifting off my nail beds and flaking away like old scabs. And my hair's falling out by the handful. But then, all of us are sick one way or the other. We like to joke that you spend the first six months of your deployment pooping your guts out, the second six months puking your guts out, and then you go home and puke and poop till you're redeployed. Some say it's sandfly fever, some say it's contaminated water. We call it the Bucca bug.

That's where we are, by the way: Camp Bucca, the biggest U.S. prison in Iraq. It's located way down south near the Kuwait border, in the poorest, bleakest part of the desert. Address: The Middle of Fucking Nowhere. It's so poor and bleak that on our way here from Kuwait, children in bare feet kept running up to our convoy, cupping their little hands to their mouths to beg for food and water, even jumping up on our trucks till we had to push them off, right into the road. Some of those kids were no more than two years old, their eyes big and black in their teeny faces. Skinny and ragged but cute as chipmunks. But when we tried to give them water, the convoy commander said we had to stop because those babies might be carrying bombs.

I'm going to collapse if I don't get some water myself, whatever Kormick says, so I take a deep breath and head over to the shack, ready to face more crap.

"Hey, Tits!" Boner calls out before I even get close. I sigh and walk up to the shack door, where he's now standing guard. He blocks my way with his rifle, grinning like the dickwad he is. Boner's called that for obvious reasons, but also because he's short and stocky, with a bony bald head like a knee. He's fresh out of high school but he acts like his brain froze back in fifth grade.

"Let me by, Bonehead. I need water. Bad."

He runs his eyes over me, making a big deal of staring at my chest. This is a popular theme among the guys in my platoon—me having big boobs—but it's all a dumb joke. I was a runner back in high school, track and long distance, and runners don't have big boobs. They're tight and lean, and that's how I'm built, only skinnier than ever now. Nothing but a scrawny little soldier, orange freckles popping out by the dozen under the desert sun.

"Gimme a squeeze," Boner says then, leering. I know he doesn't mean it, just has to try it on like the fifth grader he is. But I'm not in the mood for his bullshit.

"Let me by, mini-dick. I'm dehydrated."

He shakes his head. "Come on. One little quicky?"

"Look, I just had a dying baby in my arms. Leave me the fuck alone."

Boner just stands there grinning, still barring my way. I can see Kormick inside the shack, eating Skittles and reading some girly magazine. I'd like to avoid all this hassle and leave, but I'll faint if I don't get some water soon. I know this because it's happened to me three times already. My ears start ringing, I black out, and then I wake up with one of the guys shoving an IV in my arm to rehydrate me. After which Kormick gets on my case yet again for being nothing but a useless pussy.

"Sergeant?" I call. "Tell Boner to let me by, please. I'm about to pass out from thirst here."

"Let her by, Boner," he says in a bored voice. He doesn't even bother to look up.

Inside the shack, I grab a couple bottles and chug a long slide of water right there.

"Okay, get back out where you belong," Kormick says then. He looks up at me. "And Tits? No more leaving your post, for fuck's sake."

"Yes, Sergeant."

"THAT'S GOOD, HONEY-pie. You look just fine now, all cleaned up and smellin' sweet. Sit down here and I'll go get your young man."

The soldier slumps on the edge of the bed and stares at the hands quaking in her lap. White and puffy. Underwater hands.

What young man?

Something beeps in a corner. The ceiling light glares. White everywhere: The raised bed. The window blinds. The walls and the floor and the ceiling. Her swollen feet. Shivering hands.

A giant clock face on the TV ticks one second. Two.

"Katie?" A tall man steps into the room.

The soldier flinches.

"Don't be scared. It's only me." The man's voice wobbles.

The soldier scoots to the far side of the bed, pulls herself to her feet and backs up against the wall. Only then does she really look at him. The man is pale and young and long-haired.

"You do know who I am, don't you?" he says.

The man seems to be crying.

# [ NAEMA ]

IT WAS THE looting that finally drove my family from Baghdad. During the bombing in March, we stayed, enduring the explosions that shattered windows and cracked open the earth, that left corpses rotting in the streets and poisoned the air with the stench of burning flesh. After each attack, Papa and Mama, Zaki and I would climb to the roof, handkerchiefs pressed to our mouths, to survey the damage. The house across the street, where we used to watch five little sisters play, was now nothing but dust and bricks, every one of those children dead. The café where I would buy my tea on the way to classes had been turned into a mound of smashed stone and twisted wire. Baghdad's ancient buildings, mosques and markets, her elegant avenues of bright palm trees—all this we saw reduced to rubble and blood. Yet we were no more able to leave our beloved Baghdad than if she were our dying mother.

At the end of May, though, when the streets were swarming with thieves and thugs and the desperate and angry poor from Sadr City, released by war like wasps from a broken nest—this we could not endure.

In the beginning we thought the Americans would stop it. After all, they had their tanks and guns, their soldiers, and we had nothing since they had dismantled our army and police. But no. They lounged on their trucks in the sun, smoking and taking photographs while looters stripped our shops, our homes, our museums. Zaki could not go back to school for fear of being kidnapped or killed by criminals who would snatch anybody for ransom. (Our poor neighbor's son, a little boy of twelve, was shot dead in the street for nothing but his CD player.) And I could not go to my classes at Baghdad Medical College for fear of the same, or of being raped. Many girls and women were being raped.

"We can't stay here any longer," Papa told us one morning after we'd eaten what breakfast we could find, his thin face sad and gray. "Your mother and I have decided to go to your grandmother's house. Umm Qasr has been badly bombed, but the Americans have moved on from there now and it's more peaceful than this place. Pack up one bag each, only. We leave tomorrow at dawn."

"Tomorrow?" Zaki jumped up from the kitchen table, panic in his eyes. "But I haven't said good-bye to Malik yet, or any of the others! Can't we wait a few days?"

"No, little one, it's too risky." Papa stood and took Zaki in his arms, patting his back and stooping to kiss the top of his head. "I spent all day yesterday waiting for petrol so we could leave," he added in his quiet way. "We have no time to delay. Now go pack, children, and please, don't fuss."

But I could hear the shame in Papa's voice. I knew he thought it cowardly to run from Baghdad, even then; that he felt he was abandoning his city in her time of need.

Some speak of how hard it is to choose among their possessions when they must flee their homes like this; it is an old refugee story. But for me, it was not hard. All I needed were a few clothes and my medical books so I could continue my studies. Photographs, ornaments, childhood souvenirs—what did these matter anymore? If I wanted memories, I had them in my head. I could have jumped in the car with nothing at all, so eager was I to escape the sight of my city being smashed and pillaged.

No, the hardship for me was having to leave my friends, and most of all, my fiancé, Khalil. I telephoned him as soon as Papa finished telling us to pack and he ran right over to see me. We clung to each other in shock. "I'll count every minute until we can be together again," he said urgently, holding me tightly to his chest. "And as soon as the war ends and we're reunited, *inshallah*, we will celebrate our new freedoms, our new Iraq, right, my love?"

"Yes, God willing, yes," I replied, weeping. But when Papa gently told Khalil that he must go, I could not watch him walk out the door. I had to turn and run into another room, for I was afraid. Already I sensed that even the deepest of loves and most earnest of promises can be crushed by war.

For Mama, it was leaving our house itself that hurt the most. She had been raised in a simple village of farmers, steeped in the old peasant ways, so to her our Baghdad home and belongings were proof of how far she had come and she could not bear to let any of it go. All night long, she agonized over which tea set to bring, which scarves, which dishes and dresses and photographs and letters, until I was mad with impatience.

Zaki was also distraught. He had spent years obsessively collecting souvenirs of his favorite musicians, and more years accumulating bootleg tapes and CDs and lovingly arranging them in categories on his shelves, as if building a nest to keep himself safe from the world. He wept frantically when Papa told him he must abandon these things, just as he wept at being separated from his friends. His only comfort was that when he appeared at his door, hugging his guitar to his chest as desperately as he had once hugged his baby blanket, not even Papa had the heart to make him leave it behind.

At dawn the next morning, we climbed into our old red car to set off, Mama openly crying, Papa grim, his glasses already grimy with dust and sweat. Zaki huddled in the rear seat with me, clutching his guitar. "Don't look back, Zaynab," Papa said to our mother. "It will only hurt more. And when this is over, Allah willing, we will come home."

We knew not to count on this, but it was necessary to hope.

The drive was long and hot and excruciatingly slow. Every corner brought a tangle of traffic and soldiers shouting and waving their incomprehensible signals, their faces livid and sunburned. Checkpoints, barricades or tanks blocked every road we needed to go down, or so it seemed. People were running this way and that, their mouths contorted in panic. Along the roads, trails of looters filed like ants, carrying or dragging their stolen trophies: plush red seats torn from theaters, restaurant tables, office cabinets, vases and televisions and statues. What use do they have for all this rubbish? I wondered. Why are we tearing apart our own city?

The many roadblocks forced us in the wrong direction over and over, and once a soldier made us drive right into a market. Just as we got there, a military truck came roaring in, the gunner on top pointing his killing machine at the women selling their eggplants and melons. The soldiers were shouting and waving but we could not tell what they wanted. Stop? Turn around? Go to the left, to the right? Why did they not make themselves clear? The driver in front of us tried to turn and get out of the way, but he must have panicked and hit the accelerator instead of the brake because his car catapulted into a market stand, crushing two children and their mother. Then the soldiers began to shoot—why? People screaming, running, guns exploding, blood drenching the vegetables. Five people dead, among them a mother and her baby, the child's pink dress matted with blood, her arm a ragged stump.

Zaki put his head out of the window and vomited.

Papa set his jaw—I could see it in the mirror. Slowly, he backed up, turned and wove the car like a needle around the market stalls and out the other side. He knocked nobody down, showing it was possible to do.

It took us four hours to get out of Baghdad. Mama found her strength at last and stopped weeping. She sat forward, her slim back straining as she peered through the dust-covered windshield, on the lookout for the slightest sign of danger. Papa drove without a word, his jaw clenched, his hands gripped tightly on the steering wheel, his frail shoulders hunched with tension. Zaki huddled in my arms, trembling, the little man he so wished to be swept away by fear.

I sat up straight and fierce. It would have to be my strength that would carry us through, I knew that then. Zaki was too young, my father too fragile and my mother too stunned by loss. It was up to me now, and me alone, to make sure that my family survived.

# [ KATE ]

ONCE I'M BACK at the checkpoint with my hard-earned water, I settle into the rest of the day's work. It would help kill the long, dead hours ahead to have some kind of a conversation, but neither DJ nor Rickman, who's finally at his post, seems to feel like talking. That's normal for them, though. Whether it's because they're too damn tired or don't like working with a girl, I don't know, but most of the time they treat me like I'm not even here.

DJ, whose real name is Derek Johnson, is our team leader—our team being me, him and Rickman. DJ's this hunky black dude from Brooklyn who's already married and a dad at twenty-three, and when he isn't around Rickman or Kormick he can be okay. But the only member of my squad who really talks to me is Jimmy Donnell—that is, if he's not out of reach in his guard tower. Jimmy grew up not far from me, in Slingerlands, a suburb just outside of Albany, and he looks like a lot of Irish around my hometown—tall and lanky, with black hair, a high-cheeked face and bright blue eyes behind his ugly-ass combat glasses. (His nickname is Teach 'cause of those.) He told me he lives with his mom, who has mental problems, and his two younger brothers. He's always saying he misses those little guys real bad, just like I'm always saying I miss Tyler.

My team's routine goes like this: Whenever a vehicle drives by the base, DJ waves at it to stop and makes all the people inside get out. Usually it's some dented old rattletrap filled to bursting with families trying to get away from the war, but two of us pat them down anyway, while the other one searches the car inside and underneath with a mirror on a stick. So far we haven't found any bombs or grenades, but we have found plenty of AK-47s, which messes with our heads because we've got no way of knowing whether we're dealing with a family that owns a weapon for protection or with a bunch of U.S.-hating insurgents. We've also found hoards of jewels and dinars, the Iraqi currency that isn't worth much more than toilet paper by now. Sometimes we take the stuff, sometimes not. Then we either arrest the men or send them on their way, depending on how they behave and our moods.

The reason I was given this MOS is because only females are allowed to search Iraqi women and I'm the only female in my squad. I'm practically the only female in my whole frigging platoon, for that matter. There's me, Yvette Sanchez and Third Eye. Three of us and thirty-nine fire-breathing, ball-scratching males.

This morning I search two women. The first is this teenager in baggy pants and a long shirt who giggles when I pat her down. But the second is a middle-aged mom in traditional dress with three kids in the backseat, and she's scared shitless. I try to smile and act friendly, miming how I'm not going to grab her body or do anything gross, just use the backs of my hands, but I don't really expect her to feel happy about it. After all, she still has to spread her legs, hold out her arms and put up with me touching her all over through her robe. And she still has to deal with the fact that I'm a soldier, and "friendly" is not what soldiers do. She could leave friendly little me one minute and get shot by someone who looks just like me the next. And then I'm pretty edgy myself, 'cause how am I to know whether one of these scared or giggling ladies will turn out to be some maniac ready to blow us into mincemeat? These people are capable of anything, or so we've been told: using babies as shields, smuggling weapons under pregnant women's dresses. And the worse thing is we can't tell from looking at them whether they're innocent civilians or bad guys.

After those two women, though, nothing happens for hours. A fly crawls up my arm. Another one tries to get in my ear. The sun dawdles across the sky. But finally an old van drives up. Inside are two men who look like father and son, the older one with the usual dumbass mustache, the younger one about sixteen. We make them climb out and they act so jittery we get suspicious right away. We might not be able to talk to these people but we've gotten real good at reading their body language and smelling their fear. DJ and Rickman pull them away from the van, make them hold out their arms and pat them down, while I poke around inside, hoping the damn thing isn't booby-trapped. In the back I find a can of gas and a bunch of oily rags, which could be for cleaning the van or starting a fire, who the hell knows. Then I lift up the front passenger seat. Four Kalashnikovs.

"DJ!" I call, holding one of them out like a flag. "They got four of these fuckers in here!"

"Well, suck my balls," he says, and in a flash he and Rickman shove the men against the van and cuff them. The boy begins to cry. A wet stain seeps through his trousers. It makes me wonder if Naema's little brother pissed himself like that when he was arrested. He's only thirteen, after all, if I'm to believe anything that girl said.

"Jesus fuckin' Christ," DJ mutters in disgust. He pushes the men in front of him, his rifle at their backs, and marches them over to the shack to be delivered to the prison, leaving Rickman behind with me.

Once that bit of excitement's over, though, the rest of the day inches by slow as a slug. Just the desert sun blasting off the sand, roasting me from all directions like I'm a peanut. The sky hard and blue, a plastic lid clamped over the desert. Flies buzzing around my eyes and crusty lips. Those knitting needles still stabbing my head, made worse by the weight of my helmet. Mouth dry with a desert thirst no amount of water can quench. Stomach cramping with the Bucca bug. Itches along my spine and legs and crotch from heat rashes, dust, sand fleas and sheer, soul-shriveling boredom. And DJ and Rickman still aren't talking.

By somewhere around four in the afternoon, I've drunk so much water my bladder's about to explode. It's always like this out here—you've got to hydrate all the time 'cause of the heat (we don't drink in the Army, we hydrate), but that means you need to piss all the time, too. I try to ignore my damn bladder as long as possible, but I know I'll come down with another infection if I'm not careful. I've had two already from trying to avoid the four stinky Porta-Johns that are all my unit has in the way of bathrooms. It isn't like there are any bushes or trees to squat behind, either, except for Marvin, and Marvin's no wider than my leg. Anyhow, he's beyond the wire, surrounded by toe poppers, for all I know, the landmines left over from the last war. But those infections are a bitch. They make you feel like you have to pee so bad you can't think about anything else, but when you try nothing comes out, or if it does it burns like acid. If the infection goes on too long, you get a fever and start pissing blood.

So I go up to DJ and ask permission to go. "Sure," he says. "Take your sweet time. Ain't nothing else to do in this shithole."

Walking far around Kormick and Boner this time, I slip behind the shack, cut off the top of one of my empty water bottles with my knife, unzip my pants and stick the bottle between my thighs. It's messy but better than exposing my ass while I squat. When I'm done, I drop the piss bottle onto the ground and kick some sand over it. That's how we females do it in the desert.

Back at the checkpoint, DJ and Rickman are looking as worn out as me. Our faces are dry and shriveled from the wind and sun, and we're covered in moondust, this white powder that lies on top of the desert and puffs up at your every step, getting into your lungs and nostrils and ears, and chafing you in all kinds of places it has no business being. The sweat's pouring into my eyes, down my chest and back. My underwear's a soggy sponge and my uniform feels like a sleeping bag drenched in hot water. Why the hell we can't have some kind of shelter, I don't know. Jimmy Donnell at least has a pathetic little roof on his plywood tower. But here on the ground we got nothing.

I wish there was another girl at the checkpoint. I wish Tyler was with me. I wish I had somebody, anybody, to talk to.

I wonder whether Tyler would understand if I tried to tell him what it's like out here. I doubt it. He'd probably only say that I asked for it by enlisting because he was against me joining the Army all along. We used to argue about it a lot. He said that the military would take away the sweetness he loved in me, the part of me that was still tender as a kid. He never understood that's exactly what I wanted. I was sick of being the kind of girl people patted on the head, the Goody Two-shoes who volunteered for bake sales and church bazaars—the girl everybody smiled at but nobody listened to. So when I heard the Army recruiter at school talking about how noble it is to serve your country, I thought it sounded perfect. I wanted to do something impressive like that, something that'd make people sit up and take notice. Anyhow, half the kids in my school were enlisting—the half who got the most respect.

I couldn't wait to tell Dad the day I made up my mind. He was always proud when I did stuff like a boy: joined the track team, ran hurdles or anything like that. So soon as I got off the school bus that day, I flew into the house shouting, "Dad, where are you?"

"Shush," Mom hissed, waddling her plump self into the front hallway, where I was kicking off my boots. "Stop that hollerin'. Your father's just come in."

Dad has this routine when he comes home from work that we all have to follow before we're allowed to speak to him. Even Mom. First, he takes off his holster and gun and locks them in the dining room sideboard. "Guns don't belong in homes," he likes to say. "Homes are for rest and prayer." Then he stands, tall and lean in his gray uniform, straight-backed and silver-haired, crosses himself and leads us in grace over dinner—me, Mom and my little sister April repeating his every word: "Bless us, O Lord, and these

Thy gifts which we are about to receive from Thy bounty, through Christ, our Lord. Amen."

We've been following this routine for as long as I can remember, but it's never stopped me from being fascinated with that gun, whatever Dad says. Ever since I was small I wanted to sneak it out of the sideboard and hold it. Feel its power, its heft. Feel the respect it brought him.

Once grace is done and my family sits down to eat, we have permission to talk, as long as we raise our hands first. "Dad?" I said when it was my turn. "Remember when I took the ASVAB test?"

He nodded. "You got the results?"

"Yeah! The recruiter said I did real good. He said the test showed I'd be just right for the military police. I want to do it, Dad. And if . . ."

"Slow down, honey." He turned to Mom, who was sitting at the other end of the table, her round face pink and glossy with too much makeup. "What do you think, Sally?"

"Is Katie gonna be a policeman?" April blurted, her little blond head barely poking over the tabletop. April was only four back then.

"No talking out of turn, sweetie-pie," Mom said. "But no, your sister wants to be a soldier." Mom looked at me, frowning. "Have you prayed for guidance, Kate? Have you consulted the Lord over this? Are you sure this is the path He has chosen for you?"

"Yes, Mom. I've prayed a lot. I know this is right for me."

"Don't rush it, Katie," Dad said then. "It's a big step. But if you do choose it, I think it's a good idea. You'll grow up in the Army." This was back in March 2000, way before 9/11, so none of us was thinking about war.

"So can I do it?"

"If you mull it over real careful and you're still sure, yes. But I'll only agree if you join the reserves. You need to get an education first."

"I'm so proud of you wanting to serve your country, sweetie!" Mom crowed. "It shows you have a good Christian heart."

But Tyler didn't see it that way. "I respect that you want to do something noble, but the Army's not the place to do it," he kept saying. "Specially not for a girl." He sang me old folk songs about wounded soldiers and loves lost forever, Bob Dylan songs about the evils of war. And he made me watch all those scary movies about Vietnam, *Platoon* and *Apocalypse Now* and *Full Metal Jacket*. He even told me my parents were wrong to support my decision to enlist, except he didn't use the word "wrong." The word he used was "misguided."

"But it's different now," I said. "The recruiter said I'll be traveling the world and keeping the peace. He said I'll do things I can be proud of for the rest of my life."

Tyler looked at me a moment, his cinnamon eyes droopy and sad. "Then marry me before you go."

"Get serious! We're seventeen. We haven't even finished high school."

"I am serious."

"Listen, I'll marry you later. We need to grow up first."

So I joined the MP reserves, applied to Catholic colleges—the only kind my parents would let me go to—and went off to summer boot camp, coming back bulging with muscles and ready to fight. I thought I was so tough! I'd spent nine weeks marching for miles with huge weights on my back, singing songs about blood and bombs, learning hand-to-hand combat, jabbing bayonets into human-shaped sacks, screaming "Kill!" and "Yes, sir!" and "Hooah!" I still remember this one rhyme we used to chant while we marched:

*What makes the green grass grow?*
*Blood, blood, bright red blood.*
*What makes the pretty flowers bloom?*
*Guts, guts, gritty grimy guts.*

And you know, I liked it. I liked feeling strong and capable. I liked proving myself. What this had to do with keeping the peace wasn't exactly clear to me anymore, but I figured clarity would come. One thing was clear, though: I was definitely no longer the type of girl you patted on the head.

I started at Saint Catherine's College, up by Albany, in September 2001, the very same week those lunatic fuckers attacked the World Trade Center and the Pentagon. If I got called to do something about those bastards, I was ready! But nothing happened. The war in Afghanistan began. My freshman year went by. I hung out with Tyler, watching him play guitar and feeling sidelined and useless. My whole life seemed on hold.

Then, in February 2003, halfway through my sophomore year, I finally got the e-mail I'd been waiting for. It said that I was attached to the 800th Military Police Brigade out of Uniondale, New York, and that we were deploying in two days. What a scramble! Only forty-eight hours to quit college, pack up all my gear and say good-bye to everybody— my professors, my friends, Tyler and my family. I also had to make a will and sign all kinds of papers about what would happen if I got killed—something I hadn't thought much about, to tell the truth. After all, Mom and Dad had always taught me that it's all in God's plan when we die. Makes no difference whether we go to war or stay at home knitting booties.

The night before I left, Mom took me to church to pray for protection and be blessed by our priest, Father Slattery. "May the Lord watch over you, child," he said in his goofy Irish accent, making the sign of the cross above my head as I knelt in front of him. Then he told me to always obey the will of God with the same humility as the Virgin Mary. "A soldier is asked to lay down his life for others, just as Jesus did," he added. And after we'd said the Lord's Prayer and some Hail Marys, he cited a verse from the Psalms he'd picked out to give me courage:

*The Lord lifts up the downtrodden, he casts the wicked to the ground.*

That's what I'll be doing, I thought proudly. Lifting the downtrodden, casting the wicked to the ground. That's what soldiers are for.

On the morning I had to leave, Tyler came down to New Jersey with my parents and April to wave good-bye at Fort Dix, along with all the other crying moms and dads, girlfriends and boyfriends and kids. I could see him in the crowd even from the airplane steps, big guy that he is. Football shoulders, back straight and strong. Long brown hair blowing in the wind. And below it, his soft face full of love and sadness.

Sometimes, standing at the checkpoint here, I see his face the way it looked that day. Like he's watching me. Like he knows something I don't.

When our shift is finally over, fourteen long hours after we started this morning, Kormick drives us back to our tents. Everybody's in a crappy mood, exhausted and itchy and irritated as fuck. The one blessing is that Boner isn't with us. He's in Jimmy Donnell's team and they leave separately.

The drive back to our tents takes twenty minutes, long enough for a serious nap, so I drop my head back against the cooler behind me and doze with my eyes half open like a cat. Rickman's crammed in beside me and DJ's up front with Kormick, but none of us says a word. We're all too pooped even to move our mouths, let alone shout over the wind and the groans of the Humvee rattling over the stony desert. My neck bounces against the hard cooler as we bump along, and my knees are folded up almost to my ears because of all the crap stuffed in here—weapons and water and ammo and first aid and MREs and tools and toilet paper and baby wipes and God knows what. I ache all over and each bump feels like it'll snap my head off. But I'm too frigging wiped out to care.

"What a fuckin' dead day," Kormick finally yells over the noise.

"Yeah, I hate this checkpoint shit," DJ shouts back. "No action at all."

"I saw some action," zitty Rickman chimes in, grabbing a chance to push his way into the big-guy talk in the front. "Brady's ass, hanging out there in the breeze."

"You saw Brady's ass?" Kormick snickers.

"Yep. Taking a piss. Nice little pink thing."

"Hey, Brady." It's Kormick again.

I don't answer, even though I'd love to tell Rickman that he's a lying fuckface. "Pinkass, I'm talking to you," Kormick says.

"That's not my name," I say warily. Why's he picking on me so much today?

"That's not my name, *Sergeant*," he snaps.

I don't answer that, either.

"You wish you had a cock, Brady?" Kormick says then. "A real cock like a man, so you can piss like a man? Nobody'd have to see your little pink ass then, would they?"

"Better than having to look at all your wormy little dicks," I say before I can stop myself.

DJ chuckles.

Kormick glares at me in the rearview mirror, his blue eyes narrowed and framed by a rim of sand where his shades have been all day. When me and the other two girls in my platoon first saw him we had a fit, thinking, wow, they sent us a movie star for a sergeant, all chiseled and blue-eyed and blond. But his good looks are beginning to seem grotesque now. Brad Pitt's evil twin.

"What the fuck makes you think you can talk to me like that, Pinkass?"

"Sar'nt?" DJ says cautiously. "We've all had a long day. You think maybe we should give it a rest?"

"Shut up, DJ. All of you, watch your fuckin' mouths." But Kormick doesn't say a word after that.

We drive the rest of the way in silence.

THE NURSE TAKES the soldier gently by the arm. "Quiet down now," she says. "It's okay, honey-pie. Nobody's gonna hurt you. Come sit."

She leads the soldier back around the bed and makes her sit down. "It's a flashback," she says to the crying man. "She'll be out of it in a moment. Maybe you should sit yourself down too, hon. She might take you in better that way."

The soldier watches the man sit in the visitor's chair and lean forward, his elbows on his knees and his bangs dangling into his wet eyes. "Katie?" His voice is still wobbly. "You do know I'm Tyler, right?"

She does now. Maybe. But when she tries to nod, the pain shoots through her neck and her mouth twists into a grimace. Her face feels hard and immobile, as if somebody's glued a mask onto it. And she doesn't feel like talking.

"Is your back any better?" the man asks then. "Are they treating you right in here?" He sits up and looks around. "Seems okay. Clean. You never know what you'll find with these VA hospitals, right?"

He pretends to smile. She doesn't like that.

"I guess the food stinks, though, huh? Remember when I had my appendix out, how I hated the food?"

She stares at the polished floor. Bluish white, like the skin of a corpse. Her feet the same corpse color in their hospital slippers, only puffy, like rotting fish.

"Your mom and dad send their blessings. They'll come Friday."

That makes the soldier find her tongue. "I don't want their fucking blessings. I don't want them to come on Friday."

"Oh, Katie." The man leans toward her again, his face looking helpless. "You know you don't mean that."

# [ NAEMA ]

MY POOR MOTHER is in a state. As soon as I return from my long absence at the prison, she flies at me in a panic. "Thanks be to Allah you're safe!" she cries, clinging to me. "We've been waiting and waiting for you. Now tell me quickly—what did you find out?"

"Nothing," I say, dropping into a chair, exhausted. She hands me a glass of water and I take a deep drink, parched from my hours of standing under the sun. "They told me nothing."

Mama moans and rubs her face, her long, graying hair falling over her hands, her shirt and trousers crumpled. "Why has this happened to us? How can these Americans lock up your innocent father? How can they arrest a little boy? Zaki's not even fully grown! Can't they see this?"

"I know," I say quietly. "I know, Mama." I look about the room. "Where's Granny?"

"In her bed at last. This terrible night has been too much for her."

Mama crouches beside my chair, her face pale and drawn. Neither of us have had any sleep since Papa and Zaki were arrested. When the soldiers took them, I wanted to run after them to see where they were going, but Mama stopped me. "You can't go now, alone in the night, you'll be killed! We must wait and go in the morning with widow Fatima and the others." So she, Granny and I stayed up all night, sick with worry and fright, watching for the first light of dawn so we could leave. But by the time that light finally came, Granny was in such a bad way that Mama could not leave after all. "Go," she said to me, her voice breaking. "But, in the name of Allah, be careful."

Now she looks up at me, her brow pinched. "Naema, what do you think they'll do to your father? Will they torture him the way Saddam did? And what about Zaki? Will they starve him?"

I take her hands and kiss them. "I don't know, Mama. But I met a girl soldier today and she doesn't seem like a torturer, only a child."

"But what did you hear from the other families? Have any of them seen their men? Have any been killed?"

"No, I told you, nobody knows anything. No dead were announced, we heard nothing. We had to wait outside the huge coils of wire they've put around the prison and we were too far away from the tents to see anything."

I stand and pull my mother to her feet. "Try to keep up your courage, try not to think of the worst. The girl soldier said they'll have a list of the prisoners soon. I'll keep going back every day until I find out more, I promise."

"But it's so dangerous!" Mama steps away from me, compulsively rubbing her long fingers. "I don't know which is worse, to let you go out there, exposing yourself to who knows what, or sitting here helplessly, knowing nothing. If only I could go with you!"

I wrap her in my arms. "I know it's hard, but I can look after myself and you know I won't ever go alone. There are plenty of people for me to walk with—I've already made friends with kind widow Fatima. I'll find news of Papa and Zaki. Be patient."

But as I hold her, I too am engulfed by sorrow and yearning. For Papa and Zaki to be home again. For Khalil, my love, his comfort and wisdom. And for the simple routine of school and work and meals that was once our life in Baghdad, and that I fear is now gone forever.

I wonder how much that little American soldier I met today understands of what she is doing to us. If I see her again, I would like to ask her. How would you feel, I would say, if I tore your mother's children away from her, as you have done to mine? How would you feel if we flew over your cities and towns, dropping missiles and cluster bombs until your dead were lying in the street, shredded and putrefying? How would you feel if we dismantled your army and police, and destroyed the power that cleans your water, works your traffic lights and illuminates, heats and cools your homes? How would you feel if, having crippled your defenses, we opened the way for criminals and fanatics to come in and rob and murder and rape you—and then, when you tried to protect yourself, we arrested or shot you for being a terrorist? How would you feel if we drove you from your homes, scattered your friends and lovers and families, killed your children . . . ?

Yes, I would like to ask her all this, but I will not. For what could she tell me? She is young and ignorant. Nothing but a puppet.

# [ KATE ]

AS SOON AS grumpfuck Kormick lets us out of the Humvee, I drag myself into the tent and drop onto my rack, wishing for the billionth time I could wave a wand and make every douche bag in sight disappear. Kormick sleeps in the NCO tent, thank God, but Rickman and DJ are right here with me across the aisle, so I can never get away from them, even for a frickin' minute. They pull off their boots, stinking up the air as usual, take out their MREs and start to eat. DJ offers me his bag of chips—we're always trading food in the hopes of getting some variety—but I shake my head. I owe him for shutting up Kormick, but I don't want to deal right now. Not with him, not with anybody.

I lie on my fart sack, the sleeping bag I use for a mattress, my arm over my eyes, trying to just breathe. The tent is always hot and dusty inside because we have no floor but sand and no air-conditioning but tent flaps. It's overcrowded, too, with eighteen green cots lined up on each side and our crap stuffed into every available space in between: duffle bags and dirty underwear, helmets and rifles, boots and socks and backpacks. Even the tent poles are cluttered—fading photos of girlfriends and wives, good-luck rabbit feet and key rings, or in my case Fuzzy the spider and my crucifix. And then, of course, there are the men. The tent reeks of them. Sweat and farts, beard and balls.

"Hey, Freckles." (That's what my friends call me. Better than Tits or Pinkass, at least.) I lift my arm off my eyes, relieved to see another female at last. Third Eye walks over to me in her brown T-shirt and camo pants, looking as sand-crusted and exhausted as the rest of us, and parks her big self on her rack beside me. She's six foot tall, with a round red face like a Russian's, short dark hair and squinty black eyes. And she's built like a bulldozer. She could scoop up most of the guys in my platoon and fold them up like a handkerchief.

"You eaten yet?" she says.

"Nope."

"I figured. Eat this. Come on. You're shrinking to nothing out here."

She hands me an MRE—Meal Ready to Eat, that is. MREs come in these brown plastic sacks, and inside there's a main course of cardboard disguised to look like greasy meat, along with a bunch of artery-clogging junk food and a chemical pouch for heating the mess up without fire, which probably tastes better than the stuff it's supposed to cook. The MREs are famous for clogging up your guts like plaster—we call them Meals Refusing to Exit—and they only fill you up for about ten minutes, but they're all we have to eat, along with our equally disgusting T-Rations, because neither the fucking Army nor its fat-cat contractor, KBR-Halliburton, has gotten around to building us a chow hall yet.

I sit up and tear the packet open, pick out a cold ball of grease and force myself to take a bite. Third Eye, meanwhile, is wolfing down a solid cube of spaghetti and red sauce like it's mama's home cooking.

Third Eye got that name because of this nasty black bump that appeared one day in the middle of her forehead. It's gone down now, but it was quite a humdinger there for a while. We all thought it was a zit at first, a bad one, but then it grew grotesquely huge and turned into a golf ball with a black dot in the middle of it. She had to have it operated on. Apparently some bug had laid its eggs and was raising a nice little family in there.

Third Eye's real name is Lynnette McDougall, which doesn't suit her at all, and she's twenty-five, quite an old lady compared to most of us. She grew up not far from me and Jimmy Donnell, in Coxsackie, New York. Her dad's a fireman, but when her parents divorced, she and her mom moved down to Virginia to live with an overweight cop who beats up on her mom all the time. Third Eye told me she signed up after 9/11 to get away from them and protect the American Way, but I think the real reason is because she's a lesbian. Or I'm pretty sure she is, since she moves and talks like a guy. Lesbians love the Army.

"Hey," she says, pointing to the spider on my tent pole. "What the fuck is that?"

I glance up at its hairy legs. "That's Fuzzy. He's a present for Macktruck."

She chuckles and shakes her head.

After I've forced down a couple more grease balls, I pull out the snapshot that Iraqi girl gave me and hand it to Third Eye. "You ever seen either of these guys?" Third

Eye guards the prison tents, so she sees more of the detainees than I do.

She glances at it. "How would I know? They all look the same to me. Where'd you get this?"

I tell her about my deal. "Will you keep an eye out for them? This girl's English is amazing—she could be a real help."

"If you want," Third Eye says with a shrug, and hands the photo back. She slides her eyes over to Rickman and DJ, who are listening to our every word, as usual. "Let's go. I need to get washed."

We pick up our rifles and go out together, doing our battle-buddy thing. When we first landed in Kuwait, the command told us that no females could walk to the latrines or anywhere else at night without another female as a battle buddy, and the same rule applies here at Camp Bucca. That's so we can protect each other from getting raped by one of our own fine comrades.

The walk to the latrines is pretty far because we've built them out near the berm, this big sand dune we've bulldozed up around the perimeter of the camp as a security wall. Doesn't anybody in the Army remember what Jesus said about building a house on sand? *And the rain fell, and the floods came, and the winds blew and beat against that house, and it fell, and great was the fall of it.* Security wall, my ass.

"So what's up, glum-face? God piss in your Cheerios again?" Third Eye says as we make our way through the dark. The only light is from the moon. We can't use flashlights because that would make us a target for mortars.

"It's Kormick. He was in a shitty mood today."

"Oh come on. He's not so bad."

"Are you kidding? He picked on me all day."

Third Eye grunts. "You must've pissed him off then. What did you do?"

"I didn't do anything!"

"Sure you did. Come on, Freckles, when're you gonna learn to play along? That's all he wants. Then he'll lay off of you."

I look up at her face, but I can't see it in the dark, 'specially under her helmet. "What do you mean, 'play along?'"

"You know. Listen, you made your choice. You gotta be a bitch or a slut around here, everybody knows that, and since you won't be a bitch with that sunny little Christian act of yours, you've only got one choice left. That's why the men chase you so bad. They all want to get in your pants, Sergeant Movie Star included. But you won't put out, so they're pissed."

"So you're saying I have to sleep with him? Fuck you! Not that I think you're right about that anyhow."

"No. I'm saying you got to make your signals clear, kiddo. If you don't wanna put out, then you need to get a whole lot meaner."

"Like you?"

"Yeah, baby. Like me."

We walk on in silence while I try not to say that the only reason the men don't bother her is because she's an obvious bull-dyke and looks like the back of a garbage truck. Specially with that fucking bump on her forehead. But I don't. I'm a Christian, like she said. I'm supposed to turn the other friggin' cheek. And anyway, maybe she's right. Maybe my signals aren't clear.

Thing is, I try. All day long I try to act like a hard-ass, but it just isn't me. I can't be convincing. I sound like a clueless little country girl trying to act street-tough. And I sound like that because, well, that's what I am.

"You know what you gotta do?" Third Eye says then. "You gotta pick out a boyfriend. That's the only way for somebody like you. One meathead to fend off all the others."

"But I can't stand a single one of them! Anyhow, I'm not going to cheat on Tyler, no way."

"You know what they say about beggars, kiddo. Think about it."

We're at the latrines now, the four Porta-Johns I mentioned, which is all we've built so far for the hundred and seventy-five people in my unit. They smell like you'd expect, so we do our thing quickly and leave, trying not to gag. There aren't any bathrooms to wash in, either. For showers, we dump bottles of water over ourselves—a whore's bath, the guys call it—or once in a while hang up a poncho and get under a portable shower bag. But most of the time we're crusted with desert mud: sand and dust and sweat all mixed up into a fine brown soup and dried by the sun on our skins. Our uniforms get so stiff from sweat-salt and sand that you can stand them up on their own, like an army of ghosts.

Why it has to be like this, I don't know. Isn't the U.S. the richest country in the world? So why the hell do we soldiers have to live like we're in a pigsty? It's worse than when I go camping with Tyler and April, and we're into roughing it, too. No campsites or tents, just sleeping bags on the pine-needle floor and a roll of toilet paper in your pocket. But it's never disgusting like it is here at Bucca.

Me and Tyler love camping so much that we go all year round, even in the snow. But our favorite season for it is the fall, when the leaves are doing their flame dance and the sky's so clear it can't even hide the moon in the middle of the day. We head over to the Catskill Mountains, which are near where we live, and hike long and hard up to the high ground, jays squawking their warnings in the trees. Then we find a patch of soft pine needles and moss, settle in, build a fire and cook dinner: roasted hot dogs and ash-baked potatoes, usually, and if April is with us, marshmallows burned on the outside, gooey in the middle, the way she likes them. After we eat, Tyler plays guitar and sings while I clean up, April curled in her sleeping bag close by, little and lucky, her mouth sticky with sugar.

We wait for her to fall asleep, then Tyler slides into my sleeping bag and we lie there together, cuddled up tight, looking at the stars flickering through the trees and talking softly about whatever comes into our heads. Breathing in each other's words and scents. Silky skin, soft breath. Our cocoon.

By the time I get back to the tent with Third Eye, Macktruck is there, sprawled in his boxers on top of his rack, his blubbery belly out for all to see and a clump of chew stuck in his cheek. Just the sight of him makes me want to puke. A couple weeks ago I asked Sergeant First Class Henley, our platoon leader, to make the slob move, but he refused. "You can handle that yourself, soldier, and if you can't, you should," is all he said. So even though Third Eye's on my right and Yvette Sanchez is over beside her, on my left I've got to put up with this moron sleeping right next to me every single night—which, in our tent, means only two feet away.

"Here comes my wet dream," he calls as I walk in. He's nudged his rack over closer to mine. Again.

"Move. You're in my space." I stand over him with my rifle on my shoulder.

He ignores me. Mack's about thirty-two, hairy as a gorilla's balls and ringed with fat that not even the Bucca bug can shrink. His face is so heavily bearded that even when he's newly shaved it looks blue. Worse, he spits tobacco all day. Nobody likes him, not even Rickman.

"I mean it, fuckface. Move."

He hauls himself up, his gut sagging over his Skivvies, emitting a wave of stale sweat and tobacco. Then he bends over and pulls his rack closer to mine than ever. He puts me through this asinine routine every night while the other guys watch and snigger. His little comedy act.

"I'm gonna puke on you if you don't move away, you stink so bad," I tell him.

"Hey, Macktruck!" Rickman calls from the other side of the tent, laughing. "You gonna let Tits talk to you like that?"

Mack grunts. And then it happens. What I planned. He straightens up and finds himself face-to-face with his worst fear: Fuzzy.

"Fuck!" he yells and staggers back, this terrified look on his face. His rack catches him in the back of his knees and he falls over with a huge thump, his fat legs flying into the air.

Everybody roars. Round one, Kate.

He struggles to his feet, red and spluttering, yanks his rack over to where it belongs and climbs onto it, pretending to laugh. He doesn't look at me.

I pick up my poncho lining and tie it to some strings I've sewn onto the tent ceiling. This is the only wall I've got between me and this creep. I've been putting it up ever since he started whispering obscene suggestions to me on our second night here. Then I lie down, say my usual good-night prayer, pull the sheet I brought from home over me and change into my PTs, the gym shirt and shorts I sleep in because they're easier and cooler than PJs. But how the hell I'm going to get through yet another fire and brimstone of a night I do not know. My head hurts. Stomach hurts. Bladder hurts. It's stiflingly hot and I'm crazy with thirst again, but I can't drink more than one sip of water because if you're a female it's too fucking dangerous to go outside for a piss.

Is Third Eye right? Is it my fault things are like this?

The minute I wake up the next morning, I snatch my water bottle and chug the whole damn thing down. I spent half the night awake, moving the dust around in my mouth, and when I did finally drift off, I dreamed I was swimming in my local lake with my mouth open, drinking my way across. Only, every gulp I took turned to sand.

I shake Third Eye and Yvette awake too, so we can go for our usual run together before leaving for our separate shifts. This is our only chance to get away from all the douches we work with, and our only free moment to actually enjoy ourselves. I think it's the best moment of the day. It is mine, anyhow.

We creep out of the tent still wearing the PTs we slept in, and stretch a little before we get going. The air's cool from the night and the sky's glowing slate blue. The only other people around are a few guys running like us and the poor suckers on shit-burning detail. Since we've got no sewage facilities, they have the delightful job of dragging the barrels out from under the latrines, dousing them with gas and diesel and setting them on fire, then stirring them with a long pole so they can send black clouds of toxic stink over the camp for all of us to breathe in our sleep.

We jog along the dirt road that runs down the middle of the camp, too sleepy to talk yet. I feel my legs stretching and my body turning loose and strong, like it always does when I run. Makes me miss my track days in high school—the days when I still felt sane.

"Did that spider keep Macktruck quiet last night?" Third Eye asks me after a while.

"Not really."

"Y'know, we should teach that mofo a lesson," Yvette says. Yvette's even shorter than me, but she has this husky, loud voice that makes you sit up and pay attention. "You two got any dental floss?"

"*Dental floss?*" Third Eye says. "Why?"

"You'll see."

Yvette always comes up with the best schemes. She's a weird mix of street-tough and gentle. All her life she's bounced from one foster home to another because her mom's a junkie and her dad's out of the picture. A lot of people are like that in my unit, but Yvette's the only one I know who doesn't hate the war. "It got me outta the ghetto," she likes to say. "God bless America." If war's better than where she came from, you know it had to be bad.

I like her, though. She's a dark-skinned Puerto Rican, narrow as a broomstick, with this little old-before-her time face under super-short hair. She can curse the cock off a roach, worse than most of the guys in our unit. But if you treat her right, she's truly generous. More than Third Eye, who I wonder about sometimes.

The dawn breaks while we're running and for a moment the landscape is actually beautiful. Fiery orange streaking the sky. The dust in the air sparkling like powdered rubies. The sand glowing rose.

Sunrises and sunsets are something else out here in the desert. The rest of the time it's hideous.

I scan the sky a moment for birds, an old habit. Me and Tyler were into birds back at home, nerdy as that sounds. In the spring and summer we'd sit on my parent's back deck, right at that moment at dusk when the swallows are tumbling through the sky catching their insect dinners, and look out for birds over the long valley that stretched up to the mountains behind us. We liked to compete over who could identify the most. Every evening, a great blue heron would flop over the fields, like a commuter on his way home from the office, minus the briefcase, but he was too easy for either of us to claim, with his long ragged wings and tail like an arrow. But I was best at catching first sight of the rose-breasted grosbeak in spring, and Tyler was always the first to spot the nervous little nuthatch trying to get at our feeder before the jays and catbirds chased it away.

So I was excited about the birds I'd see in Iraq. I looked them up in a bird book before I came. One is the Eurasian hoopoe, this crazy-looking thing with a woodpecker's back, a dove's head and a sandpiper's beak, topped off by a striped crest like a clown hat. And there are supposed to be larks and ibis, eagles and storks—the kinds of birds you only see in zoos back home, never in the wild. I want so badly to see them! But so far I haven't seen a single one.

Where the hell do birds go in war, anyway? Do they fly away someplace else? Do they hide? Do they catch fire and fall, black and smoking, to the ground? Or do they breathe in the bomb smoke and depleted uranium and burning bodies and oil and shit, like we do, and crawl away somewhere to die?

"HERE, I BROUGHT something for you," the long-haired man says once he's stopped crying. He slides a hand into his jacket pocket.

The soldier starts and shrinks back again on the hospital bed.

"No, no, it's okay." Slowly, he pulls out a little pink box, as shimmery as an Easter egg. He holds it out. "It's from April. She misses you real bad. She says to please get well and come home in time for her birthday. Eight years old, can you believe it? She's growing up so fast."

He puts the box on the bed.

The soldier picks it up carefully, cradling it in her underwater palms. April is good. April is safe.

"Are you going to open it?"

The soldier looks down at the box.

"Katie?" The man leans forward again, his elbows on his knees. "Look at me, please?"

She hesitates. But then she lifts her head and eyes him warily.

"You're home now, remember? The war's gone. You're not with those people anymore. It's over now, you're safe."

The man does have the same soft face as Tyler, the same pleading, cinnamon eyes. Same flop of brown hair over his brow, too. But he's doing something Tyler never would have done.

He's lying.

## [ NAEMA ]

GRANNY MARYAM IS not well. The shock of the soldiers storming into her house and taking Papa and Zaki has affected her mind. She was already bent and shaky, her little head drooping, but at least she was sharp. Now she wanders from past to present and doesn't seem to understand that it was not Saddam's soldiers who seized her beloved grandson and son-in-law, but the Americans. All soldiers are the same to her, whatever their uniforms, whatever their justifications. All are murderers.

Mama and I try to lift her spirits by putting her to bed in the prettiest room in the house, the one she normally saves for guests, which has sweet-smelling rush mats on the floor and blue and red tapestries on its walls. We arrange her favorite cushions under the windows so their bright colors and gold threads can catch the sunbeams filtering through the shutters and send cheering sparkles over the room. And when the heat of the day has baked the house to an inferno, we carry her to the roof, where we can all sleep in the relative cool of the night.

But Granny notices none of these efforts. I take her temperature and blood pressure and feel her pulse, the way I was taught at Medical College—there's nothing wrong with her but old age and heartbreak. Yet she won't eat anything but the thinnest of gruels. She refuses to get up except to visit the outhouse, leaning on Mama's arm, or to sit at the table, bent over her soup bowl, clutching her unused spoon and sighing. She moans and frets and wrings her bony hands, her eyes clouded with hurt and confusion. And she calls again and again for Grandpa, even though he's been dead these twenty years.

I hate to see Granny like this, so changed from the lively and mischievous woman she once was. How Zaki and I loved to visit her when we were small! This little house and her animals; her soft, round body, smelling of the jasmine with which she perfumed her long hair; her secret smile, promising all sorts of forbidden treats once our parents' backs were turned.

Every year on *Eid al-Fitr*, Papa would bundle us into the car—its red paint bright and unscratched then—and drive the nearly five hundred kilometers from Baghdad to here for the holiday. Laden with the cakes and breads Mama had baked and the clumsy gifts Zaki and I had made at school— lopsided clay bowls, usually—we would arrive tired and dusty but salivating in anticipation of breaking the Ramadan fast. And Granny would always be waiting at her door, dressed in the black abaya she has worn since Grandpa was killed, her old face crinkling with joy at the sight of us.

Once we were inside, Zaki and I would wait by the window, counting the seconds until the sun dipped below the horizon. And the minute it did, Granny would bring out her special buttery date balls, spiced with cardamom and anise, which we would gobble until we felt sick. Then she would send us outside to play so the adults could talk among themselves while they prepared the night's feast: perhaps *masgoof*, fish split down the belly and roasted with herbs; or maybe *kibbe*, my favorite, spicy lamb dumplings encased in cracked wheat.

Zaki and I spent hours playing outside in those days. We chased Granny's chickens and collected their eggs. We learned to milk her goats and feed their bony kids, their fur so silky, their tiny bodies wriggling. And we climbed the neighborhood fruit trees to pluck what oranges and dates we could before getting caught, or ran over to play with the grandchildren of kind Abu Mustafa al-Assawi and his wife, who lived next door.

But our favorite times were the warm nights when we slept on the roof with Granny, as Mama and I are doing now. Zaki and I would lie side by side, watching the stars dance above, and ask Granny question after question about her life. Her past was like a history book to us, for she had lived in the old ways, far from the modern life we knew, and she had progressed from misery to happiness just like the heroine of a folktale. She had been married at fourteen to a man old enough to be her father, and for years was terrorized by his blows and the pain and horror of the nights when he came to her bed. She became pregnant before she was fully grown and almost died giving birth to a stillborn baby. But then, after five years of this misery, she was released. Her husband died, poisoned perhaps by his own cruelty, and a year later she was married to my grandfather, a man also older than she but kind and loving. "I wish you had known him, my little pets," she would tell us. "Your mama, how she adored him when she was small! On the days he did not have to work, she would make him sit all morning while she played barber, pretending to cut his hair and shave him, getting soapsuds all over his clothes, just to keep him close to her." Granny would chuckle then and patiently answer more of our questions, or tell us village gossip about the fat tobacco seller and his bullying wife until she had lulled us to sleep. Granny had a salty tongue.

When we grew older, Zaki would tear off for a game of soccer with the village boys while I stayed behind in the kitchen to help Granny cook and listen to more of her stories. I delighted in these times alone with her, rolling those delicious date balls in sesame seeds or sugar while she regaled me with the ancient tales of her village: naughty children eaten by demons, unfaithful husbands cuckolded by traveling merchants, genies rising out of earthenware pots to grant a wish.

I remember once Zaki was feeding a newborn goat just as Granny called us in to supper. He tucked the kid inside his shirt, where it fell asleep, lulled by his warmth, and came in. The kid slept unnoticed through most of the meal, but finally awoke and began to struggle and kick its tiny hooves. We all stared, but Granny did not turn a hair. She regarded the strange jumping and poking inside my brother's shirt and said calmly, "Zaki, it appears you have eaten too much."

All that is gone now. The goats slaughtered for their meat. The fruit trees shredded by American bombs. The boys Zaki played with imprisoned, exiled or killed. And Granny Maryam is too unhappy to joke or tell stories. Just as Mama and I are too unhappy to listen.

# [ KATE ]

**WHEN I GET** back from my run with Yvette and Third
Eye, Mack's still asleep. He always grabs every last second of
shut-eye he can, usually sacrificing a wash to do it—no doubt
why he stinks so bad—but it's just what we want right now.
Yvette winks at us, puts her finger to her lips and quietly
fishes out some dental floss from her duffle bag, gesturing
at us to get ours. Then, quick as a flash, she wraps the floss
around Mack's legs, tying them down to his cot, while we do
the same to his arms, stomach and chest—he sleeps like the
dead. The guys in the tent gather around silently, grinning.
In no time at all, ol' Macktruck is tied up tight as a pork roll.

The next thing Yvette does is pure genius. She points her
rifle at an open flap in the tent, screams "Attack!" And fires.

Mack's eyes fly open in terror and he tries to jump up.
But he can't, of course. The look on his face! He struggles
for a few minutes in such a panic I almost feel sorry for him.
Almost. The rest of us fall around, laughing.

Once the ruckus has died down and we've left the guys to
untie Mack, which they don't do till he's seriously late for his
shift, we females douse off our running sweat with bottled
water, ignoring the shouts of "Wet T-shirt time!" and take

out our T-Rats. Morning is the only time I can really chow down, before the heat and my nerves get too bad—if you can call T-Rations chow. Tubes of green eggs that shake like a fat lady's flab, mushes of unidentifiable—well, mush. I shovel it all in anyway, needing the strength. Then we're off to our squads, and that's the last I'll see of another female till tonight—an American female, that is.

By the time my team arrives at the checkpoint, not only are the usual civilians already there, but I see that girl Naema right away, too. I'm heading over to say hi when Kormick barks, "Brady!" At least he didn't call me Tits or Pinkass.

I turn and trail back to him, the moondust puffing around my boots like talcum powder, wondering what crap he's going to load on me now.

"Take this. See if it calms the hajjis down." He shoves a piece of paper at me, his jaw hard under the blank of his sunglasses. "Now move."

I look at the paper he's given me: a hand-scrawled column of about fifty names. That's it, the promised list? Fuck.

When I get up to the wire, Naema greets me with a cool look. She's standing in front of the crowd this time; I guess the people recognize her as their interpreter now. Her head's wrapped in a lavender headscarf that doesn't look as good on her as the blue one did. It turns her skin sallow and makes the circles under her eyes look like bruises. Or maybe she's just too worried to sleep. I would be, if it was my dad and brother in here.

"*Salaam aleikum*," I say again, and try once more to shake her hand.

She avoids it as coldly as ever, but at least she returns my greeting this time. "*Aleikum salaam.*"

We're wishing each other peace, which, under the circumstances, is pretty ironic.

"They've given me a list of the prisoners today," I tell her. "Or some of them."

Her face brightens up at that. "May I see?" She holds out her hand. I'm not sure it's protocol to actually give her the paper, so I look over my shoulder to see who's watching. DJ's my battle buddy this morning and he's standing nearby, unlike zitface Rickman. I appreciate somebody doing his job for a change, but at the same time I wish he'd back off. He looks so fierce with his M-16 held at the ready, his face hidden under his Kevlar helmet and shades. He looks like the fucking Terminator.

"Give it to me!" Naema snaps, and before I know what's what, she's snatched the list from my hand. "Yes, Zaki is here!" she says, running her eyes over it. "Thank God! But my father, where is his name? I cannot see it."

"It's only a partial list," I answer quickly. "More's coming later." The crowd's pressing around us again, making me jumpy as a rabbit. I hope that woman with the stinky baby doesn't show up again. "Read it out quick," I say. "And tell them to back off."

Naema holds up the list till the people quiet down. Then she reads all the names on it aloud.

Right away some people cry out, while others hang their heads and sob. I'm surrounded by suffering faces so worn and sunbaked and sad that the sight of them makes something crack inside of me. A certainty, perhaps, a sureness that I'm doing the right thing—I don't know. Whatever the hell it is, I feel it break.

The people are clustering around Naema now, shouting

out questions like she's the authority here, not me, which I don't appreciate at all. "They are asking what will happen to the men you have in here," she calls to me over the din.

"We have to process them," I shout back.

She gives me a blank look.

"I mean they've got to be questioned and—I'm sure the ones who are innocent will be freed." What bullshit. I have no fucking idea what we're going to do with the thousands of prisoners we've taken in. I don't think anybody knows. But if they do, they sure as hell aren't telling me.

"And the boys? What about the children you have locked up in here like animals?"

"Same thing," I reply.

Naema unhooks herself from the clutching hands and makes her way back to me. "Kate—you said that is your name, right?"

"Yes."

"Kate, I was at Medical College before the war sent me here. I am not stupid. You must not lie to me. I ask you again: What are you going to do with our men?"

"I'm not lying! I'm just telling you what they told me! I'm a junior enlisted. You know what that means? It means they tell me nothing, I know nothing. I've got no power to help you."

"Yes, this is true. You are nothing," she says calmly.

I know that should make me mad, but all I feel is tired. "Look, the only thing I can do is ask my higher-ups. They might not tell me anything, but I can try."

"And why should I believe you will do this?"

"Because I didn't make this war."

What the hell made me say that? I look around quickly, but if DJ heard he doesn't let on. I could be court-martialed and thrown in the brig my whole goddamn life for saying something like that to an Iraqi.

Naema gazes at me with her strange green-gold eyes. "You look very young to be a soldier," she says then.

That surprises me. "Well, I'm nineteen. But a lot of us are young."

"But why are you a soldier? Why, as a woman, did you choose such a path? Soldiers take life. Women give life."

I can't answer that. I don't even know what to think of it. "In my country, a lot of people have to be soldiers to pay to go to college," I say lamely. "Women and men. And we want to serve our country, too, you know? Um, did you say you're in medical school?"

"I am. In my fourth year."

"Wow, I didn't know you could do that here." It's true. I thought Iraqi girls weren't allowed to do anything except get married.

Naema looks almost amused. The whole time we've been talking, she's been standing tall and proud, her back straight, her gaze clear and hard. I feel like a hunchback next to her, dirty and sandy and loaded down with my sixty pounds of soldier's gear.

"Do you know nothing of my country?" she says then. "I come from Baghdad. My father is a professor of engineering and a poet, my mother is an ophthalmologist—or they were until your war took away their jobs. What do you think, that we are all goatherds?"

"No, I didn't mean that. Sorry." I try on a grin, but it only makes me feel more of an idiot than ever. "My mother's in medicine, too," I add, groping for some way to make this conversation go better. "Well, she's a medical secretary, anyhow. She works for an obstetrician. And my dad's a sheriff. You know, a policeman?"

"I see."

What the hell is that supposed to mean?

"You know what my brother, Zaki, wants to be?" Naema says then, her voice a little more gentle. "He wants to be a singer, like your Bruce Springsteen. He plays his guitar day and night. It drives us all crazy."

Iraqis know about The Boss? I try to hide my astonishment. "My fiancé plays guitar too," I say. And for a second there, we almost smile at each other.

"Brady, Sar'nt just radioed," DJ calls out, startling me. "Says we gotta get these hajjis to leave." I wish he wouldn't use that word in front of Naema. "He says this is a security risk." DJ raises his rifle in the air and waves it around, trying to shoo the locals away. I wish he wouldn't do that, either.

Most of the civilians duck and back off. But a few just stand there looking puzzled.

"DJ, quit that!" I say quickly. "You're gonna cause a panic. This girl here speaks perfect English. She can tell them to go, okay?"

DJ looks at Naema curiously, but she ignores him, keeping her eyes on me. "You will have another list soon?" she asks.

"Yeah, I'm sure we will. Tell these people they can come back tomorrow, but they've got to leave now."

She hesitates, frowning, like she wants to ask more. But DJ's glaring at her now with both hands on his rifle, so she steps away and says something to an old man in front of her. He repeats it to the people behind him, and soon a murmur ripples over the crowd. One by one, they turn and plod away across the desert, Naema with them.

"See you tomorrow!" I call after her. She doesn't respond.

"Don't say 'hajji' in front of them like that," I say to DJ once she's gone. "It's not respectful."

He raises his eyebrows. "And I suppose it was respectful when those motherfuckers blew up Jones and Harman last week? Jesus Christ, Brady, whose fuckin' side are you on?"

After Naema and the other civilians leave, things stay quiet for the next hour or so. Quiet enough, at least, to let me block out the sandpit and all the shit in it and float back into my memories. Tyler. Camping. The mountains. Sex. Only one car drives up the whole time, the usual rattletrap, this one driven by a little old man with no passengers. He speaks enough English to tell us that he owns a jewelry store in Basra and is trying to get to his family over the border in Kuwait. We search his car and find nothing but a bag of cheap silver rings, then send him on his way, although none of us thinks he has any more chance of getting over the border than we have of waking up in Oz.

After that, I stare out at spindly little Marvin, trying to trick myself into thinking that this eyeball-shriveling heat is nothing but a hot summer's day back at home. It's hard to believe in this hellhole, but I used to actually love the summers. Being alone in the fields behind our house. Flowers. Cows. Thoughts. Lying in the grass watching birds or reading a book.

The best summer of my life, though, was my first one with Tyler, the one after eleventh grade. He wasn't any more experienced than me at being a couple, so we were high on everything about it. Waking up in the morning and remembering there was no school, but that we didn't have to feel lonely anyway because we had each other. Lying under the warm stars, telling each other our secrets. Having a best friend you could kiss. Losing our virginity together in a field on a steamy July night full of fireflies and mosquitoes.

I remember one time we went down to Myosotis Lake to watch the sunset with a bottle of tequila, because that was the most romantic thing to do around Willowglen. We sat on top of a picnic table, drinking and watching the gulls fly over the lake. The sun was already low in the sky, the air still and windless, so the water lay flat and silent as a sheet of silver, reflecting the rose and salmon pinks of the sunset without even a ripple. Then we heard a splash and a strange munching sound. "Let's go look," Tyler mouthed, and he put down the tequila bottle and slid off the table.

We crept toward the noise, which was coming from a bank of weeds by the water. And there, under a fallen willow, we saw a beaver chomping on a branch like a hungry old man gobbling his dinner. We watched a long time, trying not to make a sound because beaver are shy. But the critter was slurping so greedily it made me giggle. Then Tyler caught the giggles too and we both spluttered into laughter, scaring the beaver into the water with a loud slap of his tail—loud as my M-16. In an instant he was gone.

We watched the glassy surface above him break into ripples, spreading its watery sunset into wider and wider circles. "Let's go in with him," Tyler whispered, and he turned and kissed me, peeling off my shorts, then my shirt and underwear, till I felt the warm, silky air of the summer night kissing me just like he was. He took off his clothes, too, and holding hands we stepped into the brilliant pink water and slid out after the beaver.

We swam quiet as we could for a while, just listening to the night sounds: peepers echoing in the woods, an owl hooting. The sky darkened, turning the water from pink to purple. The fat moon stretched its shadows across the banks. Without needing to speak, we swam up to each other and Tyler pulled me to him, skin warm and satiny. And then there was no difference between his flesh and mine, our bodies and the lake, our breath and the night.

"Hey, Freckles."

I blink and look around. It's DJ. "I been calling you for five minutes. You asleep on your feet or something?"

"What is it?"

"Sar'nt wants to see you."

"Why?"

"Fuck if I know. He says to go over there now."

"You coming?" I ask hopefully.

"Nope. I gotta stay here."

"Sure?"

DJ nods. He's seen the way Kormick's been picking on me lately—he understands. "I'm sorry, Freckles. Wish I could, but you know."

"Yeah, okay. Damn."

Kormick's standing outside this time, his chest puffed out and his chin cocked high. "Brady, new orders have come down," he barks soon as I come up to him. "You and Teach are rotating to guard duty—you'll be assigned to a new team. We're bringing in Third Eye to search the hajji bitches instead."

"Oh. All right." I don't bother to ask why we're being switched like this because there never seems to be a reason for anything in the Army, although I suspect it might be 'cause they don't like me getting friendly with Naema. But this is good news for me. It means I still get to work with Jimmy Donnell, the only truly nice guy in my squad, and it gets me away from two dickwits at once, Kormick and Boner.

"So this is your final day with us, Brady," Kormick goes on. "I'm sure you're heartbroken. Come in here, I got more instructions."

Something in his tone doesn't sound right. A shiver runs through me.

"I need to get back," I say quickly and take a step away from him. "DJ's alone out there. Can't leave my battle buddy by himself, right, Sar'nt?" I try on a grin.

But Kormick isn't having any of it. "Didn't you hear me, soldier? I said come with me." His jaw's jutting out and his teeth are clenched, but I can't see his eyes because they're hidden behind mirrored sunglasses. Sand glitters in the blond stubble on his perfect chin. He's always on edge, but I've never seen him on edge as this.

I look around to see who else is nearby. Boner's standing guard by the shack door, as usual, staring into space, flies buzzing around his numbskull head. The rest of my squad are out by the checkpoint.

"I'm real sorry, Sergeant, but I promised DJ I'd be right back," I say then, my nerves tightening. "I'll check in with you later." I turn to get out of there but Kormick grabs my arm and yanks me around to face him.

"Where the fuck do you think you're going? Didn't any-body tell you back in soldier school that you gotta do what your sergeant says, Pinkass? Huh?" And still holding my arm, he drags me toward the shack.

Now I'm really scared. Again, I look over my shoulder for help, but Jimmy and Rickman are still facing away from me and DJ's searching a truck out on the road. None of them can see me. None of them can hear me, either.

Kormick pulls me up to the shack, making me stumble. "Boner!" he barks.

Boner snaps out of his trance with a start. When he sees Kormick gripping my arm with that weird clench to his jaw, he looks scared, too.

"Want a little fun?" Kormick says to him.

"What?"

"Boner!" Kormick's even angrier now. "Come on, you know what I mean. Do it!"

"Uh, okay, Sar'nt. If you say so."

Boner steps up to me, looking embarrassed, but he reaches out anyway, aiming right at my boob. But just before he touches me, I hear this roaring sound in my head and the next thing I know I've wrenched my arm out of Kormick's grip and I'm pointing my rifle right at his crotch. "Touch me and I'll shoot your fucking balls off!" I shout.

Kormick looks mildly surprised, then throws his head back with a laugh. Boner just stands there, his jaw dangling.

"Whoa, the bitch really can't take a joke," Kormick splutters, still laughing. It isn't real laughter, though. "Put that fucking thing down or I'll slap you with an Article 91," he says to me more seriously, although he's still pretending to chuckle. "Insubordinate conduct toward an NCO. Not to mention threatening me with a weapon, tut-tut. That can get you in serious trouble, Tits, didn't you know that?"

I back up, rifle still pointing at his crotch, my eyes locked on his.

For a second, everything's still. Then something comes flying at me from the side and slams into my right breast so hard it knocks away my breath. I double over, dropping my rifle and gasping, the pain tearing into my chest. I feel myself being picked up, flung into the shack and thrown facedown on the table. I kick out hard as I can, struggle and struggle, but huge hands are gripping my neck, pressing into my trachea, the fingers squeezing so deep I can't move, can't breathe. All I can do is taste my own spit and blood.

And then I'm not me anymore. I'm a wing. One ragged blue wing, zigzagging torn and crooked across the long, black sky.

"THERE, BABY, LET me just plump your pillow for you. Isn't that easier on your poor back, huh? Now take your pills and go to sleep. It's time for this overworked nurse to get her butt home."

The nurse hands the soldier her nightly paper cup full of pills.

The soldier pulls herself upright and peers into it, picking them out one by one. An orange one to numb her messed-up back. A yellow one so she doesn't get sad. A pink one so she can fall asleep and have fun dreaming about screaming and blood. Two blue ones so she doesn't know what's hurting so much inside of her that she can hardly get from one breath to the next. And a white one—she thinks that's to stop her pissing the bed.

She swallows them all.

The room is dark now; it must be late. The nurse changes the TV channel from its usual giant, ticking clock face to some sitcom, but the minute she's gone the soldier gropes for the remote to turn it off. She keeps telling the nurse she can't handle TV, the fast-moving lights, the noise. The news. She keeps telling her. The nurse, who is kind but on automatic pilot, keeps forgetting.

The soldier lies back down in the quiet darkness, waiting for the pills to take her away again. She doesn't like it when her body empties of them and her mind begins to clear because that's when the memories come. She'd take pills all day to avoid that.

In her hand she holds April's little pink box, still shimmering like an Easter egg, but she's afraid to open it. She's afraid the innocence inside will fly out forever.

# [ KATE ]

I'M ALONE IN the shack when I come to. Crouched on the floor in a corner, knees to my chest, back up against the wall.

There seems to be somebody else's rifle in my hands. It seems to be pointing at the door.

I have no idea why I'm alone like this, or who pulled Kormick off of me just in time. All I know is the next son of a bitch who puts his head around that door is getting it blown to pieces.

The wind is moaning through cracks in the plank walls, pushing the moondust in a wave along the ground. But when it dies down a moment I hear angry male voices outside shouting, and it sets me to shaking so hard I need to rest the rifle on my knees. Then the wind rises again, drowning out all but its lonesome whistle. But the shaking won't stop.

A knock.

I jump. "Get the fuck away or I'll shoot!" My voice comes out a rasp.

"It's Jimmy Donnell. Let me in."

"I said get away!"

"Kate, I'm going to open the door now. Don't shoot. I'm coming in."

The sand edges across the floor. The wind groans. I stare at the door, heart kicking against my ribs.

The door creaks open slowly. Lifting the rifle to my shoulder, I squint through its sights. My bullets could go right through that flimsy plywood. I don't even need to see my target.

"If anybody's with you, I'm firing!" My voice is still a croak.

"No, I'm by myself, I promise." Jimmy eases his head inside. "Can I come in?"

"Swear you're alone?"

"I swear."

He steps through the door and closes it behind him without turning, watching me the whole time. I focus on his face through the crosshairs. His nose is bleeding, upper lip cut. And his glasses are cracked right across the left lens.

I lower my rifle to my knees. "What happened to you?"

"Me and Kormick had a scuffle. I saw from the tower, saw him . . . did he hurt you?"

"Where is he?"

"He's gone. Boner too. Took off in the Humvee."

I pause while this sinks in. "Boner's the one who punched me, isn't he?"

"Yeah." Jimmy looks at me, his face tight. "The fucker should be shot. It's you he should've protected, not Kormick."

"Is this Kormick's rifle?" I nod at the weapon in my hands.

"Yup. He left it here when I dragged him out. I think he's got yours."

Jimmy hasn't moved. He's still standing with his back against the door, holding it closed behind him.

"They're gonna throw you in the brig for fighting an NCO like that," I say then, each word a scrape in my throat. "I'm sorry."

"*You're* sorry?" Jimmy looks at me strangely. "Don't worry about it. If that shithead reports me, I report him. Me and DJ both. He knows what we saw."

"Did you see me point my weapon at his balls? He could get me for that."

"He wouldn't dare. It's you I'm worried about. Are you okay?"

I place the rifle butt on the ground by my foot, its barrel pointed at the ceiling. I don't want to stand up because the seat of my pants is torn wide open, I hurt all over, and because I'm trying not to cry. "I'm fine."

Jimmy steps toward me. I shrink back. "I said I'm fine."

He stops. "All right." He takes a deep breath. "Listen, we need to get out of here. You think you can get up? You're driving back with my team, don't worry. Here." He takes off his blouse and hands it to me. It's damp and smells of his sweat but I put it on over mine anyway because it's long enough to cover the tear in my pants. Then I pull my flak jacket over it so nobody can see Jimmy's name tag.

"You need help standing?" he says then.

I shake my head and drag myself to my feet, nauseated and dizzy, a sharp pain shooting again through my breast where Boner punched me. Jimmy turns and walks out of the shack. Moving stiff and slow, I follow him.

His team's waiting in their Humvee right there, all guys I know well enough to kid around with, but not as friends.

Jimmy walks me over, close but not touching, while I concentrate on staying upright, one step at a time. My ears are ringing like I'm about to pass out and my legs feel like Jell-O. Next thing I know, I'm doubled over and puking.

Jimmy stands between me and the Humvee, trying to hide me. When I'm all emptied out, he guides me over, although I still won't let him touch me. We crawl into the back. The men inside stare at us—me dressed in Jimmy's uniform shirt, disheveled and splattered with puke; Jimmy with his smashed glasses, bloody nose and lip. I can smell their curiosity filling the car like a gas. None of them speaks, though.

I look down at my hands. They're still shaking.

Once the driver drops us off at the tents, Jimmy walks me to mine—he sleeps in a different one down the row. "You going to be all right?" he asks quietly. We both know the tents have ears.

I swallow, tasting blood and acid. Then I take my scarf, the one I use to filter out the moondust so I can breathe, and wrap it around my neck to hide the fingerprints.

"Everyone's going to know about this, aren't they?" I croak.

"Probably. But not from me. Listen, if either of those fuckers or anybody else gives you any more trouble, you tell me. Promise? And if you want to report them or anything, I'll back you up."

I turn away, Kormick's rifle up against my chest like a shield. I don't want a protector, I don't want a fuss and I don't want to look like an even bigger loser than I already am. I want to look after myself. I am a soldier, after all.

Nobody greets me when I step into the tent. The teams are all back by now, the guys sitting on their racks, chewing on tobacco or MREs. Third Eye and Yvette are there, too, doing the same. I can feel every one of them stare at me as I walk past. Feel them taking in Jimmy's blouse hanging down to my knees, the scarf around my neck. I freeze my face so it won't show anything.

Sitting on my rack, I drag my duffle bag from under it and fish out my spare pants and mending kit. Macktruck snorts and rolls over on his side to face me, hairy gut hanging, his chew making a bulge in one blue cheek. "Where you been, party girl?"

I shake out a needle from its little metal coffin and try to thread it. I can't even get close. My hands are quivering too bad. I want to poke that needle right in Mack's eye.

Nobody else speaks to me for the rest of the night. Nobody at all.

# [ NAEMA ]

WE ARE IN a painful time of suspension, Granny, Mama and I. Our manless house has grown oddly still, as if the very walls know we are waiting. Nothing we do seems to matter—eat, drink, work, talk. We are unable to take pleasure in anything in the face of our fears for Papa and Zaki.

The news that Zaki is on the prison list does little to comfort us, for we do not know what it means. If it means that Zaki is alive, that, of course, is good. But what, then, does it mean that Papa is not on the list? Is it better to be on the list or no? We have no idea.

We try to alleviate our worries by making plans. "When your father and brother are freed, *inshallah*, we must leave this place," Mama says to me in the kitchen, where we are gathered to sew and clean. "I'm afraid a former colleague or neighbor, someone jealous of your father's position, perhaps, must have given his name to the Americans. Why else would they arrest him? I don't think your father will be safe if he returns here."

I nod in agreement. We are only too familiar with betrayal by friends and colleagues, with spying and denouncements, rivalry and revenge. We have been living with this corruptive poison for decades. It is what keeps the powerful secure.

"But where will we go?" I ask. "And we have to take Granny with us. She's too sick to leave alone."

Granny shakes her head, her worn face stubborn beneath her heap of white hair. She is feeling better today, her mind restored to the present, at least for the time being, so has risen from bed to sit with us at the table, where she is sewing a torn and faded blouse with her quivering hands in the hope of making it last. "I will never leave my home," she declares, her voice tremulous. "Umm Kareem left her house and immediately strangers moved in and took it over. In this war, everyone is a thief."

"But Mother, it's not safe to stay," Mama says. "Now that Halim's been arrested, we can trust no one, not even your neighbors."

"Bah!" Granny exclaims, waving her old blouse for emphasis. "I refuse to believe it. These people are good and honest, especially dear Abu Mustafa and Huda next door. We've helped each other survive for years. No, this can't be true."

Mama lays a hand on Granny's arm. "Don't distress yourself, Mother. Perhaps we're wrong about the neighbors, perhaps it was one of Halim's colleagues who denounced him. We're only guessing. What else can we do when we know nothing?"

"But where will we go?" I ask again. "And how are we to get across the border? Widow Fatima told me the Americans are blocking or arresting anyone who tries to leave."

Mama walks across the room to gaze through a small window into the courtyard where Granny keeps her few scrawny chickens. "Your father has cousins in Jordan.

They've offered to help us before. When he's released, I'm sure he'll know what to do."

Yes, we talk like that. *When* Papa and Zaki are released, not *if*. Never *if*.

"I'll ask Fatima for her advice tomorrow," I say, for I am still set on going to the prison every morning. "She's been through so much, she might know where we can go."

Mama turns from the window to face me, her dark eyes grave. "Be careful what you tell her, my love. Remember, trust no one, not even a friend who seems kind."

After that, we return to our tasks. Granny bends over her sewing. Mama puts the lentils in to soak and feeds the chickens pecking in the yard. I sweep the dust from the carpets and floors, then go to what is left of the local market for the few supplies that are available. Later, I will take a ration of the flour and sugar we brought with us from Baghdad to give to the village baker so she can bake for us our daily *samoon*, the flatbread which is all we have now to make bearable our wartime diet of watery soup and goat yogurt.

All the while I work, though, I harbor secret plans. Once Papa and Zaki are home, I will not leave Iraq with them, whatever Mama says. I will go back to Baghdad, to my fiancé, Khalil, and to medical school, for I am determined to qualify as a doctor and make something of my life.

I call Khalil my fiancé, but in truth, matters between us are too uncertain for that to be entirely accurate. He is my closest friend, and I love him and yearn for him every moment here in our exile, but we are not yet officially engaged.

We met during our second year at Medical College, for we are the same age and at the same level of schooling. As soon as I saw him, my heart began to leap about in my chest like that little goat under Zaki's shirt. His fine dark eyes, curly black hair, sturdy shoulders, these pulled me to him as the moon pulls the tides. And when I saw him looking at me, I knew he felt the same.

We began to talk whenever we could without attracting attention—between classes, on our way to lectures—sidling up to each other shyly, clutching our books to our chests in excitement. Every day I awoke with a surge of pleasure at the idea of seeing him, and every evening I stared dreamily at my books, as foolish as any girl in love. We were awkward and slow, but I knew Khalil was a good man, a man who would not hurt or betray me.

The first time he kissed me was on my roof at night, my family safely out of sight inside the house. This was before the war, so we were not too afraid of bombs to be out after dark. Khalil looked about to make sure we were seen by nobody but the stars, then took my chin in his hand, his gentle eyes asking permission. His lips were so warm, little pillows of tenderness.

After nearly two years of courtship, just before I fled Baghdad, we were again on my roof, gazing sadly at the ruins of our poor city, when he asked me to marry him. "I have a dream about our future, my love," he said. "I want us to be doctors together and set up a joint practice. And when, *inshallah*, the bombs and looting are over, I want us to open our own clinic. Look around, Naema." He swept his arm over the bloodstained rubble below us. "Think of the wounded and sick who will need our help. Think of the good we can do."

The generosity of his vision moved me, as did his eagerness to include me in it. But I also felt afraid. Yes, Khalil is kind and intelligent, and yes, I love his warm eyes and kisses, his devotion to his career and belief in mine. And our parents approve of us, so there would be no objection from them. But I am wary of the yoke of marriage and all the expectations that go with it. I love Khalil, but I do not love the idea of being a wife and am not ready for children. I am only twenty-two. Like Zaki, I have most of my life ahead of me, and, like him, I have my own ideas for my future.

So I did not give Khalil the reply he expected. "Khalil," I said, "I love you and I'm grateful for your proposal. But I need to wait. I need first to follow my own dreams."

My own dreams, yes. This is how they go: When the war is finally over and we are truly liberated from Saddam and his murderous sons, God willing, as well from the Americans and their armies of thugs, I will travel to London and Paris, to Istanbul and Rome, and there I will add more languages to my English and more skills to my medical practice so I can gain the tools with which to help my country. Then and only then will I be ready to return home, be married and open a clinic with Khalil. That is, if the war spares us both.

I know my dreams would probably seem absurdly romantic to an outsider—to anyone who does not understand what we have suffered in Iraq. That girl soldier, Kate, for example, no doubt would find them foolish. Or perhaps the very idea of an Iraqi with dreams would be too foreign for her even to entertain. After all, don't Americans like her consider us all "insurgents" now, primitive Islamists and terrorists—the sort of creatures who are not allowed dreams?

But no, I would say to her—for I would need to argue—nobody can live in Iraq and not dream of a better future.

All my life, I have watched one force after another crush my homeland. Our war with Iran started two years after I was born and lasted until I was ten. The ruthless deprivation that followed—imposed by your fellow Americans, soldier Kate, and their Western friends under the name of "sanctions"—ate at our infrastructure, our middle class, our schools and hospitals the way termites eat at a house until it collapses. The Kuwait war, which began when I was twelve, slaughtered hundreds of thousands of our people—again with your weapons. Saddam also used your weapons and your support to torture and murder us for decades. And now, Miss Kate, you bring us this new war, repeating the same lies as your predecessors, promising freedom only to bring occupation and terror, pushing us into poverty and illness, ignorance and hatred, and opening the way for violent fanatics to seize control and rule us.

What else do I have, oh comfortable, blind and selfish American? What else could any Iraqi have but dreams?

# PART TWO

# TOWER

## [ KATE ]

THE FIRST MORNING of my new job, Jimmy comes right to the entrance of my tent to pick me up. He pretends he's just here to take back his blouse, but I know he's really trying to protect me and I don't like it any better than I did last night. I don't want him escorting me to the Humvee like a prisoner, and I don't want him causing a lot of gossip, either. I want to walk around free, prove that no shitbag on earth, not Kormick, not Boner—not the whole frickin' Army—can stop me from being a soldier.

It isn't even dawn by the time I clamber into the Humvee with my new team, so other than saying hi, nobody's awake enough to feel like talking, thank God. But I lean my head back and pretend to sleep in case they try. My scarf's still around my neck to cover the bruises, the sweat gathering underneath it. My right boob throbs, and my throat feels so crushed and raw it hurts even to turn my head. As for the rest of me—my soul or whatever you want to call it—that's still flapping away in the sky.

My new team consists of three guys and me: Jimmy, who's been promoted to E5 sergeant and team leader. Our driver, a big muscled blond called Ned Creeley, with a button-nosed face that makes him look fourteen. And Tony Mosca, a.k.a. Mosquito, a hairy little Italian from New Jersey with twinkly brown eyes and a mouth as filthy as Yvette's. I know they must have heard about last night—me covered in puke and Jimmy in blood—but nobody says anything. It might be tact, embarrassment or just laziness, I don't know, but it's fine with me. Far as I'm concerned, it never fucking happened at all.

Our assignment is to guard a prison compound near the rear of the camp. A compound is what we call a block of forty or so rectangular tents, lined up in rows to make a square. Each tent is twelve feet long and holds about twenty-two prisoners. And each compound is surrounded by a corral of sand and a fence made of three giant coils of razor wire stacked in a pyramid, two on the bottom and one on top. Typically, one soldier guards each side of the block, either on the ground or in a guard tower, while a few extra, like Jimmy, are stationed at the entrance.

My post turns out to be a tower on the west side, so after button-nose Creeley drops me off, I climb up its ladder to look around. The tower's about as high as a streetlight, just a platform on a wobbly scaffold made of plywood and two-by-fours, with a flat roof no bigger than a beach umbrella. I'm only ten feet away from the rolls of wire, so the prisoners can come up pretty close if they want. But not another soldier's in sight.

This is what I have with me for the job: My rifle. Two MREs. Three one-liter bottles of water. A pack of cigarettes. A walkie-talkie that crackles but doesn't work. A radio that doesn't work either. A chair. And a headache.

I play with the walkie-talkie a while to see if I can get it to do something, but it really is a piece of crap. It looks exactly like the toy one Tyler gave April for her seventh birthday, except that one worked better than this. We let her bring it once when she came camping with us, and we had a lot of fun hiding in the woods where we couldn't see each other and being able to talk anyhow. When she lost hers and cried, because in our family that would have got her spanked, Tyler crouched down beside her and said, "Hey there, everybody loses things sometimes. I'll get you another. So no April showers, okay?"

"I hate that joke," April said between sobs, but she was smiling a little, too.

Tyler's often kind like that. His whole family is. His mom and dad take things easy, like he did with the lost walkie-talkie, even though they've got five kids and not much money. They could hardly be more different from my parents. Dad runs us like we're part of his sheriff's department. Rules here, rules there—not just about saying grace before we talk and locking the gun in the sideboard, but all day long. He even puts lists of our daily schedules up on the fridge. I think he'd make April and me call him "sir" if Mom let him. He likes posting mottos around the house, too. *Take responsibility for your actions. Don't blame others for your mistakes. If you dig your own grave, you must lie in it.*

Guess that's what I've done. Dug my own grave.

It only takes the prisoners about ten minutes to realize that their new guard is a female. At first they ignore me and wander around in their man-dresses, some of them in head rags, most not, smoking the cheap cigarettes we give them for free and kicking the bits of dried shrub that grow out of the sand. But when one of them comes up close enough to see my face, all hell breaks loose. He laughs and beckons some others over. They point. They jeer. They gesture at me over and over to take off my helmet and show them my hair. And then one guy swaggers up, pulls out his dick and jerks off right in front of me.

And this is just my first hour.

I'm shocked and disgusted, but I'm not about to show it. I look away, glad my eyes are hidden behind my shades, chew my gum and try to act like he and the other men are no more important to me than ants. All right, I tell myself, this must be a test from God, having to endure one piece of crap after another like this. I'll handle it, pray when I need to, suck it up like the soldier I am. Anyhow, I don't really blame the prisoners for being angry. I mean, look at the poor fuckers, stuck in overcrowded, stinking hot tents for reasons they probably don't understand. I know most of them are innocent because we've been told as much. Some are criminals who escaped in the war—you can tell which ones are thieves because they have a hand cut off. A lot are Saddam's soldiers who deserted soon as the war began and turned themselves in to us, skinny and ragged and desperate for food and protection. Some are real bad guys, of course, Saddam loyalists or insurgents. But most are just ordinary people who got caught by mistake. Like Naema's little brother—perhaps.

So I try to be Jesus-like and forgiving about it, the way Mom and Father Slattery would want. *Remember those who are in prison, as though in prison with them*—isn't that how the verse in Hebrews goes? It isn't me they hate, I tell myself, it's what I represent. The power behind those bombs, the foreigners who arrested them and put those hoods on their heads. And from what I've heard, all Arab men think Western women are whores anyhow.

These are the things I think about during my first few hours as a prison guard, sitting up here on my tower in a fold-up metal chair, cooking in the heat like an egg on a skillet. These, and how much I long for Tyler, for his soft singing, his eyes so full of love—for the days when I could trust people. The one thing I don't let myself think about is what happened with Kormick.

"Kate?" A voice floats up from the ground.

I peer over the edge of my platform. Jimmy's looking up at me from behind a new pair of prescription shades. They suit him a lot better than his basic combat glasses—a.k.a. BCGs. Those make you so ugly we call them Birth Control Glasses, 'cause no one will sleep with you when you're wearing them. "What're you doing here?" I call down to him.

"I got a break. There's a bunch of HHC guys working the entrance with me and we're spelling each other." He holds out a paper cup. "Ice. Can I come up?"

Ice is like gold around here, so I tell him he's more than welcome. Slinging his rifle strap over his shoulder, he climbs the ladder and offers me the cup.

"All for me?" I'm still croaking, throat raw and sore.

"No way, we're sharing." He looks at me with concern. "You sound terrible—sure you're okay?"

"Yup. Don't worry about it." We dig out an ice chip each and stand there sucking it in bliss, staring out at the sand. Ice chips in the desert: the best ice cream in the world. It helps my throat feel a little better, too.

"Can I ask you something?" Jimmy says then. He has this soothing voice, low and calm. Perhaps that's why I'm letting him talk to me.

"Depends."

"Well, no pressure, but I was wondering—now you've had time to sleep on it, are you going to report Kormick?"

I keep my gaze on the sand. "Why would I want to do that? To win myself more friends?"

"Well, in case, you know, he tries to hurt somebody else." Jimmy sounds embarrassed, but he forges ahead anyhow. "I meant it when I said I'll back you up if you do. So will DJ. We talked about it. That shitbag should be thrown in the brig, have his big-ass career ended. Boner, too."

"What did DJ have to do with it?"

"He took care of Boner while I was busy with Kormick."

I shake my head. If Jimmy or DJ stick their necks out for me like this, their careers will be fucked. I can't ask them to do that. And if I report Kormick, he'll only make my life even more fun-and-games than it already is. Anyhow, it isn't like he actually raped me, only tried to, so what's there to report? That he attacked me and I failed to be a soldier and fight him off? No, anything I say will only make me sound like one of those whiny pussies all the guys think we females are anyway.

"I'll think about it," I tell Jimmy finally.

"You're pretty tough, aren't you? Were you always like this?"

"Who, me?" I look at him in surprise. He's smiling at me teasingly. "No way. I was little Miss Innocent at home. Served the pie at church picnics. You know the type."

"You weren't so innocent. You had that boyfriend you told me about."

"I *have* that boyfriend. Fiancé, in fact."

We fish out another ice chip each.

"What about you?" I say then, happy to keep off the topic of Kormick. "You got anyone waiting for you at home?"

The age-old question. The stuff soldiers have been talking about since war was invented.

"Nope," Jimmy says, looking away from me. "I had this girlfriend, but when she found out I was coming here . . . well, you know."

"You mean she dumped you? What happened to standing by your man while he serves his country and all that shit?"

He shrugs.

"Well, that sucks. Sounds like she didn't deserve you. You'll find someone better. You've got plenty of time."

He glances at me, then gazes over the concertina wire at the prisoners.

"We're in a war, Kate. What fucking time?"

On my second morning of guard duty I get up even earlier than usual, determined to fit in a run. My throat's still bruised and aching but at least my boob feels a little better. If I put on my tightest sports bra, I think I can run without it hurting too much. But the idea of being trapped up in my tower, facing another long day of masturbating perverts without even having had my precious morning exercise is more than I can stand.

Third Eye won't come, which surprises me. She just rolls over, growls, "Leave me the fuck alone," and goes back to sleep. But Yvette's ready. I'm still pissed at both of them for not speaking to me the night after Kormick, but since I can't go running by myself—too dangerous and against the rules—I appreciate her company, at least.

The air feels thicker than usual, even though the sun hasn't risen yet, and a light wind's already stirring up the moondust, making it hard to breathe. "Looks like we're in for another frickin' sandstorm," I say while we jog down the road.

"Shit. It'll suck to have to drive in this." Yvette's been going out on convoys for weeks now, often at night, which is way more dangerous than anything I have to do. Her MOS is convoy security, which means she rides in the passenger seat of a convoy truck with her weapon out the window, scanning the desert for danger. I'm still a fob-goblin, a soldier who's never left base.

We run in silence for a time, sinking into the rhythm of it. The sand road's a pretty good running track as long as you keep your eye out for stones, but one step off it into the soft stuff on either side can twist your ankle in a flash. Ahead of us the road stretches straight as a plank till it disappears in a haze. I swear the Iraq desert must be the flattest damn place on the planet.

"You okay?" Yvette says after a while, her voice strained. "I heard some shit went down the other day."

"What did you hear?"

"Oh, the usual BS. Fuck, this moondust's hard to breathe." We run for a while without saying anything.

"Well?" she says eventually. "You ain't answered me yet."

"Oh. Yeah, I'm okay thanks."

"You sure? Your voice sounds funny."

"It's nothing. Just a sore throat."

"Is that why you're wearing a scarf in one hundred and forty-fucking degree weather?"

"Yep."

She eyes me skeptically. "If you say so. But talk to me anytime you need to, all right, babe? I mean it."

I glance over at her bony little face and for a moment I feel a flash of love for her. Or maybe it's just abject gratitude. She knows something happened to me and she's acknowledged it, which is more than anyone else in my frigging unit has done, aside from Jimmy. We never confide how we really feel—we're much too busy keeping up a front. Specially Third Eye, with that tough-guy act of hers. Some days it seems like all we do is brag, tease or lie to each other. Whatever happened to the band of brothers and sisters we're supposed to be at war, I don't know. In my company we're more like a band of snakes.

By the time we get back to the tent, the horizon's turned a dark streaky orange and the air's clogged with dust. I rinse off with a bottle shower the best I can, although it only makes the dust stick to me worse than ever, then go inside to change into my uniform. Third Eye's sitting on her rack giving me the strangest look. "What's the matter with you?" I say, squeezing my hair carefully with a towel. I have to be careful since so much of it's been falling out lately. "You're looking at me like I turned green or something."

"You been to the crapper yet?"

"What kind of a question is that?"

"You better go look. Come on, I'll go with you." She has this heavily serious expression on her face, so I guess she isn't kidding, although you can never be sure with Third Eye.

"Okay. Whatever."

I slip into my fart sack to change (no need to give the guys any more eye candy than they take already), pick up my gear and trudge out after her, the men following our asses with their eyes, like always. She doesn't say anything more.

When we get to the Porta-Johns, panting from trying to breathe through the whirling sand and pizza-oven air, she points at one. Through the dust I can just make out some writing on it in big black letters. I walk up to see.

TITS BRADY IS A COCK-SUCKIN SAND QUEEN. SIGN IF YOU'VE FUCKED HER.

Under it are fourteen names: Boner. Rickman. Mack. And close to half the guys in my tent. At least DJ's name isn't there. Nor is Kormick's—doesn't want to draw attention to himself, I guess. But Jimmy's is.

Third Eye comes up beside me and stares at the list. "All I can say, kiddo, is I warned you."

Without looking at her, I turn and walk back alone.


"Mom?" I'm behind the tent, my cell phone crackling in my ear. "I know it's late for you, did I wake you up?" My words echo back at me.

"Katie, is that you?" Her voice is delayed by the distance, so it's overlapping the echo of mine, tangling up our sentences.

"Yeah, it's me. Did I wake—"

"It's so good to hear your voice, sweetie! You know you can call any hour you want. You okay? Not hurt or anything?"

"No, no, I'm fine. But Mom?" My voice is trembling. I can hear it echoing in a pathetic whine. *Mom, Mom . . .* "It isn't going so good out here—"

"Thank the Lord."

"No . . . did you hear me? I don't know if I can hack it—"

"What? Oh yes, I can hear you now. I'm sorry you feel that way, honey, but don't give up. You're just adjusting,

I'm sure. It'll get easier. And if you just pray to the Lord Jesus, He will help you. He'll help you be strong."

"I am being strong. That's not what I—"

"Katie?" Dad's on the other extension but I can hardly hear his voice between the echoes of mine and Mom's. "Don't worry, little girl. Just hang in there. Everyone has a rough time in the Army sometimes. It was hard for me, too, when I first entered the Force. But I know you can do it. We have faith in you, sweetheart."

"But—"

"Be brave, my girl. Remember, we love you. God loves you. Make us proud."

A few minutes later, I'm in my team's Humvee again, on our way to the compound. Jimmy's in the front, as usual, next to baby-faced Creeley, and hairy little Mosquito is squashed into the back with me, cracking obscene jokes with the guys. I stare blindly through the yellow plastic side window, my arms crossed tightly over my chest. I can feel their eyes raking over me—I know they've all seen the latrine. They were probably snickering about it on their way to pick me up—the Sand Queen, the list of names, everything. Sand Queen is one of the worst things a female can get called in the Army. It means an ugly-ass chick who's being treated like a queen by the hundreds of horny guys around her because there's such a shortage of females. But she grows so swellheaded over their attention that she lets herself be passed around like a whore at a frat party, never realizing that back home those same guys wouldn't look at her twice.

In other words, she's a pathetic slut too desperate and dumb to know she's nothing but a mattress.

I'm trying to hang in there, like Dad said. I'm trying hard. But in a way, that graffiti is worse than Kormick.

When the Humvee stops on my side of the compound, I climb out without looking at anybody and set off for my tower. The sandstorm's blowing stronger by the minute, so I pull my scarf over my mouth to keep out the grit. Right now, I wouldn't care if the sand just buried me forever.

"Wait!" Jimmy calls. Normally he drives on with the others, but this time he jumps out, sends Creeley off without him and runs after me. The whole frickin' base is going to hear about that in a flash.

I ignore him and keep walking.

"Listen, can I explain something?" he says.

I speed up.

"It wasn't me put my name there. You've got to believe me. Some other fucker did it. You know I wouldn't do that!"

I keep going.

"Kate!"

He reaches out for my arm. I shake him off.

"Listen to me!"

"Go fuck yourself." I walk even faster.

"Kate, come on! Don't be like this."

I climb the ladder to my tower, refusing to answer. He stands there in the wind for a long time looking up at me. But I won't look back at him.

Only after he gives up and leaves do I drop my head onto my arms. Whatever made me think Jimmy would be any better than the other guys in this craphole? It's a boy's club and it's never going to be anything else. Bros before hos, as they like to say.

I'm such a fucking fool.

THE SOLDIER IS sitting in a circle with a bunch of female vets, who shift uneasily in their hard plastic chairs. Brightly colored admonishments blare down at them from posters on the walls:

*Love Yourself as Much as Others.*

*Listening Is the Key to Success.*

*Heal by Hugging a Friend Today.*

And the one that irritates the soldier the most: *Learn From Your Mistakes, They Are Our Teachers.*

She hunkers down in her chair and glances at the other women with disgust. They look like a bunch of washed-out alcoholics in their sloppy sweats and paper slippers, faces medication-puffy and blank. They're older than she is, too, fat and shapeless. Vietnam nurses, first Gulf War pilots. They probably *are* alcoholics, she decides.

The therapist, a stringy-faced female in glasses who sits as if she's got a poker up her ass, does the same thing she did in the last few meetings: makes the women go around speaking their thoughts like kindergarten kids. Vicky, the Vietnam nurse, mumbles something about her husband knocking her around. Nicole, the Gulf War pilot, complains that her memory's gone. But most annoying is the tiny broad who says she was an Army corporal but has the dumbest little voice imaginable. Corporal Betty Boop. Her contribution is that her head won't stop aching.

The soldier scowls and wraps her arms across her chest. She hates this fucking shit. She'd rather go back to the pills.

"Kate, would you like to take a turn sharing your thoughts with us today?" Pokerass says when the others are done, peering over her doctor specs.

The soldier glowers at her without answering. The other vets glance at each other.

"Kate," Pokerass says again, "if you don't feel like sharing, we understand. But airing our issues usually helps. That's what we're here for. Are you sure that you don't want to contribute?"

That suffocating feeling is coming on again, the one that makes the soldier panic and her breath come short and hard. She doesn't want all those eyes on her, all those loser eyes. She doesn't want to hear those women's sad-sack loser stories, either. She doesn't want to hear how, thirty friggin' years after the Vietnam War, they're still as screwed up as she is.

Anyhow, none of them was a real combat soldier like her. They have no fucking idea.

# [ KATE ]

THE SANDSTORM BLOWS harder and harder as the day goes on, and being stuck in a tower like I am, I get the brunt of it. The sky turns a spooky dark orange, and the wind scoops up the moondust and blows it around in swirling billows, clogging my ears and nostrils. The prisoners stay inside their tents but I don't have that luxury. So I cover my mouth with my scarf and hunker down in the chair, watching my sunglasses cake over with sand, wiping them, then watching them cake over again. Soon nothing's visible except brownish-gray muck. I only hope the prisoners don't try anything. My rifle, which I just cleaned, is already too sand-jammed to shoot; I'm blind from the dust, deaf from the wind. They could walk right out of the prison and I wouldn't even see them—all they need to do is dig out some sand and wriggle under the wire. They could sneak right up and cut my throat, too.

Jimmy comes back after a few hours. He calls out to me, although I don't answer, and when he gets close I can just make out the jagged brown streaks on his uniform through the dust. He's bent forward against the wind, a white scarf over his mouth and nose like mine, and for a moment it makes me think of the scene in that old movie, *Doctor*

*Zhivago,* when Omar Sharif is struggling through a blizzard to catch up with his great love, Lara. I used to watch that movie over and over in high school. Nobody minded a star with an Arab name back then.

Jimmy climbs the ladder to join me, uninvited.

I don't say anything and I don't move from my chair. What I really want to do is push him off the goddamn tower.

He sits on the platform floor beside me, knees pulled up to his chest. His face is still hidden under his scarf, and his helmet and goggles are covered in moondust. For a long time neither of us says anything. Just sit there like a couple of abominable sandmen.

"God I miss green," he finally says over the wind.

I don't answer. Fool me once, I'm thinking.

"I miss air, too," he says next.

Another silence.

"This country's famous for its date palms, you know that? Forests of date palms. I'd love to see a forest of date palms."

I shift in my chair.

"They got beautiful palm trees all over Iraq, hundreds of different species. And all we get is desert. Not a fucking tree in sight."

"We've got Marvin."

I say that without meaning to but Jimmy doesn't show any surprise. He just answers, "Who's Marvin?"

I point in Marvin's direction, although he's totally invisible right now.

"Oh, you mean Rambo."

I don't want to, but I smile.

We sit without speaking for a time, the wind and sand whirling around in a brown blur.

"I miss birds," I finally say.

"Yeah, what the hell happened to all the birds? Even the desert's got to have birds."

"I know. I've been wondering about that."

"Guess we bombed the fuck out of them, too."

"Guess so."

"What else do you miss?" Jimmy asks.

"You mean other than people?"

"Yeah."

I think for a moment. "Tree roots."

"*Tree roots?*"

"Yeah. You know when you walk through the woods and they snake around and make all those beautiful patterns on the ground, like they're trying to match the branches above? There's this lake in Willowglen called Myosotis, which is Greek for forget-me-nots. And in May and June, the forget-me-nots grow in beautiful blue clusters all around it, tucked right inside the tree roots. And even better, there are tiny butterflies that match them exactly."

"Flying forget-me-nots. Cool."

I glance at him. Is he making fun of me? I can't see him too well, but he sounds serious. "What do you miss?" I say then.

"I miss riding my bike with my brothers. I miss swimming."

"Swimming. I love swimming. I used to swim in the lake all the time with Tyler."

We sit in the dust cloud, not saying anything more for a time. Jimmy, I notice, has put a condom over the end of his rifle to keep out the sand.

"Jimmy?" I finally say. "Why do the guys here hate me so much?"

[ NAEMA ]


WE HAVE HAD a terrible night. We were sleeping on
the roof, as usual, when Granny Maryam awoke shrieking
from a nightmare. The sound was so ghastly, as if her throat
were being cut, that Mama and I jumped up straight out of
sleep, our hearts knocking wildly. We roused Granny and
tried to calm her, but she could not shake the horror from
her head. I had to grope my way downstairs in the dark to
fetch her some of the precious date juice we have been sav-
ing. Yet even after swallowing this, she took many minutes
to recall where she was.

It is not only the shock of Papa's and Zaki's arrests that
did this to her, but the fact that the war is coming so close.
Last night, the sky above Umm Qasr was lighting up in
white flashes, and plumes of black smoke were blotting out
the moon. After we roused Granny, we stood on the roof to
watch for a moment, listening to the explosions and shots,
the throb and roar of helicopters so loud they seemed to be
pounding inside our own chests. Then we quickly gathered
our sleeping pallets and took Granny downstairs, hot as it
was. No more cooling off in the night air for us; not with the
bullets and bombs this near.

Zaki and Papa must also have heard the noise in their prison. I wonder if Zaki was frightened. My golden-eyed brother, with his sweet, funny face and his little-boy fantasies of being a rock star . . . what kind of an army puts a child like that in prison? A child who would rather feed a baby goat than pick up a gun? And why couldn't the Americans at least have allowed father and son to stay together? Zaki was so terrified when the bombs fell on Baghdad, although he pretended not to be. "Don't fuss over me, go help Mama," he kept saying when I tried to hold him, but I felt his little bones quaking. Who can protect him now in a tent full of thugs and thieves? Because everyone knows that among the incarcerated are not only innocents like him, but soldiers of the Republican Guard, brutish and corrupt, as well as criminals and perverts who will rape little boys.

And what about Papa? Surely this new incarceration must be reviving his days in Saddam's prison. His legs have never recovered from being smashed again and again by Saddam's prison guards—he walks bent over and limping now, as if he is stepping barefoot on glass. How can his mind and heart, already broken by torture and starvation, bear the strain?

I have to stop thinking like this. The not knowing, this is what drives one mad. So I concentrate on keeping useful. I wash and say my morning prayers, then go to the mirror, pick up my blue hijab, a garment to which I am still unaccustomed, and put it on by the light of a candle: fold the front over my forehead, pull the sides over my ears to hide every strand of hair, wrap it firmly around my neck and pin it at the back. I never wore a hijab before this war, just as I never had to wear long skirts, and have not yet learned to move my head without fear of it slipping off. I spend all day holding my neck high and stiff until the ache burns down my back.

I look at my unfamiliar face in the mirror, a pale and tired oval framed in blue, then extinguish the candle and go outside once again to join the same handful of beleaguered citizens who accompany me to the prison every morning: Umm Ibrahim, with her stout middle-aged daughter, Zahra; wrinkled old Abu Rayya and his despairing wife; and the fierce widow Fatima. On our way I think again of asking Fatima's advice about where my family can flee once Papa and Zaki are released. But I dare not. Mama's words ring in my head: "Remember, we can trust no one, Naema."

It is so lonely not to trust.

The journey to the prison is not a pleasant one. We keep to the edge of the road and walk in single file, for any minute we might have to scramble out of the way of a military convoy barreling past and prepared to stop for no one. Already, we know of children and old people mown down by those convoys because they could not move out of the way quickly enough. I have seen the bodies myself, run over so many times they lie flattened on the road, reduced to nothing but bloody patches of organs and bones. But when we break away from the road to escape those convoys, or to take a short cut over the desert, that brings its own dangers. Hidden landmines left over from the last war. Roving dogs, mad with hunger or rabies. A stray colored ball from a cluster bomb.

I cannot think of those cluster bombs without outrage. It is forbidden by international law to use them in urban areas, yet the Americans and British rain them down on us without compunction. Cluster bombs are filled with small, colorful tin balls, many of which do not explode on first impact. Instead, they lie in the streets looking as harmless as toys, waiting for a passing vibration to detonate. Thus the child who picks one up with delight or the young mother who walks by innocently pushing a pram are turned into suicidal murderers, setting off an explosion that shreds themselves and all around them to pieces. This is one of the reasons our hospitals are filled with babies without arms and our graveyards with disembodied heads and limbs. What sort of a demon invents a weapon like this? And what sort of a population allows its armies to use it?

But then, what did we do when Saddam gassed the Kurds with his own demonic weapons? And what did we do when he slaughtered the Shia, my mother's people, stole their water, dried up their fields and destroyed their livelihoods? We, too, can be sheep.

My companions and I reach the prison just as the sun comes up, joining all the other anxious families who, like us, have come once again to find their loved ones. They usher me to the front, as has become our custom, and press their photographs into my hands so I can give them to the girl soldier. Then we wait, as the powerless must always wait, no more effectual than asses swishing away flies with their sleepy tails.

The dawn suffuses our faces, first with rose and then burnished gold, the sun as resplendent as if this were a time of celebration, not horror. And finally, when that same indifferent sun has risen high and hot, the soldiers exchange shifts and I can look for the little Kate with her silly, ignorant face. I wonder what she believes she is doing here—serving God? Or is it her president she is serving, with the same cowed obedience with which our soldiers served Saddam?

But I am disappointed, for the soldier who comes toward us is not Kate. Instead it is another woman, a tall one, with wide, heavy shoulders and full breasts filling her uniform. Her face is round and red but hidden behind the usual sun goggles, so I cannot judge her age. But her mouth is grim. I brace myself for the worst.

"Good morning," I say to her in English.

"Get back!" she snaps and waves her rifle at me.

"Excuse me, but I am only trying to help. I can interpret for you."

She runs her eyes over me, this tight-mouthed Amazon, her jaw set hard. "Yeah, I heard about you. Well, I got news: there's nothing to interpret. Now leave, and tell the rest of your buddies to leave too. Go!"

"But where is the other soldier, the one called Kate?"

"Didn't you hear me?" She raises her gun and points it at my heart. "I said git!"

I draw myself up and look at the woman with disgust. She does not frighten me, for she is too obviously frightened herself. "You have no right to talk to me like that," I tell her in my very best English. "You come here, invade my country for no reason, lock up our children. What kind of people are you?"

"Naema, in the name of Allah, stop!" Umm Ibrahim says, pulling at my sleeve. She cannot understand my words but my tone is unmistakable. "You mustn't quarrel with the soldier like this, she'll kill you! Come away!"

The soldier stares at me coldly, her rifle still pointing at me. On her chest I see the word McDougall. For some reason, this word makes me laugh.

"Come!" Umm Ibrahim urges again. "You're going mad. Come!"

I allow her to pull me away, for there is obviously no point in staying. But I cannot refrain from looking back over my shoulder and shouting, "You should be ashamed!" to satisfy my stubbornness.

Mama has always said I am as stubborn as a goat. Perhaps it comes from being the eldest, or perhaps from having had to help her cope when Papa was in Abu Ghraib during my school days. Saddam had him arrested for writing a poem about the death of a young soldier in our war with Kuwait. Papa's accusers said he had "committed an irreverence toward His Excellency, our Venerable Leader" by portraying the death as a tragedy rather than a triumph of patriotic martyrdom. But we knew the real reason was that Papa had refused to join Saddam's Ba'ath Party. Papa is a free spirit and hates despotism, as do Mama and I. But Saddam, of course, punished anybody who would not bend to his will.

"I knew this would happen," I remember Mama crying to me just after Papa was taken. "As soon as your father showed me his poems when we were courting, I knew they would bring him trouble one day." She looked at me, her dark eyes wide and frightened beneath her glossy hair, which was still a deep black in those days. "Your father's a good man, but he wears his heart for all to see. His poems hide nothing if one is not blind. You know what I said to him when I first read his poetry?"

"What, Mama?" I looked at her warily. I was sixteen at the time and terrified that Papa would die. I was not at all sure I wanted to hear what she was about to say.

"Your father and I were in my uncle's parlor. That's where we did all our courting because, with my mother in Basra and Father deceased, may Allah have mercy on him, I was under my uncle's protection while I went to college in Baghdad. Uncle kept a strict eye on us! Your father hated it—he wanted me all to himself." Mama smiled, forgetting for a moment the present and all its miseries. "We were sitting side by side . . . not too close . . . on the sofa, his soft eyes looking at me. Your father was so handsome in those days, like Zaki, such a gentle face. A poet's face." She paused, at peace for a moment within her memories. "Then he handed me the poem, blushing. 'Be merciful, Zaynab,' he said. 'Please don't think me a fool.'

"I took it and read, feeling his eyes watching me anxiously. It was a young man's poem, full of flower imagery and longing. It makes me smile now to think of it, and I know it embarrasses your father. But even then I could see that this juvenile effort was dangerous."

Mama shook her head and sank to a chair by the window. "You know what I told him, Naema? 'You bare your heart in these poems, my darling,' I said. 'It's a good heart, but I fear it will bring you sorrow.' Yet he kept writing those poems anyway. And now, you see? I was right."

But Mama was not angry with Papa, only frightened, for we had no idea if he was alive or whether and when he would be released. Once a person disappeared into Abu Ghraib, the family was told nothing. One was forced to wait in ignorance until the prisoner was released, perhaps without fingers or a hand, perhaps crippled or mad. Perhaps dead.

The Americans at least have lists.

Mama tried to stay strong for me and Zaki while Papa was gone, but it was not easy being two women alone with an eight-year-old boy to feed. Our relatives did what they could to help us, but Mama had to keep going to the hospital to see her patients or else lose her job, so I was forced to stay home from school to look after Zaki, go to the market, cook and clean. How I missed school and my friends! But I read my books when I could, went with Mama to bribe and petition this or that official for Papa's release, and when he suddenly appeared at our home eleven months later—alive, praise be to Allah, but with his legs bent and crooked from torture, his skin torn, his body emaciated and his heart fluttering weakly in his chest—I nursed him for months. What choice is there but to grow stubborn under such circumstances?

Once Papa had recovered from the worst of his pain and shock, my stubbornness had other uses. I went back to school determined to catch up, and each day when I came home I made poor little Zaki sit and listen while I played teacher and repeated what I had learned. If he fiddled or whined or tried to run away, I rapped his knuckles with a stick. It was only when Papa caught me that Zaki was liberated. Papa was so angry! "How can you torment your own little brother?" he said. "This is not the way to be strong. The truly strong are gentle and merciful, they don't exploit the weak."

If only.

That was a calm time for our family, though. Papa was home at last and teaching again at the university, after paying who knows how much in bribes and joining the Ba'athists after all. (Not even he was able to be a hero in those dire times.) Zaki was popular with his little gang of boys at school. And I, now seventeen, was studying hard at school and had my friends Farah and Yasmina, with whom I giggled over film stars and boys.

My favorite of these times were the evenings, when, after Zaki and I had finished our long hours of homework, we were allowed to curl up on the sofa with our parents to watch the latest soap opera on television. We liked to play at guessing and reinventing the plots, and Zaki, who so loves to clown, would introduce the silliest twists: the hero would turn out to have chicken legs, or the heroine to have two husbands and two heads, one for each; ideas I am sure he gleaned from Granny's stories. He would jump up and stalk about the room, jerking his head and picking up his thin little legs with just the same comic delicacy as chickens do. I find myself smiling at the memory as I walk from the prison back to the house, poor Umm Ibrahim wheezing at my side. How beautiful the most ordinary of times seem when they are gone.

These times will come again. They must.

But with the little Kate soldier removed from the check-point, how am I to find out anything of Papa and Zaki? How am I to know whether the Americans are as brutal in their prison as Saddam was in his?

[ KATE ]

TWO WEEKS HAVE crawled by since I started guard duty and my days are so much the same now that I can't tell one from the other. I take my morning runs with Yvette, if she isn't out on a convoy. Third Eye sleeps in most days, which is fine with me—I've been keeping my distance ever since the unsympathetic bitch pulled that I-told-you-so crap at the Porta-John. The rest of the time I'm up in my tower staring at the prisoners while they wander around in their pathetic sand corral, or get down on all fours to pray.

I've got to admit, it freaks me out when they do that. They line up in rows facing southwest, which I guess is the direction of Mecca from here, spread out their little rugs, if they have any, get down on their hands and knees and stick their foreheads right into the dirt. I don't like watching them grovel like that, their butts in the air. I know they don't see it like I do, cultural differences and all that, but I don't think God wants us to act so undignified—aren't we supposed to be formed in His image, after all? And it bugs the hell out of me that all that praying doesn't stop those same guys from acting like assholes the minute they're done.

A whole bunch of them are throwing stuff at me now. Snakes and scorpions they find in the sand. Spiders, dead or alive. Beetles and bugs in all shapes and sizes. They love it if they can make me jump or squeal, so I have to use up all my energy trying to look unfazed when a scorpion lands on my shoulder or a snake falls wriggling at my feet.

There are a lot more prisoners to deal with now, too, because Bucca's growing so fast. Every day, more are brought in. The tents are so overcrowded that we've been ordered to go out after our shifts and put up more compounds, even if we've already worked fourteen bone-draining hours that day. Why the prisoners can't build those compounds themselves I will never understand. In MP training we were taught to discipline inmates by making them work for rewards and privileges. Not at Camp Bucca. "It's too hot for the detainees to work," the command keeps telling us. "Now get out there and sweat." That sucks enough, but it really bugs me that the prisoners get fine meals and free cigarettes, whether they've been trying to escape, jerking off at me or saying their prayers like good boys. Some days it feels like they're hotel guests and we're their goddamn maids.

At least we have a few more amenities for ourselves now. DJ and three other guys in our tent stole some plywood from an engineering company and built us a floor to cut down on the rats and bugs. There are more latrines and even a shower trailer. And we also have e-mail, although there are so few computers and they're so damn slow that I get too frustrated to bother with it. I don't really care, though. I don't much want to write or call home anymore, not after that last conversation. What's there to say? I can't tell Mom or Dad about guarding prisoners who jerk off and throw dead spiders at me; that's not their idea of what a soldier does at war. I can't tell them about Macktruck reading porn all the time, or what Kormick did, either. All they want to hear is how noble and heroic I'm being. The first thing Dad's always said the few times I have called is, "Kate, I'm real proud of you." And the last thing he's always said for good-bye is, "That's my girl, brave and strong."

Thing is, I do still want to make him proud. I do want to be brave and strong.

Mom's approach is different. "Have you been saying your prayers every night and going to chapel?" she likes to ask, after telling me she prays for my safety all the time. "Are you setting a good example to those poor brave soldiers over there?"

It was Mom who made me bring the crucifix with me, the one I tacked to my tent post right above Fuzzy. That crucifix is incredibly important to her because she was wearing it when she had this terrible accident back in high school and she's always believed it saved her life. "Make sure you keep it by you all the time, okay, sweetie?" she said when she took it off her neck and gave it to me the night before I left. "Trust in Our Lord Jesus to watch over you, like He did me." I was touched. I'd never seen her let the thing out of her sight before.

She told me about the accident when I was fifteen, same age as when it happened to her. "Katie?" she said in the kitchen one summer day, while I was rooting around in our freezer for a Popsicle. "You have a moment? I need to talk to you."

I pulled out a lemon pop and turned to look at her. It was hot, so I was in bare feet, cutoffs and a bikini top, and I remember itching all over from mosquito bites. Robin, who was already my best friend by then, and a couple of cute boys from school were out in the front yard, splashing in our above-ground pool and waiting for me.

"Now?" I said itchily. "Can't it wait?" But Mom looked so weird and sad that I shut up and sat down. "What's wrong? Am I in trouble or something?"

She pulled a chair right up to my knees, folded her pudgy little hands on the lap of her yellow skirt and fixed her watery blue eyes on me. "No, it's not you, honey. But there's something I've got to tell you. It's about what happened to me when I was your age. It's time for you to know." And then she told me the whole horrible story in this strange, detached voice, like she was talking about somebody else. Didn't spare any of the gruesome details, though. The five girls getting drunk on stolen whiskey. Piling in a car, giggling, even though every last one of them knew better. Careening into an oncoming pickup at sixty miles an hour. Dangling heads, twisted backs, smashed faces. "I lay in the hospital for six months, thinking about why the Lord let my friends die and not me," Mom said, "and that's when I realized He was giving me a second chance, calling me to spread His love. *Be the doers of the word, and not the hearers only.* That's why I want you to trust in Jesus and Mary, Katie. They'll look after you as long as you heed Christ's teachings. And that's why I don't want you seeing those boys outside again. They're not the kind of boys you should be with. I know their parents. They're hard-drinking, ungodly people. Dangerous people. You understand?"

I nodded, feeling all weird and knotted-up inside. Then something cold hit my knee. My pop had melted clean off its stick.

But even if my parents were willing to hear the truth about my life out here in the desert, what would be the point of telling them? It'd only make them scared for me, and I know they're already living in dread of seeing that military car drive up, the two stiffs in dress uniform coming to the door—angels of death. Even April has some sense of the danger I'm in. "Katie?" she said one time on the phone. "I saw a program on TV about soldiers dying in the war. Are you gonna die? 'Cause I don't want you to."

Tyler's the only person who's come close to guessing what's really going on, though. When I called him the second day after I started up in my tower, he said, "Are the men treating you okay out there?" I thought he was asking if I was cheating on him, so I answered, "Don't worry, they're all dickheads."

"That's what I meant. Are you safe?"

I could hear the need in his voice, the need to know I was all right. But I wasn't about to repeat the mistake I made with my parents and come across as whiny and pathetic. So all I said was, "Tyler, I'm fine." That was the first time I ever lied to him, and somehow, since then, I haven't felt like calling him any more than I've felt like calling Mom and Dad. The command's banned us from using our phones now anyway, so if Tyler or my parents ask why I don't call anymore, I've got an excuse.

Tyler wrote to me for my birthday, June 6th. He must've planned real carefully when to mail the letter because it arrived today with a package, only ten days late. Normally, snail mail doesn't get here for months.

*Happy Birthday, Katie-pie!*

*Wow, 20 years old! One more year and we can go to bars and get hammered, and you can get into the clubs I'm playing without a fake ID. It's crazy that you're old enough to fight but not drink.*

*I miss you so bad there are no words for it. I ache for you every day, all day, and every night too. I keep going to our places, like the drive-in and Myosotis Lake and The Orange Dog, thinking it'll make me feel better. But without you I can't stand them. It's like you're walking beside me, but you're invisible.*

*Keep safe, brave girl. I'm counting the days. Hope you like the present! Listen to track three. I wrote it for you.*

*Love and more love,*

*Tyler*

In the package is a portable radio and a home-recorded CD of his own songs, their titles written out in red marker. I push the CD to the bottom of my duffle bag. I appreciate how sweet and careful his letter his, and how much work he put into that CD, but I can't face listening to it right now. The sound of Tyler singing, especially about us, would turn my whole self inside out.

I'm glad to have the radio, though. Gives me something to listen to in my tower other than the frigging detainees. Two guys in particular are getting under my skin. The first is this dipstick in a mustache, about thirty-five or so, who comes up to me every damn day to beg for cigarettes in English. He has his own fucking cigarettes, but no, he wants mine. "Soldier girl, gimme smoke. Come on pretty baby," he starts. Then, when I won't give him any, it's, "Come on, cunt," and other such charming phrases he must have picked up from American porno movies. After he's finally given up on begging and insulting me for the day, he stands in the same spot for hours staring at my face. I've tried yelling at him to go away, but that only makes him laugh and stare even more. I've tried ignoring him, but we both know I'm pretending, so that doesn't work either. I've tried staring back at him, too, but then he acts like I'm flirting with him and strips me with his eyes. Maybe he was a torturer under Saddam or something because he's scarily good at this game of his and I'm not on the winning side. It's ridiculous: I'm the prison guard here, I have the weapon. But those burning eyes of his won't leave me alone. They even get into my dreams.

The other prisoner who drives me nuts is the jerk-off. I think he's genuinely crazy. Every time I face his direction, he whips out his dick and starts beating it, leering at me with the most obscene expression I've ever laid eyes on. He shouts at me, too, but I don't understand what he's saying, thank God, although it isn't too hard to guess his gist. He wears western clothes, gray pants and a white shirt, which are getting dirtier by the day, and he has a beaky face and graying black hair. I don't think he can be a political prisoner; he's too disgusting. He's probably some nutcase sex offender who was locked up under Saddam, let go when we fired all the Iraqi police, and then locked up again by us.

One day, though, he tries something new. He doesn't just jerk off. He drops his pants, squats in the sand and does his business. Then he wipes his ass with his left hand and throws his turd at me.

When he does that, I almost shoot him. He misses me but it hits the platform right by my boot, and the stink of it makes me gag. I raise my rifle and aim it at him but it doesn't faze him at all. I think he doesn't believe a girl would shoot him. I think he doesn't believe a girl is worth any more than the shit he's just thrown at me. I aim right at his chest while he jeers, my finger on the trigger, the whole of me yearning to shoot his fuckass head off. The only thing that stops me is remembering how much trouble I'd get into if I killed an unarmed prisoner cold.

I lower my rifle and kick his turd off my platform, and when Jimmy comes for his usual visit he finds me down on the ground, rubbing my boot in the sand, my face screwed up in disgust and my hands shaking even worse than usual.

"What happened?"

"See that fucking hajji over there?" I point at the jerk-off with my rifle. He's strolling around the compound, trying to look innocent.

Jimmy looks. "What about him?"

"He just threw his own shit at me."

"Jesus Christ!" Jimmy shakes his head. "It's much worse for you females out here than for us, isn't it?"

It's true. Those prisoners really hate having female guards. But that isn't the only reason it's better for Jimmy than for me. He doesn't have to work directly with the detainees like I do, 'cause he's posted at the compound entrance, not right by the wire. And he doesn't have to spend all frigging day alone, either—he shares his post with those guys from Headquarters. He doesn't know how lucky he is.

Every time Jimmy comes to see me, he brings me some kind of treat: soda and a bag of Doritos or Skittles from the PX. I think he's worried I'm getting too skinny. But we don't normally talk about the crap-throwing prisoners or anything else that goes on in that toilet bowl. It's too damn depressing. We both feel, without needing to say it, that the whole point of each other's company is to forget. So we talk about other stuff. Books we've read, movies, his past girl-friends, Tyler, our families, our plans for when we get back to college. Jimmy wants to study physics so he can invent things. I'm not sure what I want to be—maybe a teacher, maybe a TV reporter, or maybe one of those scientists who spend most of their lives alone in the forest studying bird-calls. Anything, really, so long as it isn't a soldier.

I'm the one who does most of the talking, though. Jimmy likes to speak about his little brothers, who are living with their aunt while he's deployed, but he never says much about the rest of his life at home. I think it makes him too sad, partly because of his mom—I gather she's been in and out of loony bins most of her life—and partly because his dad skedaddled when Jimmy was a kid, leaving Jimmy to pretty much raise himself and his little brothers on his own. I think that's why he worries about those brothers so much.

So when we talk, it's mostly me blabbing on about how Tyler's studying music at SUNY New Paltz, about Robin moving to New York City to be a model, or about some cute thing April did once. Bullshit, really, since that's not what I'm thinking about. What I'm thinking about is when I can next take a piss, when I'm going to run out of water, when can I sleep and when can I shower. It's like my brain has shriveled to the size of one of Rickman's zits.

As for reporting Kormick and Boner, Jimmy doesn't bring that up anymore. Once, he says, "Kate, no pressure, but if you ever want to talk about what happened with those fuckers, or if you want to do anything about it, tell me. But if you don't, it's okay. I won't bug you about it anymore."

"Thanks," I answer, and I do appreciate how kind that is. But there's no way I'm going to tell him about it, or anyone else either. That's not what soldiers do.

"HI, SWEETIE," THE mother says timidly, standing in the door of the hospital room with a big yellow bouquet in her arms and a quavery smile. "Can we come in?" She's small and puffy, like a pigeon, and so loud with colors she makes the soldier squint. Hair stiff with copper dye. Eyelids powder blue. Lips neon pink to match her dress.

The mother has a right to be nervous after what happened, the soldier knows this. So she nods and tries to smile. "Sure," she says. "There aren't enough chairs. You can sit on the bed if you want." She moves over to stand by the window, the bed between her and her parents like a berm.

The mother comes around the bed for a hug, but the soldier steps out of the way. The mom stops, disconcerted. "How's your back, honey? Still hurting?"

Shrug.

"Well, you look a lot better, thank the Lord. Where can I put these flowers?"

The soldier points to a vase on the sink. The mother tiptoes back around the bed as if she's in church, which annoys the soldier to no end, and fills the vase with water. Then she unwraps the plastic around the bouquet with a deafening crackle and shoves the yellow flowers in, fussily arranging them before she puts them on the bedside table. A rotting, musty smell fills the room.

"I brought you these," the father says then, stepping around his wife. He reaches across the bed and hands over two books. One a Bible—no surprise there; the other a collection of nature essays by Annie Dillard. The soldier used to love Dillard. But the idea of reading anything that pre-cious and preachy right now makes her sick.

"Thanks." She puts the books down on the bed and looks at her dad. He's still as upright and trim as ever. Wide shoul-ders, silver hair cut military short. Clint Eastwood creases around his light-blue eyes. He looks exactly like what he is: a God-fearing, law-enforcing American bully.

He hands her a manila envelope. "I think you might want to look at this." It's from the Army and it's been opened.

"You read this already? My mail?"

"Open it," is all he answers.

The soldier obeys, hands trembling even more than usual. Inside are her discharge papers. Medical, along with "fail-ure to adjust." That means she's been booted out for being a fuckup.

"You can fight it, you know, appeal," the father says. "They tell you how right there."

She looks him in the eyes, the exact same washed-out blue as hers. "Why would I want to do that?"

"It makes it sound like there's something wrong with you."

"There *is* something wrong with me."

"Oh, Katie." The father looks at her sadly. "You know what I mean. You don't want that smear on your record all your life, do you? It's not right after what you've done for this country."

"I don't give a shit. The last thing I ever fucking want to do is go back in the Army. They can smear me all they frig-gin' want."

"Katie, your language," the mother says weakly.

The soldier sits on the bed, her back to them, and drops her face into her hands. They don't understand that she's got no patience anymore. Not for their bullshit, not for their hypocrisy, not for their total goddamn dangerous ignorance. So her parents can't be proud of her now? Can't boast about her being a hero, as brave as any son might have been? So fucking what.

Nobody moves. The soldier can hear her mother's wheezing breath. The mom stopped smoking years ago, but she's so fat and out of shape she breathes like a Pekingese.

"Where's April?" the soldier says once she's calm enough to speak. She stands and turns to look at them again.

Her mother glances at the father. "We thought it was still a little too soon." She swallows. "Next time."

"Well, shit! How am I going to make it up to her if you won't let me see her?"

"Well, you know what happened. You know what you did."

The soldier nods, mouth clenched. "Yeah, nobody's hero, me. Scared my little sis. Embarrassed you all. I've got no right to act like that with my nice little family, do I? God forgive me and all that crap."

"Sweetie, please," the mother says, reaching out a hand so plump it looks like a little balloon with fingers. "You can't hide from the Lord, you know that. If you would just pray with me a moment it would help. Just one little prayer?"

"Mom. Stop."

"Sally, leave it," the father says. "Let's all get ahold of ourselves here and sit."

He waves his wife to the one chair in the room and plunks himself down on the corner of the bed. The soldier backs up until she's standing as far away from them as she can get.

"Tyler told us he came last week," the father says then.

No answer.

"He said you weren't doing so well. He said you acted like you didn't know him."

*I didn't.*

"Looks like you're doing better today, though."

"Yeah. I know exactly who everybody is now."

The father and mother look at each other again.

"Katie, are they treating you right in here?" the dad says next, trying to soften his voice. "Do they know what they're doing? Are they giving you too many of those drugs? Maybe you'd be better off at home, huh?"

"No."

"No what?"

"I'm not going home."

"Don't be ridiculous. Of course you are. You need to be with your family."

"No, that's not what I need. But you can't understand that, can you? 'Cause for all your tough sheriff shit, you've never seen anything. What do you deal with all day up there in small-town land? Drunk drivers? 'Domestic incidents?' Teenage pranks? So don't try and tell a soldier what she fucking needs, okay?"

The father closes his eyes. "Maybe you should stay here a little longer. But Kate . . . " He opens his eyes again and gives his daughter the severest sheriff glare he can muster. "The Lord helps those who help themselves. You've got to want to be better, you've got to try. Otherwise nobody can help you at all."

Not only are her hands shaking, now her whole body is. "Just go!" the soldier shouts. "Get the fuck away from me!"

Sheriff Daniel Brady rises to his feet. "I know it's been hard, I know you've been through a lot, but you need to stop behaving like this."

"Leave!"

And the soldier picks up the father's Bible and throws it as hard as she can at the vase, sending yellow petals and shards of glass flying all over the room.

[ KATE ]


A FEW DAYS after the jerk-off threw his shit at me, Yvette tells me she's been relieved from night convoys for a while, so is back on the same schedule as me. I'm real glad to hear this, not only because I miss her when she's away but cause I'm still not getting on so good with Third Eye. We talk when we have to because you can't *not* talk to someone who sleeps two feet away from you. But ever since that Sand Queen graffiti, she's been either ignoring me or letting fly with a mean remark. Third Eye, I've decided, is turning into one of those Army females who'd rather stab you in the back than watch it. Either that, or she's swallowed Kormick's crap about me being a skank.

"What's the story with you two?" Yvette asks me one morning during our usual run to the berm and back. "You and Third Eye are skulking around each other like a couple of she-cats fighting over a tom. And I know that ain't the problem." She gives me a wink.

I concentrate on running a moment. Running is getting pretty difficult these days, what with the Bucca bug draining my guts, the lousy food and the heat killing my appetite. It annoys me. I want to be growing stronger, not weaker.

"It started over that fucking graffiti," I say reluctantly.

We both hold our breath a second while we run through a particularly fragrant cloud of burning latrine fuel.

"Why, what happened?"

"She acted like I deserved it and she's been treating me like shit ever since."

Yvette looks over at me. "Well, fuck her! What's her problem? I mean it's one thing being a dyke, I can live with that, long as she don't hit on me. But why's she have to be twice as bad as the boys all the time, huh?"

I shrug. I'm out of breath and my legs are aching already. "She's even worse now that she's started working with my old team. She hasn't said anything to you about them, has she?"

"Nah, she just said they suck. How're your new guys?"

"Not too bad. Mosquito's pretty funny. Creeley's a kid. But they're all right."

"What about Teach?" Yvette grins at me, bouncing along the sand road with no effort at all.

"What about him?"

"I hear he visits you up in your princess tower every single day."

I don't answer that, just concentrate on breathing through the burning sewage and getting my aching legs along that road and back again without collapsing. To my relief, she doesn't push it.

A couple nights later, I'm reading on my rack when Third Eye comes in looking even more pissed than usual. She throws her big body down on her cot and stares up at the roof a long time, her red face clenched so tight she's turning white around the mouth. I try to ignore her and keep reading, but she looks so miserable that I figure I better do the Christian thing and see if I can help, even if she is a hard-assed bitch. Mom would be proud.

"Something wrong?" I ask.

No answer. She just lies there on her back, mouth clenched.

"Smoke?" I offer her my pack. She shakes her head.

"How about water?" I hold out an open bottle.

She nods at that and props herself up on an elbow to drink. And to my shock I see that her narrow black eyes are filled with tears. Third Eye—that tough dyke—crying?

I pin up my poncho curtain in case Macktruck comes back, sit down and lean toward her. "Wanna talk?" I whisper. "Did you get some bad news or something?"

"Leave me the fuck alone!" She rolls over to face away from me.

I gaze at her broad back a minute. Yvette would be much better at this 'cause she and Third Eye still get along fine. But Yvette's out on a convoy, so I'm the only option.

"Look, don't bite my head off," I whisper, hoping the guys around us aren't listening. "Is it Kormick? Did he do something to you?"

But even as I say that I think, come on, Kate, be real—this chick's built like a wall. Even that fuckhead couldn't pull anything on her.

But then, ever so slightly, she nods.

"He did? What . . ."

"Shut up." She rolls onto her back again and wipes her eyes with her wrist. "I fucking hate men."

"Shh!" I look around quickly. This is not a conversation that should be overheard. Luckily, far as I can tell, most of the guys are tuned out over their DVD players and earphones. Maybe one's actually reading a book. Still, you never know who's eavesdropping.

"If I tell you, you won't say anything about it, right?" Third Eye whispers then. "Nothing to nobody, ever? You swear?"

"I swear."

"If you do, I'll kill you. I mean it."

"I know you do." I lean closer. "Did he hurt you? Are you all right?"

Third Eye swallows and looks away from me. Then she says in a hoarse whisper, "He raped me. Him and Boner together. Of course I'm not 'all right.'"

"Oh God! They tried to do that to me, too!"

Third Eye stares at me angrily. "I'm not talking about your fucking problems, Sand Queen. I'm talking about mine."

[ N A E M A ]

GRANNY MARYAM'S NEIGHBORS, old Abu Mustafa and his wife and sister, have invited us over again to watch television. We have only one or two hours of electricity a day now, if any at all, but Abu Mustafa says that as soon as it does deign to visit us, we are welcome. We have taken to talking about the electricity like this, as if it were a malicious trickster. After all, it switches us from modern to primitive life and back again at will. Some people try to outwit it by buying a private generator, but we cannot afford such a luxury because the few dinars we managed to bring with us from Baghdad have so lost their value that they buy almost nothing. So we are left with no more control over our light and communications, or whether we bake or freeze, than we have over the glow of the moon.

Mama goes to watch the neighbor's television whenever she can, eager to hear news of the war and our poor battered Baghdad, and Granny goes with her on the increasingly rare days she is well enough, but I hardly ever go at all. There is too much to do while the electricity lasts to waste time on television and its lies: heat the water for washing; clean the stubborn dust from our clothes; cook some rice to last us through the next few days of blackouts; soak myself from the pump and stand by the fan to cool off, the day's only respite from the suffocating desert heat. And most urgently of all, recharge my cellular telephone in the hope of reaching Khalil and the other friends from whom I am so cruelly cut off. That telephone is my lifeline here in Granny's remote little house, for we have no computers or Internet, no landline and we receive no letters. This war has isolated us as effectively as if it had sent us to Mars.

Many of my friends fled Baghdad at the first whiff of the invasion, having had more foresight than my family did, and where they are now I do not know. But those with less money or no contacts stayed behind and it is from them I particularly hope to hear, even though I know they will bear terrible tales. But the person I most long to talk to, of course, is Khalil. He and I have managed to speak only once in the nearly three weeks since my family left, during a rare moment while my telephone was working, and it was then that he told me he had decided to stay in Baghdad, no matter what. "I'm going to wait for you, my love," he said. "I want you to have somebody to come home to."

"Khalil, you mustn't! It's too dangerous!" I was replying when the telephone cut off, and ever since we have missed each other again and again, foiled by power outages, bombs and the wanton destruction of war. Now I no longer know where Khalil is, or whether he is even alive.

So the minute my phone has charged enough to work (and it only works at all down here because we are so near Kuwait; the Iraqi power lines have been bombed), I try to reach him, as I have tried so often already, punching in his number while my pulse thrums in my ears. All the other times I've called him, I have met only silence. But this time, a ring! My heart jumps so violently I can hardly breathe.

But then the ringing stops.

I try again. One ring . . . two . . . then nothing. Again I dial—the same thing. Over and over I try, but the telephone either rings and cuts off, or will not ring at all. What does this mean? Is Khalil's phone simply not working, or has something terrible happened to him? I keep punching in the numbers, faster and harder, my hand flying in a frenzy. But already I know it is futile. The telephone has become nothing but an inert object, no more communicative than a stone.

I pocket the useless thing and drag myself through the rest of my chores, my limbs weighted with disappointment. Then I walk over to Abu Mustafa's house to join Mama and Granny. They are inside with his wife Huda, and his sister Thoraya, who are good friends to Granny, drinking tea in front of a fan and sitting around a little television set, watching it in grim silence. I settle down to watch with them, too discouraged even to speak. But the minute I sit, the trickster blinks and kills the electricity once again, instantly smothering us in blackness and heat.

I should be used to its capriciousness by now, but at this particular moment I cannot bear it. I sit in the sudden darkness, unable to stop my eyes from filling with tears. Everything about this war conspires to make us helpless. Why was I so naïve as to believe that girl Kate when she said she would look for Papa and Zaki? It is much more likely that she has forgotten us, no more interested in our fate than the electricity trickster is in our needs.

Khalil, I think as I wipe my eyes and rise to light a lamp, I will marry you after all. My dreams of traveling the world seem absurd now. They seem to come from a time and place as remote and innocent as when I was an infant. Yes, I will marry you, and yes, we can be doctors together, if that is what you still wish.

Just be alive, *habib*, be safe. That is the only dream that matters now.

[ KATE ]

**THE MORNING AFTER** Third Eye tells me what happened to her, I have a little talk with Marvin. "How you doing today?" I ask him from the top of my tower. Nobody can see me talking to a tree up here, except maybe a few of the prisoners, but since they're crazy as me by now it doesn't matter. "As for me, I'm not so good."

When Jimmy comes by in the afternoon, I ask if he knows anybody who works at the boys' compound. "Yeah, Ortiz. Why?" He's chewing on a mouthful of potato chips, his helmet tilted back like a cowboy hat and his high-planed cheeks sunburned and sweaty. All of us sweat so much out here we crave salt all the time.

"Because I promised that Iraqi girl I'd look for her kid brother. But then I forgot all about it."

"So why do it now?"

"Just something Third Eye said. Could you arrange for me to talk to Ortiz?"

"Sure." Jimmy squints at me from behind his shades. He's sitting on my tower floor, as usual, his long legs dangling over the edge, his rangy body managing to look relaxed even in his bulky battle-rattle vest and jacket. I'm on the chair, scanning the prisoners, dodging shit and snakes—doing my job.

"Speaking of Third Eye, how's she managing out there with those fuckers?" he asks then.

I glance at him. "Why?" I say cautiously. "You heard something?"

He pauses. "'Fraid so."

"What?"

He stares down at his scuffed-up desert boots. "You don't want to know."

"I know I don't. But tell me."

He sighs. "Well, that asswipe Boner was bragging in the tent last night that she'd blown him and Kormick. A cozy little threesome, he said."

"And people believe that? *Third Eye*?"

"People'll believe anything in the Army."

"Fuck." I don't know which is worse, the guys thinking she did that voluntarily, in which case she'll get harassed to death. Or them knowing she was raped, which will get her treated like a leper. Either way they'll say she's a tramp, just like they say about me.

"I should've reported them, like you said. They wouldn't be spreading crap like that about her then. I'm such a friggin' coward, Jimmy."

"Don't say that! It's not your fault. Nothing you could do would stop those guys from being the shitheads they are, don't go blaming yourself. But is this anything to do with you wanting to find that boy?"

"Yeah. I just want to do something right for a change. I'm such a fuckup."

Jimmy moves over to crouch beside my chair and takes

off his shades. "Look at me. Come on, take your eyes off of those pretty prisoners a second and look at me."

I do. His bright blue eyes are staring right into mine. Forget-me-not eyes.

"Now listen," he says. "You've got to stop thinking that way. You're only coping, like all of us. You haven't done anything wrong."

I shake my head, too sick to speak. I can't even begin to tell him how angry I am at myself right now. Didn't I promise to "lay my life down for others," and "lift the downtrodden and cast the wicked to the ground," like Father Slattery said? But along comes my first test, the chance to turn in Kormick and protect Third Eye. And I flunk.

The rest of the week stinks. I can't talk to Yvette because she's back on her night convoys, so either doesn't get in till I'm at work or doesn't get in at all 'cause she's sleeping at some other base. And Third Eye's gone into shutdown and won't speak to me or anybody else if she can help it. Once I try to get through to her by saying, "Listen, if you ever need me, I'm here." But all I get in reply is, "Cut the crap, preachy-ass." It's like she's wiped her memory clean, the way a computer does when it crashes.

But seeing her like that makes me realize something. She still has to work with those fuckers every single day—what if they're still attacking her? What if they're raping her over and over again? And even if they aren't, how can she stand being with them all day after what they did to her?

When that thought dawns on me, I can't sit still any longer. If she isn't going to do anything about it, I have to. I won't tell anyone what happened to her—I don't have the right. But I can get off my ass after all and tell someone about what Kormick and Boner did to me. Yes, it'll risk Kormick's anger and make me mighty unpopular with the command and most everybody else, too. But if it gets the bastards transferred so they can't hurt Third Eye anymore, or anybody else, either, it's worth it. Anyway, it's the righteous thing to do and the only way I can live with myself.

The question now is who to tell. I could go to the EOO, the Equal Opportunity Officer, but that'll risk making my story public and turning the whole fucking platoon against me as a snitch. Or I could tell our platoon leader, SFC Henley, in confidence. Not that Henley is Mother Teresa or anything, but perhaps he can figure out a way of dealing with Kormick and Boner more quietly. Platoon leaders have to figure out shit like that all the time.

So, soon I get back from my shift at the end of the day, I walk down the narrow alleyway between our tents and over to the NCO quarters, only a few rows away from mine. It's a spooky walk at this time of the evening, all shadowy and gray, the tents snapping in the wind, the dust blurring in the twilight till you can't tell whether the figures you're seeing are soldiers, hajjis or hallucinations. I clutch my rifle, the only battle buddy I've got right now, my hands trembling more than ever. Kormick will probably be at the NCO tent, since he sleeps there, and the last fucking thing in the world I want to do right now is face him. But I have to risk it—for Third Eye, and for myself.

Sure enough, I see him right away. Lounging outside, smoking and shooting the shit with an officer, a lieutenant with red eyebrows and rabbit teeth who everybody calls Pat-the-Bunny behind his back. It's the first time I've seen Kormick since he attacked me and the sight of him makes me sick and cold and weak. But if I run now, I'll never for-give myself.

"Well, look who's here," he says as I walk up. "You come all alone, Specialist Tits?"

"Yes, Sergeant." I can barely get the words out.

"You like breaking the rules, don't you? Aren't you going to salute the lieutenant?"

I salute, hoping he won't notice my quivering hand. Pat-the-Bunny runs his eyes over me, bored.

"Good girl," Kormick says. "Now, what do you want?"

"Request to see Sergeant First Class Henley, please."

Kormick stares at me a moment, his perfect face set hard. "What the fuck for?" he says quietly.

I hold myself stiff, looking ahead in true soldier fashion, trying not to show how frightened I am. "Sar'nt, if I can't see Sergeant Henley, I'm going to JAG."

JAG, which stands for Judge Advocate General, is the last resort for a soldier with a problem and we all have the right to go there, no matter how low we are on the totem pole. Saying what I just said is pretty much like invoking the right to pray.

Kormick eyes me uneasily, then jerks his head. "In you go then. Just don't let me see your fuckin' ugly mug for a while."

"Thank you, Sar'nt."

Shaking worse than ever, I step inside the tent, which is set up like an office, with plywood floors and a couple of knocked-together tables that serve as desks. SFC Henley is sitting behind one of these, staring at a computer.

I stand in front of his desk, adrenaline pumping, waiting for him to notice me. Henley is tall and upright, with a sun-dried face and thin white lips—he always reminds me of the first President Bush, the daddy of the monkeyface who got me into this war. Henley talks like he went to Harvard, although I don't think he's ever been near the place in his life.

"What can I do for you, Specialist?" He flicks his eyes up from the screen.

"Request a private conversation, Sergeant."

He yawns. "All right, sit." I take the chair facing his desk. "What is it now, more trouble with your roommates?"

"Request to speak frankly, Sergeant," I reply.

"Go ahead."

I swallow. "I want to file a complaint."

"What kind of complaint? Someone filched your nail polish?"

I flush. "No, Sergeant. Um, it's, um . . ."

"I don't have all day, soldier."

"No. Sorry." I look down at the floor. "It's assault," I mumble.

Henley shifts in his chair. "What? Speak up, for Christ's sake."

I lift my head, my mouth dry. Speaking up in that place is like screaming your secrets through a megaphone. We aren't even alone in the tent.

"This is confidential, Sergeant," I remind him, my voice low. "But PFC Bonaparte punched me. And, and, Staff Sergeant Kormick. Um. Assaulted me."

Henley looks at me steadily. "What kind of assault, Specialist? Make yourself clear."

I flush again. "He tried to . . ." I stop. *Come on, idiot, say it.* "He tried to strangle and rape me."

Those are the hardest words I've ever had to say in my life.

Henley holds up his hand. "Wait a moment. I need to take this down." He rifles in a box and pulls out a form and a pen. "Date?"

"Date? You mean today's?"

He gives me an exasperated look. "No, Brady. The date of the incident."

"Oh." I think back. When was it? This month? Last month? All the days have blended into one long sand-colored smear. "I'm not sure. May, I think. Um, May 28th. Or 29th."

He puts down the pen. "Specialist, we're not going to get to step one here if you can't even remember the date. You are talking about a noncommissioned officer, remember, an officer with a fine reputation and a solid career. These are serious allegations. You better know what you're saying, you better get your story straight and you better damn well be telling the truth."

"I am, Sergeant."

"Well, then?"

My hands are trembling so much now that I have to pin them between my knees so he won't notice. Sweat's running into my eyes and down my neck. Why is this so hard?

"May 29th," I say randomly.

"All right. So what happened?"

Slowly, I tell him. Every word feels like I'm pulling my guts out through my mouth with a fishhook.

Henley writes it all down without looking at me once. "Did you report this at the time? Is there any physical evidence?" he says when I'm done.

"No, Sergeant."

"What about witnesses?"

"Uh, none." I can't bring Jimmy or DJ into this, whatever they say. It'd kill their careers. And I haven't let anyone see the bruises around my neck, which have faded to faint yellow splotches by now anyway, invisible under the dust and grime that stick to me like a second skin.

"No witnesses." Henley writes that down, too. "And you want to press charges against these two gentlemen, even though you have no evidence, no witnesses and you can't be sure of the date. Is that what this is about?"

"No, Sergeant. I was just hoping you could transfer these men somewhere else where they can't assault any other females."

"And have you reason to believe they have assaulted other females?"

I hesitate. "I'm not at liberty to say."

"I see." He puts his pen down carefully on top of the report, now covered in his scrawl. "First we have to hear the gentlemen's side of it, of course. Staff Sergeant Kormick is right outside, I believe. Go call him in."

I stare. "You mean you're going to interview him about this now? With me here?"

"Of course. He has a right to hear the accusations against him and to defend himself."

"But not with me here, Sergeant! I . . . I can't! Isn't there some procedure so I don't have to go through that?"

Henley leans over his desk, looking at me hard. "Soldier, in case you forgot, we're at war. The cohesion of our unit is of paramount importance, and my job as platoon sergeant is to preserve that cohesion. We have a common enemy, and that is the hajji. We can't waste our time or diffuse our energies on internal strife, and especially not on whiny snivelers like you. Now, either you pull together with your comrades like a real soldier, or you at least have the grace to give them a fair shot. I don't know what your problem is, but I've heard enough about you already. Now call Staff Sergeant Kormick in or shut the fuck up and go away."

I pull myself upright on the chair and stare right back at Henley's prune of a face. His words make me so angry they drive away my fear and fill me with outrage instead. The same outrage that made me lift up my rifle and point it at Kormick's balls.

"Sergeant, not one of those things you hear about me is true. Kormick and Bonaparte are sick maniacs, as everyone knows, and if you won't do anything about it, I'm going to the EOO and JAG and I'm not going to shut up till somebody listens."

Henley sits back and runs his eyes over me slowly, just like the prisoners do all day long. "I see. Well, I'm happy to file a report to the proper authorities for you, Brady, if that's what you want. But I have another report here, from Staff Sergeant Kormick himself, as a matter of fact, that you should know about. He reported to me, on May 30th, not the 29th, actually, that while you were on checkpoint duty, you followed him into the shack, threw your rifle in the sand and behaved, shall we say, in an indecent manner."

Henley folds his hands on the desk, his face as blank as the desert, while I stare at him in shock. He goes on.

"Sergeant Kormick, who, I might add, is a fine and dedicated soldier, kindly declined to press any charges in the hope you would not repeat this unacceptable behavior. But he did enter it on the record in case there should be a reoccurrence. He also mentioned that you committed other infractions that could come up if necessary, including insubordination. Therefore, as happy as I am to accommodate your wishes, you should know that any further action on your part will be met, at the very least, with charges of destruction of government property—you don't treat your weapon like that, Specialist—and indecent behavior, all of which will lead to trial by court-martial. This information will, of course, be given to JAG and the EOO. Now, do you still wish to fetch Staff Sergeant Kormick and bring him in here for an interview?"

I can't speak.

"Need time to think about it, Specialist?"

"Yes, Sergeant," I whisper.

"Then get your ass out of my face."


*Dear Katie,*

*Hello, sweets, I hope you get this before the end of June. I've been thinking of you so much I had to write again. I had this amazing dream I need to tell you about. You better read this alone, now! No horny soldiers peeking over your shoulder, OK?*

*Well, we're skinny-dipping in the lake at midnight, nobody around. Our limbs are glowing white from the moon, the water looks black. We swim a ways out, moon shining a silver path across the waves. An owl hoots. We're not cold at all cause we just drank a bunch of tequila. And then I swim up and pull you close to me and soon we're making love—remember? Cause when I woke up I knew it wasn't a dream at all, it was a memory.*

*I love you so much, Katie. I want you back so bad. I*
*pray every day that you keep safe.*
*With all my heart,*
*Tyler*
*P.S. Did you have a chance to listen to my CD yet?*

I fold the letter up tight and shove it to the bottom of my
duffle bag, along with his untouched CD. His words make
me feel exposed and humiliated and sick. They make me
want to puke.

*Dear Tyler,*
*Thanks for your letter. I don't have time to write much*
*now, but could you not write stuff like that anymore?*
*You never know who reads our letters before we get them,*
*there's no privacy here. If anybody saw what you wrote,*
*I'd never hear the end of it.*
*Thanks,*
*Kate*

Now I can't sleep. My head keeps screaming all the things
I wish I'd said to Henley but didn't. Burning, furious sentences shouting inside my brain. I should have known that
he'd close ranks with Kormick and buy all his lies to protect his own kind and his own fucking career. But why am
I letting him intimidate me like this? Why don't I report
Kormick anyway, no matter what he says about me? I picture myself at a court-martial, giving noble speeches about
how all I want is to protect the good soldiers by rooting out
the bad. See myself as a martyr being marched off to prison
with my head held high because I've followed my heart and

my faith. *Blessed are those who are persecuted for righteousness'*
*sake, for theirs is the kingdom of heaven.* When you get up
tomorrow, I tell myself, you better get your head out of your
cowardly ass and fix this mess.

The tent is hotter than ever tonight, which doesn't help,
and noisy as a frat house, too. A bunch of guys are playing dice down one end, gambling away their paychecks,
and they aren't exactly being quiet about it. And the prisoners are hollering and chanting their spooky Arab songs. I
lie on my cot, staring at the droopy ceiling, sweat crawling
over me like bugs, my head banging and clanging with the
racket inside it and out. It feels like somebody strapped me
down on an electric stove and is screaming in my ears and
cooking me alive all at once.

When dawn releases me at last, I make Third Eye come
with me to the latrines. The Sand Queen graffiti is gone,
thank God—somebody's scraped it off, most likely Jimmy.
But almost every day something obscene is up there about
females, words or a crude pornographic drawing. I will
never understand how guys can act like your brother one
minute, then hit on you or write shit like that the next.
What makes them do it?

My plan is to get Third Eye alone so I can ask her to join
forces with me against Henley and Kormick. Even if she
doesn't want to tell them about the rape, maybe she can
at least report harassment. But as we struggle through the
thick sand and our sleepiness, I look over at her screwed-up
face, tight and wary, and I see how hard she's working at
shutting out the pain. And all my courage drains away.

Back at the tent, everybody's buzzing with news because
a huge escape tunnel has just been found under one of the

prison tents. Seems the detainees have been digging it for weeks. DJ tells us it stretches from the tent all the way to the wire, underneath the berm and out into the desert, its exit camouflaged with cardboard and burlap. Pretty damn smart, we have to admit. Not only that, the bastards smoothed the inside walls with the milk rations we give them, and put little flashlights in there and air holes so they don't suffocate while they're escaping. It was only discovered because some satellite photos happened to show changes in the color of the sand.

"I can't understand it," Jimmy says to me when we talk about it later on my tower. "Our guys go in there all the time to do inspections. They throw the detainees out of their tents every morning so they can rummage through their shit. And they find plenty. Homemade knives, drugs. But they never found that tunnel. Why?"

"I guess you can hide anything in the sand," I say listlessly. I'm still so sick over my interview with Henley and my umpteenth fuckup with Third Eye that I can hardly speak.

Jimmy glances at me. "You okay?"

"Just tired."

"Here, want some chips? Barbecue, isn't that your favorite?"

"No thanks."

We fall quiet then, gazing out at the prisoners drooping around in the sand.

"See that man?" I say at last, pointing to the jerk-off. He's lurking near the wire under my tower, as usual, waiting for Jimmy to leave so he can whip out his dick again. "That's the one who threw his shit at me. He jerks off in front of me almost every day. Wish I could get my hands on those ragheads sometime, instead of sitting up here like a doll on a shelf."

"You could."

I look over at Jimmy, who's glaring at the man himself now. "What do you mean?"

"I could get you inside the compound if you want."

"Oh, I don't know. What's the point? I see their ugly mugs enough as it is." But then I think, you know, it would be satisfying to punish that guy. Just once. Show him that I'm not the pathetic piece of female flesh he clearly thinks I am. Show him who's boss. "Well, okay," I add. "Why the hell not?"

What I don't tell Jimmy is that more than one man's jerking off at me now, and throwing their shit, too. I don't tell him because he can't do anything about it. Anyhow, he's heard enough of my stupid damn problems.

"I talked to Ortiz, by the way," Jimmy says a few minutes later. "He can meet you after his shift if you want. He told me they had a riot over at the boys' tent last night."

"Anyone get hurt?"

"Not that I know of. I think Finley—the girl in Pat-the-Bunny's squad? I think she got her head cut open or something. Nothing too serious."

"No, I mean the prisoners. Any of them get hurt?"

"Oh. I don't know. Ask Ortiz."

So that evening I do. Jimmy brings him over to my tent right after our shifts, and the three of us stand outside sharing a smoke and talking for a few minutes before we have to turn in. Ortiz turns out to be this Nicaraguan guy with a strong Spanish accent, who enlisted to get his citizenship. He's nice-looking, with a broad face and big brown eyes, but he can't be more than five feet tall, even shorter than me. I'm amazed the Army let in such a squirt. He seems all right, though, so I tell him how Naema interprets for me and show him the photo of her dad and brother. "You ever seen this kid?" I ask.

He squints at the photo in the evening light. "He does look familiar. But I do not know."

"If I give this to you, could you try to find him? And tell me if he got hurt in the riot last night?"

Ortiz looks puzzled, but he agrees, so I carefully tear the photo in half and give him Zaki's side. Naema's dad, with his long, sad face, I put back in my pocket. "The kid's name is Zaki Jassim—it's written on the back. And his sister's Naema. Okay?"

Ortiz nods. He doesn't look too happy, though.

"Do you have any way of talking to the kid if you see him?" I ask then.

"Yes, maybe. The interpreter for our platoon, he comes sometimes to spend time with the boys."

"Great! Will you get him to tell the kid that his sister comes every day to ask about him and their dad?"

"I do not understand," Ortiz bursts out, squinting at me angrily. "Why am I doing this favor for hajjis, huh? The boys in my tent, they are fighters, not innocent babies. They hate us."

"I know," I say quickly. "But this kid isn't like that, I'm sure. And I figured it would keep the girl translating for us if we did her a favor. You think you could get a message from the boy for her?"

Ortiz shakes his head. "This is crazy! How do you know she is not using you to send secret codes? How do you know to trust her?"

"She hasn't given me any codes." This squirt is pissing me off. "She just wants to know if her little brother's safe. No big deal."

"Yeah," Jimmy chimes in. "Don't worry. It's part of the whole 'winning hearts and minds' thing, you know?" He smiles at Ortiz reassuringly.

Ortiz hesitates a second, then shrugs. "All right. If Teach here says it is okay, I will do it." He still looks pretty unconvinced, though. He stuffs the photo in his pocket and walks away.

I've got a pretty strong feeling that's the last I'll ever hear from him.

The next day, right after my shift, I tell Third Eye what I've done. "Naema is still showing up every morning, right?"

"Yeah," Third Eye grunts in her usual get-the-fuck-out-of-my-face way.

"She still interpreting for you?"

"Sometimes, when we get the lists. But I hate dealing with those friggin' sand jockeys. They're a bunch of hysterics. And they stink."

Naema doesn't stink, but I decide not to point that out. I just want to do some tiny bit of good for someone here, that's all. Something, anything, other than hiding my head in the sand. "But if I get any news about her brother, will you tell her for me? Please?"

"All right! Jesus effing Christ, Brady, you're such a fuckin' nag." Third Eye sits down to pull off her boots. She's moving unnaturally slow these days, and speaking in a low monotone, too—that is, if she speaks at all. Most of the time she stays by herself, lying on her rack and staring into space.

She doesn't even read or listen to music. She won't go running anymore, either, even though I keep inviting her. I'm running with Jimmy every morning now, Yvette joining us when she's around. But anybody can see from a mile off that Third Eye's depressed as shit. And I know why.

"Third Eye?" I say quietly. "I need a shower before it gets dark. Come with me?"

She can't refuse battle-buddy duty, so she heaves herself off her cot with an annoyed sigh and follows me out of the tent. I do want a shower, but mostly I want to try again to say what I lost the courage to say before, even if it does mean breaking open her shell.

"I got something to ask you," I say when nobody's close enough to hear. "No pressure though, I promise."

"What's your problem, Brady? Why can't you leave a person alone?"

Her insults don't bother me. I understand them now.

"Look, I know it's hard, but I want to report Kormick and Boner, and I wondered if you'd do it with me. You don't have to say anything you don't want to, but I just can't stand the idea of you having to work with those fuckers every day. Maybe with the two of us reporting them, they'll take us seriously and get rid of them, you know?"

Third Eye doesn't answer. She just thumps along, her big feet stirring up the moondust. But then she stops and swivels to face me, her eyes black and narrow in her big, round face. "I don't know what the fuck you're talking about. There's nothing wrong with those guys. I don't need you mixing up more shit for me, okay? Now drop it, and keep your sick little fantasies to yourself."

THE SOLDIER IS back in the therapy circle, refusing again to talk. This is her new strategy, her way of protesting. If they're going to force her to listen to all these other losers, she, at least, isn't going to join in. It's none of their goddamn business anyhow, what she's been through. Why she's here.

"Kate," Dr. Pokerass says then, turning to her with a smile like an anaconda's. "We heard about the problems you had with your parents when they visited last week. I wondered if you would like to share your feelings about what happened?"

The soldier can't believe her fucking ears. This is just like being back in her platoon, everybody knowing everyone else's friggin' business.

"It would be more productive if you would join in once in a while, Kate," Pokerass goes on. "We only want to help. Perhaps you have feelings of anger toward your parents because they supported your decision to enlist? It might help you to talk about it."

Dr. Pokerass has the soldier's whole sorry history right there in a file on her lap. So, since she's got the answers already, why bother to talk?

"My parents were the opposite," Corporal Betty Boop chimes in, although nobody asked her squeaky opinion. "My mom said she'd let me sign up over her dead body. So I waited till I was eighteen and she couldn't do anything about it."

"Mine, too," says the Vietnam nurse whose hubby knocks her around. "They didn't want me to join at all. Said it was only for boys. They were damn right, too."

That's when the soldier gets her idea. She's going to escape. They can't keep her here, torturing her like this. It's not a prison. She can leave whenever she wants.

The thought cheers her up so much she decides to talk after all.

"You're an asshole," she says to Betty Boop, and stands up. "You're all assholes."

And she walks out.

## [ NAEMA ]

AT LAST, GOOD news! I am so excited that I burst into the house shouting, "Mama, come quickly!"

She runs in from the back, where she has been scrubbing our clothes in a barrel of muddy water from the village well, which is all we have to wash with now. "What is it? What's happened?"

"That girl soldier kept her promise at last! I thought she was lying to me, but no—she's found Zaki!"

"Praise be to Allah!" Mama cries. She grasps my hands and shakes them up and down. "Tell me!"

"The other girl, the big rude one, you know?" Mama nods eagerly. "She gave me his message—she read it from a piece of paper in English. He says he's fine, only bored. He's made friends in his tent, two boys from Basra. They have rice to eat, chicken too. He says he misses his guitar."

"And us? He doesn't miss us?"

I laugh, I am so light-headed with relief. "Of course, I'm teasing you. He says he misses us terribly . . . and his guitar."

"Do you have the paper, may I see it?"

I shake my head. "No, Mama. The soldier said she was not allowed to give it me."

Mama wipes her chafed hands on the torn sheet she has tied about her waist for an apron. "And he said nothing about them being cruel to him? They don't beat him?"

"No, he said nothing like that. It was a cheerful message, Mama."

She wraps her arms around me then, her cheeks wet with tears. "Blessed is Allah! Thank you, thank you, my love!"

I hold her close, stroking her hair. Mama was always so reserved before this war, so dignified. She never used to call to Allah all the time, or walk about so disheveled. How she has changed.

At last she pulls away, blotting her tears with her rag of an apron. Then she looks at me, a new fear in her eyes, and begins to knead her hands frantically, pulling at her fingers and rubbing her knuckles, as she has been doing more and more often of late. "But what about your father? Has Zaki seen him?"

"No, I'm afraid not. No news of Papa."

Her face falls again, deepening the lines across her brow. She looks so much older than when we arrived here and has grown terribly thin. Her body, once so graceful, has become gaunt, the sinews in her arms and legs shadowed and protruding. Her cheeks have sunken, making her black eyes too large for her face, and the lines around her mouth are carved deep and harsh. She is only forty, yet she looks more like Granny every day.

I, also, have grown too thin. There is almost nothing to eat. The local farmers can no longer irrigate their fields because there is no electricity to drive the water pumps. The truck drivers who bring us food from the north are being kidnapped or killed, their trucks looted. And all the beautiful date groves near here have been ploughed under or bombed by the Americans for who knows what reason; to punish us, I suppose, for not loving them. So we are lucky when I can find a little salty cheese or yogurt at the market to buy, or if a local peasant woman sells me a cucumber or watermelon she has managed to coax from the dry, dying earth.

"I wish we could hear from your father. Why don't they let the prisoners write to us?" Mama says then, wringing her hands again.

"I don't know. When I met that girl soldier, Kate, she told me the Americans have thousands of men and boys in that prison. They don't even know all their names, Mama. Maybe when they are more organized, we will get Papa's letters."

Mama looks at me sadly. "In Saddam's prison they didn't let him write letters, either. But when they locked him alone in a cell for months, you know what he did to keep himself from going insane, my little one? He wrote letters and poems to me in his head and memorized them, every word. Only a poet would do that, no? Then, when he got home, he wrote them all down for me. Look, I brought them here."

She goes to the bedroom we share in the back of the house and pulls out a large envelope from her clothes drawer. "Read them," she says, pushing the envelope at me. "I've been reading them every night since your father was taken. They help to bring him closer. Maybe they will help you, too."

I sit at the table and take out a bundle of letters, already yellowing and brittle. I have never heard about these letters before and the thought of poor Papa locked in a cell with no paper or pen, working so hard to memorize these lines for Mama, wrenches my heart. "But these are yours," I say shakily. "He didn't write them for me to see."

"I know, but it doesn't matter now. He wrote them to prove that the corrupt have no power over love or art. They contain his spirit, Naema. You should read them." She waves her hand at them eagerly. "Go on!"

So I pick up a letter, unfold it carefully, and, with an ache in my chest, begin:

*May Allah keep you well and safe, my lovely Zaynab. I think of you all the time in here, of you and your flowing, scented hair. Of our intimacy and the ways we have grown together. Of our children and my gratitude to Allah for their strength, their beauty, for being all a parent could want. Memories of you and our little ones are my way of protecting my mind and body from the blows.*

I put the letter down quickly. "Mama, I can't read this." What I do not say is that it does indeed bring Papa back, as if he were here beside me, whispering of his suffering right into my ear. It is unbearable.

But Mama will hear none of my objections. "No, go on," she insists. So, reluctantly, I do.

*I receive no letters from you, dear soul, but I am sure you are writing them. The guards here are no doubt burning them, for they do their best to use you as a way of torturing me. They tell me dreadful things about what they have done to you and the children, things I will never repeat. But although they succeed in steeping me*

*in fear, deep down, far away from their cruel words, I
know, somehow, that you are safe. I feel it with a father's
instinct, and that of a husband. I feel you and Allah giving me strength.*

*I wish I could know how little Zaki is faring. Is he
managing at school? Is he being a little man for you at
home? It must frighten him so to have his Papa gone, but
I am sure that Naema, in all her grace and strength, will
cheer and distract him. And you, my darling Zaynab, I
hope you are not too sad or frightened for me. Do not be.
I will keep myself strong for you.*

*The guards are shouting. They turn us out of the cell
all the time to look for hidden weapons or money. It is
absurd, for how are we to hide such things here, where
we have nothing but stone floors and walls? I think it
is only another method of stopping our sleep. They keep
bright lights on us all night for the same reason, hang us
naked by our arms for days. But I hear the guard opening
the cells down the row from me. In a second, I shall be
turned out with the others.*

*I leave you with a poem, my love, albeit a rushed,
unpolished one. It is a prison poem, written quickly in my
head as the shouts and foul language of the approaching
guards clash in my ears like sharpening knives. Here it is.
Please forgive its roughness.*

*A flower trembles in the prison shadow
Struggling to blossom,
One pale petal at time,
Just as I, in this exile,
This graveyard of hope,*

*Struggle to remember you,*
*One pale kiss at a time*

I fold the letter, too shocked to speak. Papa never told me exactly what they did to him in Abu Ghraib. I knew they broke his legs many times and starved him, but I did not know about the other tortures he describes here. I am sickened.

But Mama is merciless. She thrusts yet another letter at me and points to a paragraph. "Read!" she urges. "Read it, Naema!" I do not understand why she needs me to do this, but, again, I obey.

*Zaynab,* habibati, *O you of the deep black eyes and silken skin. O you of the scents and softness, my woman, my wife. I ache for you like a young man newly in love.*

"You see how he loves me?" Mama says then, leaning forward, her eyes gleaming with tears. "You see how he kept his love for me alight?"

"Yes, Mama, I see." And I understand now. She needs to see me recognize Papa's love for her so she can feel it again herself—so she can keep it near and alive.

She sits back, satisfied. "Read the letters whenever you want, my sweet one. They will teach you." But then she sighs and begins again to knead her hands, rubbing her fingers, chafing the skin. "How I wish I knew what they're doing to him and Zaki in that prison. It's so painful knowing nothing! Do you think they have enough to eat? Can they wash and pray?"

I lean over the table and place both my hands on hers to still the kneading. "I don't know, Mama," I say quietly.

"But I'll go back every morning until I find out more. My patience has paid off for Zaki, hasn't it? He sounds well fed and safe. We must keep hoping, that's all."

I do not tell her how few of us are left with hope among those who accompany me to the prison now. Umm Ibrahim has grown too sick and despairing to come, so stays at home staring at the walls and praying to Allah to save her husband and sons, her daughter Zahra tells me. Old Abu Rayya and his wife have also stopped coming, too weak from lack of food to walk and stand for hours under the scalding sun. Now only two other women go with me every morning: Zahra, always so stolid and grim; and old widow Fatima, who even at eighty keeps up an extraordinary strength and courage. But we know that each day our journey grows more dangerous. Our local militia, under the control of Shia cleric Muqtada al-Sadr, whose anti-American army multiplies by the day, has decreed that any male who is Shia must join their gang or die, and anyone who is Sunni must flee or be killed. And the militia's imam has declared that women are no longer allowed to leave the village unaccompanied by men. Furthermore, we not only have to cover our heads every time we go out, but our legs and arms, too, lest we tempt unclean thoughts or rape. If we do not obey, the imam has warned, we will be captured and beaten.

We are sliding backwards in my country. We are becoming narrower than we have been for decades. Soon we women will be forced to live the life Granny had to lead—married off as little girls, beaten by our husbands, shrouded, enslaved—our rights as human beings obliterated. I know that some fundamentalist clerics, who have taken advantage of the current chaos and fear to gain new power, are already trying to obliterate the rights that Iraqi women have had for fifty years. They want to put us under the Sharia laws that treat us as slaves. If this comes to be, how are we women—how is our culture—to survive?

It makes me miss my old life in Baghdad more than ever. Yes, we were confined and fearful under Saddam, and yes, I will never forgive what he did to Papa and so many others. But at least I was able to go to school and Medical College as boldly as any boy, wearing jeans and a shirt. I was not forced to think about whether I was Shiite or Sunni, or half and half, as I am, because among the people I knew it did not matter. And I was free to become a doctor, hold a job, marry as I wished and walk through the streets alone without putting my life in danger from men who have nothing better to do than stamp upon the freedom and joy of others.

To escape these bitter thoughts, and recover from Papa's letters, I leave Mama for a moment and go into a small room in the back of Granny's house. This is where we are keeping Papa's and Zaki's belongings for the day they come home. Zaki's guitar is hanging by a string on the wall, the way he has always insisted it be hung so that no one in his clumsy family steps on it by mistake. I lift it off, sit on a cushion and try to tune it as he once taught me, then strum it randomly. The sound is jarring, for I have no idea how to play, but it brings Zaki back nonetheless. He is so funny about his guitar, so serious. I remember when he called us in to hear him once, all excited because after months of studying traditional *oud* music with his tutor, a distinguished but conservative man, Zaki secretly taught himself to play a Beatles song on his guitar. He made us sit in a row, cross-legged on floor pillows like a real audience: our parents, me and four of our cousins. Then, slowly, his tongue between his teeth, his Beatle hair flopping into his eyes, he plucked out a song he said was called "Good Day Sunshine." He taught us the chorus and the harmony and soon he had us all singing and swaying from side to side. Mama and my cousins understood nothing of the words, of course, but it felt wonderful to sing together anyway, that melody of happiness and love. And when we applauded at the end, Zaki stood up and bowed, trying to look indifferent, the way he thought a rock star would. But he could not keep a straight face for very long and broke into a big, beaming grin.

Zaki, if only I could summon you home with this guitar the way Aladdin summoned the genie with his lamp. Come home, little brother, and be a child again. Come home, Papa, and take us in your arms. Come home and bring with you peace and an end to all this fear and suffering.

# [ KATE ]

IT TAKES ME all the way till July—five months in this fucking dust bowl—to finally see a bird in Iraq. I spot it from my tower, but at first I assume it's a chopper far in the distance because you can't measure the size of anything against this hard, blank lid of a sky. A fly can look as big as a plane, a plane small as a fly. But when the thing comes spiraling down, I see it has wings like shaggy black sails and I get all excited because I think it's an eagle.

Then it comes closer and I notice its long skinny neck and hooked beak. It isn't an eagle at all. It's a vulture. And I know what it's looking for.

A lot of firefights have been going on in Basra the last few days, as well as over in Umm Qasr, this port only two or three miles away from us. We've been hearing the booms every night, close enough to shake us in our racks. Last night a bunch of us ran out of the tent to take a look and we saw the black sky flashing red and orange, and bullet tracers like strings of pearls shooting up to heaven. It was ridiculously beautiful for something that only means death. Plenty of Marines have been getting killed in those fights. Civilians too, of course.

Vultures go for your soft parts first, you know that? Eyeballs and lips and genitals. I read that back in high school, in a book about some other fucked-up war. Then they burrow through your asshole and pull out your guts. War brings out the worst in animals, I guess, just like it does in humans. In the convoy here from Kuwait, we saw a dog eating a human hand. Just chewing on it, like it was a rubber toy. DJ was so disgusted he shot the dog's head off.

I wouldn't mind shooting a dog myself, to tell the truth. Not that I have anything against dogs, unless they're eating humans, of course, but I need some way to get out my frustrations. For two months now I've been stuck up in my tower like a scarecrow on a broomstick while those prisoners fling shit and spiders at me all day, and I'm sick to death of it. I feel like Hester Prynne in that book we read in high school, the girl who had to stand up on a pillory so the whole town could jeer and throw things at her 'cause she slept with a priest or something. Only I'm not noble and long-suffering, like her. I'm mad as a pit bull.

It doesn't help that I've been hearing some pretty scary rumors about the prisoners lately. Apparently, the ones on clean-up duty have been rifling through our garbage, finding our letters from home and copying down the addresses so they can send people to the U.S. to kill our families. I don't know if it's true, but if those maniac terrorists could take down the Twin Towers, why shouldn't they be able to find our families and murder them too?

Truth is, we never know what to believe around here, since nobody tells us anything. The Army is like a cross between high school and prison, all gossip and scuttlebutt and rules that make no sense. One day we're told to shoot escaping detainees on sight, the next never to shoot the fuck-ers at all. And now that the Red Cross ladies have arrived, things are even more confusing. They're always yelling at us about the Geneva Conventions and accusing us of doing all kinds of crap I know can't be true. For example, they said four guys from the 320th MP Battalion beat up a prisoner, spread his legs and kicked his balls to mush. That has to be bullshit—our soldiers know better than that. And they made us stop using the steel containers off the backs of our trucks for solitary confinement because they said there's no ventilation. But how else are you going to punish a prisoner with solitary when everyone's in a fucking tent? The Red Cross is so busy trying to make us look bad that they never even acknowledge the good stuff we do. Like the fact that we feed the prisoners much better food than we get, that we built them showers and crappers way before we built our own, or give them blankets for free when we have to buy ours with our own frigging money. Nor do the Red Cross ladies give a shit about how those prisoners treat us—poop-ing in the sand, exposing themselves. Why do those guys act like that, anyhow? Is it just because they hate Americans? Or is it because their culture doesn't give a damn about toi-lets and cleanliness and behaving like human beings instead of filthy monkeys? I have no idea. But it's getting to the point that all I can think about is ways to take revenge. Poisoning their cigarettes. Burying toe poppers in their compounds. Shooting off their fingers, one by fucking one.

At least the radio Tyler gave me distracts me a little. I found a Kuwaiti station that plays country and classic rock, which gives me something to listen to other than all the sick thoughts wheeling around in my head like that vulture wheeling in the sky. But then "Tears in Heaven" comes on this morning, that Eric Clapton song about when his four-year-old son fell out a window and died, and it gets me real upset. It makes me think about April and how I'd never be able to keep going if anything like that happened to her. Never. And then it makes me realize how little kids like her belong in heaven, like the song says. But fuckups like me definitely don't.

"Hello? Excuse me?" It's a prisoner standing under my tower, calling out to me in English while I'm listening to the song. I hate it when those bastards interrupt my private thoughts like this.

"Get your ass away from me!" I point my rifle at him. "And no, you can't have my fucking cigarettes."

The man shakes his head. "No, no. I only want to hear the song. It is a beautiful song, yes?"

I peer down at him through the dust. He isn't the starer or the jerk-off. He's some other guy I don't recognize, a decrepit old geezer in hajji pajamas. He speaks creepily good English, too, not that I give a shit. "Shut up and back off!" I raise my rifle again.

He lifts his hands in a shrug, palms out. "I only wanted to ask if you would turn up the volume so we can hear the music."

"I said back the fuck off!"

The man drops his arms and trudges away, head hanging. Who the hell does he think I am, the Prisoner Entertainment Committee?

After that, though, the prisoners try to mess with my mind even more than usual. The starer shouts threats at me in broken English. "I kill your father! Fuck your mother in the ass!" That kind of thing. The jerk-off does every obscene thing he can think of. The other guys throw their usual snakes and scorpions. And so it goes on, hour after hour after frigging hour.

By the end of the day I'm in such a pissy mood that I don't feel like talking to anybody, so I lie on my rack reading *Pride and Prejudice*, which I brought here to keep myself from going brain-dead, and try to ignore everything around me: The rows of guys sprawled on their cots in their underwear, reading porn or playing video games, scratching their balls and belching. The usual group of gambling addicts in the corner, playing cards and dice. The sand-covered plywood floor that bends like a trampoline when you walk on it and shoots splinters into your feet. The sagging walls and ceiling, snapping in the wind and grating on your nerves. The stink of unwashed bodies, dirty socks, cooked air. The restlessness. The boredom. The heat.

Yvette walks in about twenty minutes later, back from her mission up at Baquba after a three-day absence, and I'm so relieved to see her in one piece that I actually get up, tired as I am, and give her a hug. Every time she goes out on a convoy, I worry that she'll never come back—it gnaws at my guts all the time. She's so bony that hugging her feels like squeezing a bag of clothespins.

"You don't wanna hug me, I need me a shower bad," she says, pulling away. She looks like hell. Lips cracked and eyes red and puffy, circled with blotchy dark patches. "I gotta relax a second." She collapses onto her rack.

I sit on Third Eye's cot—she's still out at the checkpoint—and look at Yvette with concern. "Was it hell out there? You get any sleep?"

She shakes her head. "You didn't hear what happened?"

"No, what?"

"A fuckin' IED hit our lead truck, that's what. Killed Colonel Borden outright. Blew off both of Halberg's legs and his right arm. I never seen so much blood."

She rubs her red eyes, hard. "I don't know if the poor sucker's gonna make it or not. And if he does, he's only gonna have half a body." Her voice trembles. "He's got a new baby back home, Kate. He showed me her picture. How's he gonna play with that baby now?"

"Jesus."

"Yeah. Wish He'd fuckin' been there."

I glance up at Mom's crucifix on my tent post, right above Fuzzy, who's all shriveled now, his pale legs dry and curly. I don't know which of them looks more useless.

"You ready for that shower?" I say. "Might make you feel better. I'll go with you."

"Yeah. I guess." Yvette heaves herself off her cot and the two of us pick up our rifles and helmets and head outside.

"You know somethin'?" she says after a few minutes, while we're tramping through the sand. "I made myself a decision out there in that truck, waiting to see who was gonna die next."

I look over at her, expecting to hear her say that she's changed her mind about the Army, that she's going to quit the minute her time's up and never look back. That's what most of us are saying these days.

"I made me a bargain with God," she goes on. "I said, Lord, if You get me out of this war in one piece, I'll go to school and train to be a medic. And then I'll sign up to come back to this sorry-ass place so I can put poor bastards like

Halberg back together. I mean it, Lord. You listenin'?" She looks over at me, her dry mouth set tight.

"I guess He was, since you're still here." I smile at her. But at the same time I feel this sheet of ice drop through my chest. Because while Yvette was out there in all that danger, making her sweet-hearted deal with God, I was sitting up in my tower, snug as a bug, dreaming about shooting people's fingers off.

After we get back from the showers, I lie on my cot trying to sleep, but it's hopeless. The prisoners are making an unbelievable racket, much worse than usual. Screaming, chanting, shrieking. But it isn't only that. On my left, Mack's fiddling with himself and grunting in the most disgusting way. On my right, I can sense Third Eye wide-awake, tense and miserable. And over beside her, tough little Yvette is lying with her face in her pillow, trying to muffle her sobs.

The next morning, Yvette has to leave on an early convoy— no rest for the weary in war. But before she goes, I lift Mom's crucifix off my tent post and hand it to her. "This is to keep you safe out there, okay babe?" What I really want to do is wrap my arms around her and make her stay with me.

"You sure? I thought it was real important to you."

"Yeah, but you need it out there more than I do. I'm stuck in my tower all day. Come on, take it."

She hesitates. "I don't think I should. It's yours."

"No, I really want you to have it. Please? It'll help me feel better when you're out there. Do it for me, Yvette, okay?"

She studies my face a second, her tired eyes serious. "Okay, Freckles. Thanks." Pulling a length of string from her pocket, her expression solemn, she threads the crucifix on it like it's a precious jewel, not just a piece of crappy white plastic. Then she hangs it around her neck, gives me a wave and leaves.

What I don't tell her is that I can't stand the sight of that thing any longer. Can't take Jesus looking down on me while I fill up with hate. Specially not Mom's Jesus.

After Yvette leaves, my team picks me up as usual and we drive to our compounds. "You all hear that ruckus the hajjis were making last night?" Jimmy asks us once I'm squeezed into the back next to Mosquito.

"Yeah," Creeley answers, steering us bumpily down the sandy road. "What the fuck was their problem, nothing good on TV?"

Jimmy chuckles and shakes his head. "Henley said the whole fucking compound was out of control. Throwing rocks and hollering. One of our guys got hurt, couple prisoners got shot. So now we're in deep shit with the Red Cross." He turns to face me and Mosquito. "But it means Hajji's real riled up today, so you two need to keep an extra eye on your compounds, okay?"

"Got it, Sar'nt," Mosquito says. "Moral: don't shoot a fuckin' sand nigger while the Red Cross is watching."

Sure enough, soon as I get to my tower I sense that the tension's much worse than usual. The starer's glaring at me like a snake, and the other prisoners keep bursting into angry shouts, although mostly aimed at each other. I scan the compound, doing a quick count. Forty-four of those suckers are out here today, two entire tents' worth, and every last one of them is strung tight as a slingshot.

Settling onto my chair, I lay my M-16 across my knees and stare down at the corral of sand between the tents and the wire. I know each grain of that sand by now, each pathetic tuft of dried shrub, each spot of rust on the wire's razor blades. Our little world.

The squabbling goes on a while. Sometimes it dies down for a few seconds, but then it flares up again worse than ever. The prisoners keep gathering in clumps, too, waving their arms and yelling, which I don't like at all. I can feel the mood tightening around my skin like a rope. Gripping my rifle, I move to the edge of my hot seat.

A second later, two of the prisoners start a furious argument. They thrust their faces up nose-to-nose, hollering and shoving and jabbing at each other, until a bunch of other guys come running up to join in. One punches another in the jaw and in a flash the whole damn pack of them erupts into a full-scale brawl.

I jump to my feet and yell into my walkie-talkie, telling the MPs inside to get their asses out here and break up the fight, but the stupid piece of crap isn't working, of course. All I get is static. I try yelling at the prisoners at the top of my voice, too, but that doesn't do anything either—they can't even hear me, they're making such a rumpus. They're out of control now. Noses bleeding. Guys rolling on the ground, punching and clawing, kicking in ribs, stamping on hands. I don't know what to do except stand up here waving my arms like a retard. So I flick the safety off my weapon, point it up into the air. And fire.

It's only a warning shot but it stops them dead. All the prisoners duck and freeze, searching the sky for where the shot came from, looking scared and confused. And, well,

I know this sounds bad, but they look so ridiculous for a moment, like a bunch of Chicken Littles trying to see the sky falling, that I burst out laughing.

*Wham!* Something hits me on the cheek so hard it spins me half way around on my feet. I drop to my hands and knees, stunned. Am I shot? I don't feel anything except a scary numbness on my face. I touch my cheek—blood! But before I have time to react, a hail of stones comes flying at me, pelting me hard all over, banging off my helmet like bullets. Where the hell are the other MPs when I need them? Where's my team? Fucking bastards!

I lift myself to my knees, the stones still coming at me, close my eyes. And fire again.

But this time I don't aim into the air. I aim right at the compound.

Then I drop to the floor, cover my head with my arms. And wait.

Silence. Not even the echo of my shot, since there's nothing for it to echo against. No sound but the ringing of it in my own ears. No more stones. Nothing. I try to make myself open my eyes and look. But I'm too scared.

*Please God, don't let me have hit anyone. Not even the jerk-off, not the starer, none of them. I don't want a body on my conscience. I don't want to get into trouble. Please.*

I wait and wait. The stillness is eerie. Nothing but the desert whistle and the crack of the shot still pulsing in my head.

Finally, I force my eyes open. Stand up and look.

No dead body. No pool of blood. Only a few MPs, who've appeared at last to see what the hell's going on and are herding the prisoners into their tents.

Ah, the power of a gun.

Jimmy turns up a few minutes later, carrying a can of Coke. "You okay?" he calls from the ground. "I heard the ruckus. They got the whole compound on lockdown now, giving them the third degree." He climbs up the ladder. "Jesus, what the hell happened to you?"

I'm sitting on the tower floor, rifle right next to me, trying to stem the bleeding on my cheek with my sleeve. "The fuckers hit me with a stone."

"Shit. You all right?" He crouches beside me.

"Yeah. But where the hell was everybody? Why'd the MPs get here so late?"

"They were dealing with some trouble on the other side. Sure you're okay?"

"Uh-huh. You think the hajjis'll come back out soon?"

"Not for a while. Here, let me take a look." Jimmy puts down his Coke, takes off his shades and peers into my face. His breath smells of Coke and tobacco, but somehow it's kind of pleasant. He lifts my jaw gently, turning my wounded cheek toward him. Nobody's touched me like that for months.

"You better go to the medic and get that stitched. Let me put some disinfectant on it. Does it hurt?"

I shake my head. I don't seem to be able to speak.

He digs into the green Combat Lifesaver bag he carries on his back. A lot of soldiers have those. You take a course for four days or so and they give you a bag to carry with you all the time, with an IV in it, catheters, bandages and so on. In Jimmy's case, he also carries condoms for soldiers to put on the ends of their rifles or dicks, whichever happens to be required. I almost took that course too, once, but when I heard you had to learn how to put needles in people's veins, I gave up. Too squeamish.

"Hold still." He tilts up my chin with one hand—that gentle touch again—and carefully wipes off the blood and dust with some cotton. He's bent real close to me now, his forget-me-not eyes only a couple inches from mine. I look right into them, can't stop myself. And he looks right back.

"It's not as deep as I thought," he says, dabbing my cheek with antibiotic gel. "I'll put a bandage on it. That's probably all you need."

"You think I'll have a scar?"

He smiles. "I doubt it. But even if you do, it'll only make you look like a sexy pirate. You want me to send someone to spell you so you can go to the medic, just in case?"

"No, it's okay."

"Sure?" He touches my cheek again, below the cut, and lets his fingers linger there a second.

"Yeah," I breathe. "I'm sure."

We're still looking in each other's eyes.

"I brought you a Coke," he says after a pause, almost whispering. "You want it?"

I nod. He breaks our gaze at last, yanks a second can out of his pocket and hands it over. Still shaky, I take a swallow. It's warm and nasty, but at least it's wet.

Jimmy settles down next to me on the platform floor, so close his arm's touching mine. Then we sit in silence a while, staring at the empty compound. A rare wisp of cloud wanders across the sun, its shadow crawling along the sand like a giant crab. I watch it every inch of the way.

"Jimmy?"

"Yeah?"

"I . . ." A flush rises over my cheeks.

"What?" He turns to face me, his eyes warm and kind.

"I shot at them."

"So?"

"I mean they were throwing stones. Fighting. But . . . I tried to kill them."

"Of course you did. You're a soldier. That's what soldiers do."

"But they're unarmed!"

Jimmy takes both my hands in his. "And if they weren't, don't you think they'd kill you in a flash? Look at what they just did! Don't make yourself feel bad about this, Kate."

"But suppose I'd killed one of them?"

"It's them or us out here, you know that. You're just doing your job."

"I am?"

"Of course you are. They asked for it, don't worry."

I look down at his hands holding mine. I want to believe him. But if what he says is true, why do I feel so dirty?

"WHOA," SAYS THE nurse when the soldier comes stalking back into her room. "They send you back here already? What you do, insult that poor therapist lady?"

*What's so poor about Pokerass?* "No," the soldier says aloud. "I just didn't want to be there." She throws herself on the bed.

"You'd feel better if you cooperated a little, honey-pie. They only wanna help you."

"Some help. Look, am I allowed to use this phone here?"

"Sure. Just pick it up and dial nine first. It's only cell phones they don't allow."

"Thanks."

"I'll leave you to have some privacy. But I'll be back soon. You can't get rid of Nurse Bingham that easy."

The nurse waddles toward the door while the soldier takes her first really good look at her. The nurse is short and wide and on the cuddly side of fat. Skin a rich, dark brown, like Yvette's. Face as round as a frying pan. The soldier realizes she hasn't been taking things in much lately.

"Nurse?" she says. The nurse turns to listen. "Thanks. Thanks for everything. You've been real kind."

"Never mind that, honey. Looks like you feeling better now, talkin' an' all. That's good. I'll be back."

After the nurse has gone, the soldier sits upright on the edge of the bed and looks at her hands again. They're shaking as badly as ever. Then she looks at the phone, trying to make herself move.

At last, she forces herself to pick up the receiver. Slowly, she punches in the numbers she's been chanting in her head for weeks. The phone rings five times, each ring shooting through her nerves like an electric shock.

She doesn't even know if he's back yet. If he's alive. If he's whole.

He finally picks up. Even before he's said anything, she senses it's him.

"Hi," she whispers.

No reply.

"You there?"

Nothing.

"You want me to hang up?"

"No," he says. "Don't do that."

At the sound of his voice, she closes her eyes. She never knew missing someone could hurt this much. A metal claw gouging at her chest.

"What do you want, Kate?" He sounds tired.

She squeezes her eyes shut even harder because his words hurt too. But then she knew they would before she called him. "Just to know that you're back and safe. If you're okay."

"What do you think?" He's angry now.

"I miss you. I miss you real bad."

Silence.

"Are you home?" he says finally.

"No."

"Where the hell are you, then?"

"Albany VA Center. Inpatient. It's my back and . . . you know, stuff."

"That's why you sound so dopey. They put you on those fucking pills, didn't they?"

"Come get me, Jimmy. Please? I can't stand it in here. It's making it worse."

"You know I can't do that."

"No, I mean it. Please."

# [ KATE ]

ONCE JIMMY'S GONE back to his post, I stay on my tower floor, still too shaken up to move—after all, it's not every day that a person gets stoned by a bunch of hysterical hajjis. I feel safer down here than on my chair because I'm less visible, but I wish Jimmy could've stayed anyhow. The heat closes in tighter and tighter, tension cramping my neck and shoulders while I wait for the prisoners to come back out. Who knows what they'll do to me next? It's real war between us now.

But the prisoners don't come back out. They stay inside their tents so long I figure they're either still on lockdown or they're having one of their meetings. Each tent of detainees is allowed to elect a leader among their own to hold meetings, take down grievances and keep some kind of order. That's the theory, anyhow. My guess is all they do is plot how to escape or kill us. They escape all the time at night. Not only through that tunnel DJ told us about, but because any fool can scoop out the soft sand we're living on, slide under the rusting wire and run. I mean, building a prison on sand—are you kidding? Still, the delay gives me time to push Jimmy out of my mind, move back up to my chair, do a quick clean of my rifle and get myself ready in case they attack again.

Finally, a few prisoners do appear, shuffling back out into the corral, muttering among themselves. Some are in man-dresses, some in loose shirts and pants, all of them dusty and unshaven and slumped. Out they file, like a herd of scruffy goats. But not one of them looks at me.

Then I hear a scream. A terrible, desperate scream. I jump to my feet. What the fuck is happening now? A prisoner bursts out of one of the tents, clutching his head and howling like he's in horrible pain. I stare at his dirty Western clothes, his gray-streaked hair, and I know exactly who it is: the jerk-off. A few prisoners run up to him, but he pushes them away and flings himself onto his knees. Still howling, he throws sand over his head, grabs his hair and begins tearing it out at the roots. I can see the blood on his scalp, even from here. I can see clumps of his hair scattered in the sand, too.

Again, the other prisoners try to calm him, and again, he shakes them off. Then he staggers to his feet, and before anyone can react, he runs at the razor wire and hurls himself against it, smack into the jagged blades. Over and over he flings himself at it, ripping his arms and hands and belly to shreds.

"Stop!" I holler and rush to the edge of my platform. "Stop that right now!" But my voice floats away in the desert air, no louder than a whimper. I'm still standing there shocked when I hear my name called.

"Kate, come down quick!" It's Jimmy again. "Now!"

I scramble down the ladder, rifle over my back, and follow him, although I've no idea why. He runs around the corner to the entrance of the compound, where a couple of MPs I only know by sight nod at me and beckon me inside. Next thing I know, I'm running with them across the same sand corral I've been staring at for weeks, till we're right up behind the jerk-off.

Four MPs are holding him now, his arms twisted behind his back. His hands are torn and bleeding all over his dirty white shirt and he's bent over, limp. But he's still sobbing and moaning.

One of the MPs hands me a pair of zip strips, these plastic handcuffs that look like giant versions of garbage bags ties. "Be my guest," he says.

Then I get it. This is the revenge Jimmy promised me! I don't even hesitate. I grab the jerk-off's shredded hands, cuff them behind his back and pull the cuffs tight, just like I was taught in MP training. Then I kick the back of his knees so he falls, put my foot on his shoulders and shove his pervert face right into the sand. "Eat dirt, fucker!" I yell. I want him to know that a girl is doing this to him, one of those females he thinks is no better than the shit he's been throwing at me. I want him to know how it feels to be treated like you're not even human. So I stamp my boot down on the back of his head and grind his face deep into the desert.

It feels great.

The MPs are laughing. "You go, girl!" says a big sergeant with the name Flackman on his uniform. "Anything else? The crazy fuck's all yours."

"Yeah," I say. "One more thing." And I bend over and pick up the jerk-off's head by his blood-matted hair so I can look right into his evil eyes and show him who I am.

I stare at him a moment, seeing his face close-up for the

first time: his eyes streaming tears, his nose and mouth filled with snot and blood and sand. He's struggling for breath, choking, his chest heaving.

I drop his head and back away. *Oh God.*

"Something wrong?" Flackman asks. The prisoner's still on his stomach, gasping, his face pressed into the sand. Ragged hands leaking blood all over his back.

"What's his name?" I say, my voice wobbling.

"How the fuck should I know?"

"Ask him. I need to know . . . don't hurt him."

Flackman looks at me like I've flipped, but he shoves the man with his foot. "Hey, you! The lady wants to know your fucking name."

The man moans.

Forcing myself to move at last, I push Flackman aside and crouch next to the prisoner's head. It isn't the jerk-off at all, I know that now. "Is your name Halim al-Jubur?" I ask shakily. But I know the answer. I know it just as well as I know his name and face from Naema's photograph.

Very slightly, he nods.

Frantically, I start clearing the sand from Mr. al-Jubur's mouth, his eyes, his bloody cheeks with my bare fingers. I think I'm saying something to him, too, something about Naema, but I don't know. I brush off his blood-caked hair, his shoulders, and lay his head gently back down on the sand, sideways so he can breathe. Then I try to undo the handcuffs around his flayed wrists. He lies there, eyes closed, his cheek pressed to the ground, breath shuddering. His face is gray.

"What the fuck are you doing?" Flackman says.

"He's the wrong man," I gasp, wrestling with the cuffs. "I

thought he was someone else. He's innocent! We have to get him a medic, get him help."

Flackman grabs my arm and yanks me to my feet. "Are you nuts?"

"No!" I wrench out of his grasp and try to help Naema's dad up, so that at least he's sitting and not lying at our feet like a kicked dog. But Flackman stops me.

"Jesus fucking Christ, that's the last time I'm letting some bitch in here. Who do you think you are, Mary Poppins? Hawkins, get her out of my sight."

One of the other MPs grips my arm and drags me back across the sand. "No!" I yell. "You've got to listen! I know who this man is! I know his daughter! You mustn't hurt him! He's got heart problems. Listen to me!"

But nobody's interested in listening to me. They just curse and march me out the entrance. "Hey Teach!" one of them calls to Jimmy, who's standing at his post with no idea what's happening. "Get the bitch out of here. She's a fucking lunatic." And he runs back inside.

Jimmy looks completely bewildered. "What's going on?"

I stand in front him, trembling.

"Kate, what is it?"

"Oh Jimmy," I manage to whisper at last, looking up into his face. "What have I done?"

[ N A E M A ]


MAMA'S SPIRITS HAVE grown much lighter since
we received the message from Zaki. Today, she even goes
down to the village to see what she can swap for the eggs
from Granny Maryam's sickly old hens, the first time in
weeks she has ventured out anywhere but Abu Mustafa's
house, plagued as she is by fear and suspicion. It is such a
relief to see some of her old courage return at last.

While she is gone, I look in on Granny, who sleeps nearly
all the time now, then take from Mama's drawer the packet
of Papa's letters. I feel ashamed, as if I am spying, and am
apprehensive about the sorrow and pain they will reveal,
but Mama wants me to read them so badly that I try to over-
come my reluctance and comply. I sit at the table, covered
at the moment in an old and yellowing embroidered cloth,
draw out a letter at random and, with trepidation, unfold it.

*Last night in my uneasy sleep, dearest Zaynab, I
dreamt of Naema and Zaki when they were babies, a
sweet dream that allowed me to awake with a smile on
my lips. My dreams, like my memories, protect me from
this hideous place.*

*Zaynab, do you remember what Naema said when
you first brought Zaki home from the hospital? She was
eight years old and so proud of being a big sister, remember? That is until she saw his little red face and squirm-
ing body, his tiny hands squeezed into fists. She took one
look into the bundle in your arms and blurted, "But it's so
ugly!"*

*I think she expected a baby like a plastic doll, pink with
batting blue eyes and red lips. But instead of being angry,
you laughed. "He will not be ugly long, little one," you
said. "The more love you show him, the faster his beauty
will come."*

*You are such a wise mother, Zaynab. Allah has been
great in giving you to me.*

*I have no doubt that Naema is doing what she can
for you and Zaki now. She has a spirit I admire, our
daughter, fierce and loyal and, at sixteen, wise beyond her
years. I only hope she remembers to also look after herself.
Please kiss her for me, and little Zaki, too. Oh, Zaynab,
my heart aches for them so!*

I put the letter down and close my eyes. I am so afraid for
Papa. Wasn't it enough that he had to endure such misery
under Saddam? Why has it been his destiny to suffer like
this yet again? But after a moment I pull out another of his
letters, for his words draw me too strongly to resist.

*It is hard, my dearest, to keep up one's spirits here. I
try—for you, for the children, for my own survival. But I
am plagued by my helplessness. I am a father, yes, but at
times even that thought is bitter to me, for what sort of a*

*father can I be locked up in here? I cannot teach my chil-*
*dren, I cannot protect them. I cannot be a husband to you.*
*I cannot even bring you a loaf of bread or an embrace.*
*These brutes have made me weak, Zaynab, and I was*
*never a man who imagined being weak.*

*All I have to offer you are my poems, these invisible*
*letters and my love. All are abstract, all are silent. And yet*
*they keep me alive, for you.*

Enough. I cannot bear this. Hurriedly, I return the letters
to Mama's drawer. I know Papa must be feeling that same
despair now, only worse, for this time his son is imprisoned
with him, so close and yet out of reach. To know your child
might be suffering and to be unable to do anything about
it—that must be the worst punishment of all.

It is the business of war to be unjust and cruel, I realize
this. To imprison and kill the innocent. To crush hearts and
families, cities and lives. And yet we humans seem no more
able to stop waging war than we are able to stop breathing.
Why?

Mama returns not long after I have put away the letters
to find me preparing tea for Granny. "Look!" she exclaims
as she comes through the door, her basket heavy, and she
pulls aside its cloth to reveal astonishing bounty: three fresh
cucumbers and a large pot of goat yogurt, even some onions
and cheese—much more than I have ever found in my for-
ays for food. She also brings back a jerrican of kerosene,
with which we have to cook and light our homes now that
the electricity trickster is being so ungenerous. Kerosene is
foul-smelling and dangerous. Families are dying because it
so easily explodes. But it has become our lifeline.

"Mama, where did you find all this?"

She shakes her head, smiling. "I put my trust in Allah, my love."

I know, however, that what has really given Mama this new courage is her effort to believe that Papa and Zaki will return any day. Even as she cooks, she pretends she is cooking for them. I can tell, for this is the only time she seems happy. Sometimes she even hums as she busies herself at the stove, her graying hair knotted in a bun at her neck, her thin body wrapped in one of her makeshift aprons. She hums because, for a few precious moments, she has forgotten that her husband and son are not in the next room, waiting for supper.

Yesterday, when we were pummeled by yet another dust storm, she betrayed this dream again. Silt covered every inch of the house—the furniture and window ledges, the floors, even under the carpets and all over the walls—as if the desert had picked itself up and moved inside. Mama made me wipe and scrub with her all day long, until every speck of sand and dust was gone, even though these storms come all the time in this summer season. For whom could this effort be, except Zaki and Papa? Granny Maryam has sunk back into her illness and lies all day in her room, her dim eyes darting about in fear, her breath wheezing and labored. Mama and I spend our days scrounging for food and water and fuel. We are long past caring about dust. No, this frantic cleaning is Mama's way of showing her hope is not defeated.

I, too, am holding onto hope, tenuous as it may be, trudging to the prison every morning with my three remaining companions. The McDougall soldier whose name made me laugh is still there, but she no longer bothers to talk to us.

She only stands with her rifle raised, her red face obscured by her helmet and sunglasses, staring at us without really seeing us, until we grow tired of trying to get her attention and go home. The only change in this routine is when she has a new list of prisoners for me to read out, or that one time she read me the message from Zaki.

I have begun to wonder about that message, though. At first I was too happy to question it, but now a worm of doubt is eating at my heart. I would never point this out to Mama, but Zaki does not speak enough English to tell the Americans that he has two friends from Basra, let alone that he misses his guitar. And why would the soldiers bother to find an interpreter for an insignificant little boy? Then there is the fact that I myself told the soldier girl Kate that Zaki plays guitar. Could she have written this message herself to trick me into continuing to interpret, or as some sort of perverse joke? These Americans seem capable of anything. And if she is cruel enough to have fabricated the message, how, then, God help me, can I have faith that Zaki is even alive?

I lie awake for many hours at night, fretting over these questions, but it does me no good, for the only person who can answer them is Kate. And I never see her anymore.

The morning after Mama's success at the market, while the widow Fatima, Zahra and I are walking through the village on our usual way to the prison, we are startled to see men in the street for the first time, even though it is not yet dawn. Usually the streets are empty at this early hour, except for the odd wandering goat or hen. The men stare at us as we walk by. They are followers of Muqtada al-Sadr. I know this because they wear black and wrap scarves around their faces to disguise their identities. I consider them cowards and brutes but nonetheless hesitate at the sight of them, for they are frightening like this, dark and faceless, just as they mean to be.

"Keep walking and don't look at them," Fatima whispers. "And stay close to me."

I keep my eyes to the ground and hurry beside her, for I am the youngest by far of we three women and thus the clearest target of the men's reprobation. But it is hard not to stare into their eyes and challenge them. I long to say, "Why must you be so destructive? I, too, want the Americans to leave, but not at the expense of even more hatred and murder among our own people, and not at the hands of fanatics like you."

"You walk like a whore alone in the streets!" one hisses at me as I pass. "You offend Allah and you will be punished." And he spits at my feet.

I hurry on, shocked and afraid, but Fatima stops and glares at him. "She is not alone!" she cries in her ancient, crackling voice, shaking her fist at him. "She's with me, her own grandmother! How dare you call my grandchild such names! Have you no respect for your elders?"

The man scowls and turns away.

I am grateful for the lie and ashamed of Mama's and my suspicions of this kind old widow. But for how long I can depend upon her fragile protection, I dare not guess.

By the time we arrive at the prison some forty minutes later, still shaken by this encounter, we find the usual thirty or so determined but exhausted citizens already there, clustered together in the dust and heat. The McDougall soldier is there, as well, but this time accompanied by a man

I have never seen before, a uniformed man, tall and dark. She escorts him up to us and stands beside him, glaring at us and holding her rifle across her chest, her legs straddled wide, as if the desert rocks beneath her like a ship. The man steps forward.

"Good morning and Allah be with you," he says, and a murmur of surprise runs through the crowd because he is speaking Arabic. "Forgive me for my imperfect Arabic, but I hope you can understand me."

Another murmur moves through us, one of assent. His accent is American and his dialect not Iraqi, but his words are clear.

"I am here to explain the condolence payments the U.S. government is offering citizens who have lost a family member through accident." Before we can decipher quite what he is talking about, he goes on to say the Americans will give twenty-five hundred dollars to any family whose father or mother or child they have "inadvertently killed"—as long as the victim was innocent, that is. "This is your *di'ah*," he says. "Reparation for accidental death."

Why is he telling us this? He must have bad news.

After he has finished talking in this insulting way about money, his voice drops and he begins to fumble with a piece of paper.

"Speak up!" somebody shouts at him. "We can't hear you!"

The interpreter clears his throat. "I have to inform you of an unfortunate incident in the prison that occurred yesterday," he begins.

Ice fills my veins.

"As you know, we treat the prisoners well here. We bring

in special food to meet their dietary requirements. We have built for them all the amenities—"

"Shut up and tell us what you came to say!" an old man beside me calls out. "Are you so cruel you want to burn us on coals?"

The interpreter looks startled and the McDougall girl steps forward, her rifle swinging in our direction. Her mouth is clenched in pure hatred.

The interpreter waves her back. "To continue. Yesterday, at twenty-three hundred hours, the detainees in compounds three and four rioted and attacked our soldiers unprovoked. Stones and illegal homemade knives were thrown, wounding several of our guards, and the detainees then began attacking one another. In an attempt to rescue the victims, our soldiers entered the compound and subdued the assailants, but were again attacked. In the conflict, ten detainees were wounded, six later deceased. I will read the names of those we have identified so far."

A great moan rises from the crowd.

The man continues, his tone expressionless. "When I read the names, if any members of the family are present, will they please step up so we can arrange to return the bodies for proper burial."

He fumbles with the paper again, while the air around us grows as still as a tomb.

"Falah Hasun."

Silence. Nobody comes forward. Nobody knows him. My hand creeps to my throat.

"Saadi al-Ramli."

"No!" cries the old man beside me, the same one who berated the interpreter. He totters and falls on me. "My son!" And he breaks into such sobs I fear they will tear open his chest. I and two others hold him up, but I cannot look at him. I am looking with fire in my eyes at the interpreter, waiting to hear him read the third name—fire, and the piercing cold of dread.

# [ KATE ]

"WHY'S IT LIKE this?" I ask Jimmy one day in my tower. "Why's everything so fucked up?"

"Which particular everything do you mean?" We're sitting elbow to elbow on my platform floor and he's chewing a toothpick, his long legs pulled up to his chest and his beautiful eyes hidden behind the usual shades.

"You know. Watching the useless hajjis all day like this. Living with pervs like Kormick and Macktruck. At Fort Dix, they told me we'd be building schools and good shit like that. Not sitting here like cats in a litter box."

"Yeah, they told me that too. But the Army doesn't give a fuck about what they say to us, you know that. Far as they're concerned, we're just robots. GI stands for Government Issue, right? Says it all."

A prisoner shuffles by the wire just then, head dangling. I scan him and the other prisoners in the corral to see if I can spot Naema's dad. I haven't seen him since I ground his face into the sand. Haven't told Jimmy what I did to him, either. He still thinks Mr. al-Jubur was the jerk-off, and that I was just feeling bad that day for roughing him up.

We sit in silence a while. Both of us know that sometimes we're too sick and tired of this hellhole even to speak. The most we can manage is to stare into space and blink. A couple of MPs come into the corral right then to usher the prisoners inside for chow, so once they're gone there's nothing to look at anyway.

An actual cloud shows up a few minutes later, wandering alone across the sky like a lost goose, so I watch it change the color of the ground as it moves. The desert often shift colors like this. Under the clouds, when there are any, it's dark tan, like a camel. During a sandstorm it's gray, unless it's raining at the same time, when it turns muddy brown. At dawn and dusk it's slate blue to near-black. And under the high sun of the day, which is most of the time, it's blinding white.

"You're right, it is fucked up," Jimmy says suddenly, like we never stopped talking. "I wish we were doing something out here we could feel good about. Rebuilding towns or something, y'know?"

"Yeah." I wince, seeing Mr. al-Jubur's blood-covered face again. "The only worthwhile thing I've done since I got here was getting that message to Naema. It was cool of Ortiz to find an interpreter. I didn't think he wanted to help."

"Yeah, I knew he'd come through. Ortiz is good people." Jimmy turns to look at me. "There's another thing I wish, too," he says then.

Something flutters in my chest when he says that. Something soft and warm. He edges a little closer.

"What?" I say shyly.

"I wish I could spend the whole day with you here, every day."

"You do?"

"Uh-huh. I'd rather be with you more than anybody else in this whole damn desert."

The fluttering in my chest grows so loud I'm afraid he'll hear it. "Same with me and you," I whisper.

Jimmy leans toward me and takes off his shades. And then he does something I never expected. He looks around to make sure no other soldiers are in sight—there aren't, of course. Then he reaches over, lifts off my shades as well and wraps his arms around me, right there on top of the tower. And he holds me for a long time.

I rest my head against his chest, breathing his smell of sweat and tobacco and dust, the sweetest smell I could ever wish for. And for a wonderful few seconds, the hate and disgust that sit stinking inside of me all the time dissolve into nothing.

"There's one more thing I wish too," Jimmy whispers then, pulling back a little so he can look into my face.

"Jimmy, I . . ."

"No, wait. Listen. I wish I could kiss you. I won't if you don't want me to. I know you've been through a lot, so I'll understand. Honest. But . . . do you want me to?"

I nod. Because I do. More than anything in the world.

He pulls me close again, and, very slowly, touches his lips to mine. He feels so tender and welcoming, he feels so kind. I wrap my arms tight around him, and a huge surge of wanting him washes through me. We kiss deeper then, and for the first time in months, I'm thinking maybe I'm not such a terrible person after all.

But just as I'm getting all swoony, closing my eyes to let go, I feel my foot stamping down on Mr. al-Jubur's head, see the blood and sand clogging his mouth, feel myself enjoying every second of the man's pain, and I jerk back with a shock, like somebody hit me.

"What's the matter?" Jimmy says, startled.

I push him away, shaking my head. "I can't do this. I just can't."

"Why? I'm not going to hurt you, Kate. You know that, don't you?"

"No, it's not that." I look at him helplessly. "It'd be okay if we were somewhere else, you know? In a different situation? But . . . I just can't handle it."

Jimmy searches my face. "You sure? Maybe if we give it more time?" He keeps looking at me, his eyes pleading. It hurts so much.

"Yes," I make myself say. "I'm sure."

His face closes down. "Okay. I understand. Forget it then." He stands up and walks to the ladder.

I want to say more, so much more. I want to tell him that it's not his fault, that he's the only person in the world I trust now — and that I want him real bad. But nothing comes.

"Oh," he says, pausing halfway down the ladder. "I'm playing poker with Ortiz and some guys tonight. Want me to ask if there's any news of your kid?"

"Yeah. Please." I can barely get the words out.

Then he's gone.

When Creeley drives us back from our shifts that evening, I take my usual place in the rear with Mosquito and shut my eyes, pretending to doze. But I'm alert to Jimmy's every move. Usually, he turns around to talk to me, or manages a friendly signal of some kind, a wink or a touch, something to set us apart, to tell me he cares. But when Creeley drops me off this time, Jimmy doesn't even look at me or say goodnight.

I stand there like an idiot anyway, watching the Humvee drive away, then turn and drag myself into the tent, almost bumping into DJ, who's right inside the entrance, beaming like he's Santa Claus. "Mail's come!" he announces soon as he sees me, and sweeps his arm grandly at the boxes and letters piled around him. "Two for you, lucky Freckles." He hands me a box and an envelope. DJ's taken to being super kind to me ever since he beat Boner's ass for punching me in the boob.

"Thanks," I mumble, and take them over to my cot. Letters and care packages are a real treat around here, something all of us pathetic sand fleas normally get hyperexcited about. But I don't even feel like opening mine. Don't feel like doing anything except sitting here, numb.

Eventually, I make myself cut the box open. It's full of stuff I asked my parents to send months ago. Gum, sunscreen, ChapStick, bug repellent, deodorant, skin lotion . . . along with a couple of printed prayers I didn't ask for from Mom. A drawing by April is in the box too, red marker on a big piece of pink paper: a little stick girl holding the hand of a big stick girl, the two of them standing inside a heart. I shove it and Mom's prayers to the bottom of my duffle bag, along with all the other letters from home. I can't handle that stuff right now. It'd be easier if they stopped writing to me altogether.

The envelope is from Tyler. I take a deep breath and open it.

*Hi Katie-love,*

*Boy, do I have news for you! The MOST amazing thing happened. It's the best thing that's happened to me my whole life! Besides you, of course.*

*I was playing Moondog—you know, that bar in Albany? And it was packed! Maybe 150 people squeezed in just to hear yours truly. And at the end of my set, this guy comes up to me and says he runs this indie label called Lizard and he wants to sign me! And he wasn't just talking, either, because . . .*

I stop reading, fold up the letter and stuff it into my duffle bag too. Good for you, Tyler. But right now, right here, I don't give a shit.

After that, I lie on my rack, pick up *Pride and Prejudice* again and try to read what I can before it gets too dark. Macktruck's back from his shift too, unfortunately, lying on my left, reading a porn magazine and picking his nose. Yvette's still away on her convoy. But Third Eye's here on my right, stretched out on her cot with her usual dead-woman stare. I can sense her lying beside me, still as a log, and it bothers me so much I can't concentrate. So I put down my book and look at her.

"Hey," I say quietly. "You okay?"

She doesn't answer, but I expected that. Shrugging, I go back to snooty old Darcy. A couple minutes later, though, she surprises me and actually speaks.

"Your hajji girlfriend freaked out today. Went berserk, screaming at us that we're murderers and shit. We almost arrested her."

I sit up. "What do you mean? Why?"

"Fuck if I know." Third Eye puts her arms behind her head and stares at the tent ceiling. "All I can tell you is that this interpreter showed up this morning and told the locals about those prisoners who got themselves shot. Your girl-friend and the rest of them went nuts. If you ask me, we shouldn't be telling them any of that shit. It only makes our fuckin' jobs harder."

"But it wasn't her dad or brother who got shot, was it? He didn't read out the names Zaki Jassim or Halim al-Jubur, did he?" My voice is wavering. I can't help it.

"Jesus, Brady. Calm the fuck down. No, I didn't hear either of those names. She's just a loudmouth. Trying to be some kind of hero or something. And she's been even worse since I passed her that message. Annoying bitch."

"Way too many of those around here," Mack comments without looking up from his porn.

"Did she say anything else?"

"Nope. We chased her away. Now shut up and let me get some frickin' sleep." And without another word, Third Eye puts a pillow over her head.

"Hey, Tits, take a look at this," Mack says then. He leans over and sticks his magazine under my nose, forcing me to see a woman with her legs spread and her finger in her ass. "You ever try that?"

I shove the magazine away in disgust and turn my back on him. Then I dig out a notepad and pen from my duffle bag and sit on the edge of my cot to write.

*Dear Tyler,*
*I'm so glad to hear about your success. It's what you've*

*always deserved. It's nice that you're making people happy. Wish that was true of me.*

*I know this is going to hurt, and I'm sorry because you've been so great to me. But I think we should call it quits. So please don't write anymore.*

*Kate*


"Tits?" Mack says again. Ignoring him, I read over my letter, a weight collecting in my chest.

"Hey, I'm talking to you!" Mack shakes my cot. "Turn around and listen to me for once!"

I fold the letter carefully, slide it inside an envelope, seal it, and then write the address slow and clear.

Mack reaches over and grabs my arm. "Hey!"

"Get off!" I jab my elbow backward into something soft and crunchy.

"Ow!"

"Leave her alone, Macktruck," Third Eye says dully from under her pillow. "We all gotta live together in this toilet. No need to make it worse."

"I didn't join the Army to live with a bunch of crazy whores!" he sputters, clutching his nose. And he buries his head back in his porn.


The next morning I wake up at the usual time and go outside to wait for Jimmy to join me for our run. I don't know whether he'll show up or even speak to me again, but what else can I do but hope? I can't make it out here without him, can't get through the days and hours and minutes that stretch ahead of me like a prison sentence. He's the only reason I can get out of bed anymore and face what I have to face.

I don't need to wait long. He does show up, and only a couple minutes after I've stepped out of the tent. I'm so relieved I'm tempted to fly into his arms after all—make it easy on myself and pretend I really am the person he thinks and let him love me. But I don't deserve that. And I don't think I ever will.

"Hi." He smiles warily. I try to smile back but my mouth goes limp. I can't find anything to say. So we do our stretches without talking and take off down the sand road.

We run for a long time stuck in silence. And it isn't the comfortable silence we used to have, the no-pressure, companionable kind. It's a thick silence, full of words that can't be said, full of hurt and longing and shame. A silence that makes me feel suffocated.

At last, though, Jimmy does speak up. "Looks like fuckin' Jupiter out here." His voice is flat, neutral. I look around, and it's like I've never seen the desert before. He's right. Everything's dark gray this morning: the sand, the sky, the tents, our clothes. The twilight, or maybe our moods, has sucked all the color out of the world.

"Aren't you sick of this place?" he says then.

"Oh yeah." But again I can't think of another word.

"You know the first thing I'm gonna do when I get home?" he goes on, panting slightly from running in this heat. "I'm going to grab my little bros, find a field and lie down in the thick green grass and just breathe. Then I'm gonna get us some brick-oven pizza and drink me a whole pitcher of beer." When I don't answer, he adds, "You still miss tree roots?"

He's trying so hard. Oh Jimmy. "Yeah," I say quietly. "Yeah, I do."

We fall back into the silence after that. Run all the way to the berm and back again, like rats in a maze, without speaking once. I just can't talk. All I can think about is how the ease and trust between us has suddenly gone; how if Jimmy knew what kind of person I really am, he'd hate me. And those thoughts hurt so bad they stop up my words like a plug.

When we're nearly back at my tent, I remember one thing I do have to say, though. So I force it out. "Did Ortiz have any news for me last night?"

Jimmy shrugs. "Tell you later." And without even looking at me, he runs off to his tent.

But he doesn't tell me later. He doesn't say anything to me in the Humvee, and he doesn't show up for his regular afternoon visit, either. For all fourteen hours of my shift, I sit trapped in my tower alone, hoping and hoping he'll come. But he never does. And at the end of the day, when he and Creeley pick me up in the Humvee, he spends the whole ride kidding around with the guys and acting like I'm not even there.

THE HOSPITAL PHONE is ringing and ringing, but all the soldier does is watch it suspiciously. She's standing pressed against the far wall, doing the careful leg lifts the rehab doctor insists will strengthen her back. That phone brings a lot of unwelcome shit these days. Parents. Tyler. Clueless civilian friends. *Please don't be any of them*, she prays. *Please be Jimmy instead so I can get out of here*. But she knows it won't be.

It rings five times before she can finally force herself to cross the room and pick it up. "What?" she snaps.

"Katie, is that you?"

It's April! The sound of her sister's breathy little voice makes the soldier's throat swell. She has to swallow hard and sit down on the bed before she can speak. "Hi there, sweet bug, how are you?"

"I fell off my bike," April says.

"Oh no! Are you hurt?"

"I got a big yellow bruise on my knee and I scraped up my elbow. It stings a lot when I take a shower, like a bee bite."

"Ouch. No broken bones though, huh?"

"Nope." April goes quiet in that natural way little kids have on the phone. If there's nothing to say, there's nothing to say.

"You out of school yet?" the soldier asks then.

"Of course not! It isn't even Halloween."

"Oh." For some reason the soldier thought it was spring. Maybe those yellow flowers she spattered all over the room. "So, have you decided what's your costume going to be?" she says, trying to cover up her mistake.

"Guess."

"Hmm, let's see. A princess?"

"That's stupid. That's for little kids."

"Oh, sorry. A marshmallow?"

April giggles. "No, silly. I'm gonna be a soldier like you. Mom found the costume in CVS."

The soldier can't talk for a moment. She swallows again.

"Did you like my present?" April says then.

Oh God, she forgot. She never opened it. She has a hard time keeping track of things these days. Time. Objects. People.

"Yeah, hold on a sec." Tucking the phone under her chin, the soldier opens her bedside drawer, takes out the little pink box and pries off its lid. Inside is a mood ring and one of those woven friendship bracelets that kids make all the time at school.

"I love them!" the soldier says, cramming the ring on her swollen finger. Luckily the ring is adjustable. "The ring fits real well and it's so pretty. Did you make the bracelet all by yourself?"

"Yeah, but Lizzy helped me. She made the middle and I made the ends."

That's when the soldier remembers what happened the last time she saw April. How she came home from war broken and hurting, unable to stop the faces and the blood. How she took her dad's gun from its sacred place in the sideboard and shot out the dining room windows because those faces were staring in. Kormick's face, the jerk-off's face, Mr. al-Jubur's face. How April huddled in the corner, screaming, because she didn't understand that her sister was only trying to protect her. How the dad threw the soldier into the car to take her here.

"Hey, April?" she says quietly. "I'm sorry I scared you like that when I came home. You know I wasn't well, right? You know I love you and will never hurt you? You know that, don't you?"

"Poo, you didn't scare me. I'm not a little kid anymore. I'm eight years old now!"

Shit. The soldier forgot her sister's birthday, too.

"What color's your mood ring right now?" April says then. "Mine's red. I think that means I'm happy."

The soldier closes her eyes. She can't talk because she's crying. Crying and crying, and she can't stop.

[ N A E M A ]

SO, THEY ARE killing our men in that prison! I knew it! As soon as the interpreter began to talk, I knew that soldier girl had lied to me. Why have I allowed myself to believe her? Now I am sure she fabricated the message from Zaki. How could anybody be so heartless?

All the way home with my companions, after the McDougall woman has chased us away as if we are no better than stray dogs, I mull over what I have learned. The prisoners are rioting, no doubt because they are being starved and beaten. The Americans are shooting them, murdering them, yet they do not even know the names of all the dead. How can little Zaki survive this? And poor Papa with his heart? If they have survived at all.

What fools we have been, my companions and I, coming to this prison day after day with nothing but photographs and prayers. We should have been coming with guns.

But as soon as I enter the house, bracing myself to tell Mama this dreadful news, she rushes at me in a panic. "Quick!" she cries before I can speak. "Come!"

I run after her into the bedroom. Granny is lying there rigid, her eyes rolled back in her head and her mouth stretched and gaping. I seize her hand, as bony as the corpse of a bird. Her pulse is nothing but a faint fluttering.

"What's wrong, Naema, what's happened to her?" Mama asks, her eyes pleading.

"I think she's had a stroke," I say, touched by her faith in my meager knowledge of medicine. "She needs a doctor right now!"

"Go to the neighbors—go quickly and get help!"

I place Granny's frail hand on her chest and run next door, where I find Abu Mustafa working his vegetable garden, trying to cajole some sign of green out of the baked blond earth. He looks up in alarm as I fly toward him, straightening his old body with a wince. "What's the matter, child?"

"We need a doctor! My grandmother's dying!"

He gazes at me pityingly. "Don't you know, daughter, that our doctors and teachers fled months ago?"

"Where can I go then? Isn't there anyone here who can help?"

He shakes his white head. "You must take her to the hospital in Umm Qasr, if it hasn't been bombed. You have your father's car, I believe. Do you know how to drive?"

"Yes, but we have no petrol."

"Come." He leads me around to the back of his small, yellow-mud house and points to a five-gallon tin. "Take this. I hope it'll be enough."

"But surely you need it? And I can't pay you for it, at least not yet."

He lifts his hands in resignation. "Your grandmother's been our neighbor and friend for fifty years or more. Huda and I have no need of this petrol. Where are we going to go at our age? No, take it, and don't argue."

So now I find myself clutching the wheel of our battered old family car, just as Papa did only a few weeks ago, making my way toward Umm Qasr. Mama is in the back, holding Granny in her arms and trying to keep her comfortable, but my poor grandmother has no idea where she is. Her eyes roll and her breath comes out in rattling gasps. Mama can barely contain her panic as she murmurs prayers and verses from the Qur'an—I even hear her urge Granny to pray for forgiveness from Allah, as the dying must do, although Granny is much too far gone to pray for anything. As for me, I cannot help but wonder if there is any point at all to what we are doing, if we will ever reach this hospital or even find it operating if we do.

Umm Qasr is only five kilometers from Granny's house, but the drive takes hours. The road is clogged with American tanks and trucks, sometimes blocking both lanes, sometimes roaring so fast down the wrong side I have to swerve the car wildly to escape with our lives. No traffic lights are working because of the lack of electricity, and everybody is so frightened that their cars careen in all directions with no order at all. And then a chain of convoys drives by, forcing us to the side of the road to wait. We have to sit immobilized under the ferocious sun, our fear for Granny's life mounting while one enormous American truck after another rumbles past, belching fumes into our faces.

Mama keeps trying to force water down Granny's throat, but we can both see her life ebbing away with every minute we are delayed. Yet each time I try to pull back onto the road, the soldiers in those convoys wave their guns at us and shout until the veins stand out in their sunburned necks.

Those soldiers. They look so inhuman standing up in their gun turrets, leaning out of their windows, weapons bristling, their bodies hidden behind sunglasses and helmets and those ugly camouflage uniforms that match nothing. What do they want with us that they look like this? What do they think we have done to them?

Finally, after nearly two hours, a break appears between convoys and I am able to pull back onto the road and continue our drive. The air is thick with dust and fumes, yet I can see women working the fields on either side of us, bent double in their black abayas as they dig and pluck at the dusty ground. What do they find to grow in all this desiccation? Children stand by the side of the road, their bellies distended with malnutrition and hunger, their legs scabbed and spindly, their clothes ragged, begging the soldiers for food. Some even run right up to the American trucks, so close I fear for their lives. Are these the people the Americans have come to help? If so, how does it help to drop bombs on their houses and imprison their sons and fathers? To destroy their villages, already so poor, and slaughter their babies? To murder them and not even know their names? Is this the way to liberate a people from a dictator? Or has the world gone mad for the taste of oil and blood?

When, at last, we reach the outskirts of Umm Qasr, I am shocked yet again, for here, too, is pandemonium. Cars stuffed with impossible numbers of people clog the road, blasting their horns. Camels lumber through the traffic, their thin legs in danger of being crushed. Pedestrians fling themselves between vehicles. Donkeys and carts become entangled in fenders and car wheels. I have to weave through all these people and animals, trucks and carts as best I can, praying I hit nobody. And all around me the crowd presses inward with a frenzy I do not understand.

Peering through the dusty windshield, my shoulders tense, my neck craned and aching, I steer the car painstakingly toward the hospital. But as I approach, the crowd only grows thicker and the confusion worse. We are forced to a stop in a jam of vehicles, all pointing in different directions, with no lights or policemen to tell us how to untangle ourselves. I lean out of the window and call to my neighboring driver, "Excuse me, sir, but what's going on here?"

"A team of British doctors has arrived at the hospital to help," he calls back. "My baby has shrapnel in her chest. She's dying!"

And then I understand who it is that surrounds me. A father carrying a blood-smeared infant, tears rolling down his careworn face. A boy, limp and emaciated, pus oozing from the gashes on his leg. A dust-covered pickup with an unconscious teenaged girl in the back, her chest and neck charred and blistered. All about me are the wounded and dying, the victims of cluster bombs and machine guns, of mines and explosives, of poisoned air and filthy water. And, like Mama and me, every one of them is frantic to reach the hospital and those British doctors before it is too late.

[ KATE ]

WHEN I GET back to the tent after my long day of point-less waiting for Jimmy, I find Yvette home from her latest convoy, pacing the aisle, wired, hungry and pissed. "I can't eat this crap," she says soon as I walk in, kicking her MRE across the plywood floor. "I'm going to the PX to get some other kind of junk food. Wanna come?"

"But it's almost dark." I'm glad to see her back in one piece, but I don't feel like being with anyone right now, not even her. All I want to do is lie down and block out what happened with Jimmy.

"Don't be such a pussy! *Almost dark.* Shit." She glares at me with her big eyes. "Come on, Freckles. I'm starving."

"All right. Jesus." Sighing, I turn to follow her.

The PX is a good twenty minutes from here across the base, and since the walk is dangerous for females, we hold up our rifles and keep our eyes peeled. The tents look like animals crouching in the darkening shadows, their sides heaving in the wind like they're breathing. The blades on the concertina wire glint in the twilight, sharp and jagged. The air's filled with its desert whistling and the creepy cries of the prisoners. It's like walking through the land of the fucking dead.

For most of the way Yvette grumbles and swears about one thing or another while I tramp beside her in silence, only half listening. "You know we got the shittiest damn base in this whole sandpit?" she's saying. "Those other FOBs I go to, like Mortaritaville and Scania? They got chow halls, computers, Ping-Pong tables. Damn. Just half an hour away from here there's a base with all that good stuff, while we . . . you listenin'?"

I grunt.

She looks over at me, her skinny little face blending into shadow. "You're mighty quiet. What's up? More shit with Third Eye? Or is Teach giving you love trouble?" Like everybody else, Yvette thinks me and Jimmy are an item now. She's always ribbing me about it.

"I told you, we're just friends," I answer. Although it looks like even that isn't true anymore.

"Well, girl, all I can say is, if a friend of mine looked at me like Teach looks at you, I'd be wetting my panties."

"It's not like that! He's a nice guy, that's all."

"And for that matter, the way you look at him."

"Give it a rest, will you?"

"Oh. *Excuuuse* me."

"Look, I'm sorry. I'm just tired."

Yvette glances at me. "I'm your buddy, Freckles. If you can't talk to me, who you gonna talk to, huh? You can trust me not to blab, you know that. But don't treat me like I'm Third Eye, and don't treat me like I'm some bitch out to get you, okay?"

That touches me, and for a moment I'm tempted to tell her everything. What I did to Naema's dad, how I feel too filthy ever to accept Jimmy's love. But then I throw that thought away. If I told Yvette what I did, I'd lose her, too.

She wants to be a medic and put wounded people back together, not grind their faces into the sand and love every minute of it.

"You're right," I say quietly. "I'm sorry. But I swear it's true. Me and Jimmy aren't involved like that. Never have been."

She doesn't answer. But I know she still doesn't believe me.

We're in sight of the PX by now, which is nothing but the open back of a truck and a couple of civilians selling junk food, pirated DVDs and knockoff watches made in China. (They'll sell you porn and pills and their sisters too, from what I hear.) A few guys are there already, and when we walk closer I see who they are: Kormick and his usual sidekicks, Boner and Rickman. I stop in my tracks.

Yvette keeps walking a few steps before she notices. "What's wrong?" She looks back at me.

"Can we wait till those bastards leave? I don't want to talk to them."

"Be a soldier, baby. Don't let 'em worry you."

But the shaking's started up again and my hands have gone cold. "I just don't want to deal with those jerks right now. Let's go."

"No, man, I'm hungry! Don't be so yellow." She strides off without me.

I've never told Yvette what Kormick and Boner did to me, or to Third Eye, either. She doesn't know that if I go up to those fuckheads voluntarily, they'll think I'm asking for more.

I stand there, shivering. All of me wants to turn around and run. But, like Yvette said, I've got to be a soldier. I can't let them make me hide and shake every time I lay eyes on them. I have to get over it.

So I pull out the knife on my belt and flick it open. Holding it behind me, I take a deep breath and force myself to walk up to them.

"Hey, look, Sar'nt," Boner says. "It's Pinkass coming to say hello."

"Pinkass and Bonyass," Rickman adds with one of his retarded guffaws.

"What's your problem, cocksucker? Your pussy hurt or something?" Yvette says to him calmly.

Kormick ignores all this. But he stares at me, his mouth pressed into a tight angry line. This is the first time we've faced each other since I reported him to Henley. I grip my knife harder, trying to control the shivering.

"So," he says. "It's Specialist Tits Brady. How you doin' this lovely evening, Specialist?"

"Fine," I mutter.

"Good, good." He turns to Boner. "Keep an eye on Bonyass here. Me and Tits have a little business to take care of. And Private Sanchez?" he says to Yvette. "Don't use that language with my soldiers, if you don't mind. It's vulgar, even coming from a fine little lady like you. Come on, Tits. This way."

"I'm staying here." My voice comes out weak and quivery. Still, I said it.

Kormick steps up close enough for me to smell him. "Are you bucking a direct order, soldier, *again*?"

Yvette looks from him to me, and suddenly she clicks. I see it happen in her eyes, the switch from dark to light. "Sar'nt?" she says quickly, moving up beside me. "SFC

Henley's orders are that we can't separate for no reason, so I'm afraid Specialist Brady is unable to leave with you. Apologies." She takes my arm and we walk away fast.

"Get back here, you fucking bitches!" Kormick yells after us, but we keep moving, sure he's right behind us. We don't run, not wanting to attract attention, but we walk fast as we can. My ears are roaring so loud with fear I can't hear anything else. I expect to feel Kormick's hand clamp down on my shoulder any minute, his rifle stick into my neck. But I don't dare look behind me once till we get all the way back to the tents.

When I do, he's nowhere in sight.

"I can't believe it!" Yvette sputters when we stop. "I can't believe he talks to you like that!" She points at the knife in my hand. "You better put that away, girl, 'fore you hurt yourself. You were gonna use it on that mofo, weren't you?"

"If I had to, yeah." I shove it back in my belt. My hands are trembling so bad I can hardly get the damn thing in.

"You okay?" Yvette says, looking at me hard.

I nod, turning my eyes away from her.

"Why you shakin' like that, then? Listen, you better tell me what happened. This shit looks serious."

"It doesn't matter." I'm still avoiding her eyes.

"Fuck that. Of course it does. Look at me." I do. Her hands are on her hips and she's staring at me, her little face grim. "Come on, babe. Spill it out."

So, at last, I do. Kormick, Boner, even Henley—I tell her the whole sorry story.

"Those low-down motherfuckers!" she says when I'm done. "I knew there was something going on. No wonder you're so jittery, girl. What about Third Eye? They doing this shit to her too?"

I can't betray my promise to Third Eye, even now. But I do say, "You've seen how she's acting. What do you think?"

Yvette frowns at her feet a moment, kicking the toe of her boot against the sand. "I tell you what I think," she says at last. "I think you and me better go to the EOO and get this shit stopped right now. If anybody tries to shut you up again, they got me to deal with this time. And we'll start with what I witnessed tonight."

"But the EOO won't listen! You know the officers care more about covering some sergeant's ass than protecting any of us females."

"Look, before it was just you against Henley and his homeys. This time there's two of us, we're going to a different officer, she's a female and nobody has a fuckin' thing they can pin on you. Let's go."

"Now? But it's so late."

"Yeah, now. Before we talk ourselves out of it. Come on Kate, you know this is right."

I'm not so sure I do, but I follow her anyhow, two voices inside of me arguing the whole way. One's saying I'm only going to get myself into more trouble and bring Yvette down with me, because there's nothing a platoon hates more than a tattletale. The other's saying here's my chance to help Third Eye at last; here's my chance to stop being a yellow-bellied, piss-ass coward.

We find the EOO sitting behind a plywood table in her makeshift tent office, looking as bored and hot as the rest of us. Her name is Lieutenant Sara Hopkins and I don't know her at all, even though she's half of all the female officers in our entire company.

My experience with female officers up until now hasn't been too good, to put it mildly—at boot camp, AIT or here. Every one of them has been a ruthless, ambitious bitch ready to cut down any other female who got in her way. So I don't feel exactly encouraged at the sight of this one. She's tall and narrow and tidy, with a heart-shaped face and big brown eyes. And her dark hair is pulled back so flat and shiny it looks painted on, like the head of a wooden doll. She makes me realize how dirty and scrawny I've become, all bones and sunburn. Nails bitten, camos stinky, nerves shredded. A total fucking mess.

After we've saluted, given our names and ranks and all that other rigmarole, I tell her my story. It's torture to have to describe it to a stranger again, although not quite the torture it was with Henley. Still, it's hard to look her in the face as I tell it, because even while I go through everything that's happened—Boner punching me, Kormick attacking me in the shack—I keep thinking, *You could've fought back harder. You could've been tougher. You gave the wrong signals, admit it. What kind of a soldier are you, anyway?* And I'm sure this officer is thinking exactly the same thing.

But then she surprises me. "This is appalling!" she says. "You should have come to me weeks ago."

"I know, Ma'am. I'm sorry."

"Have you told anyone else about this? The chaplain or anyone?"

"No, Ma'am."

She frowns down at her desk a moment. "I'm going to follow this up, don't worry. It's too late to do anything tonight, but I'll look into the appropriate measures and send for you. I'll do my best, soldiers, to make sure these men don't get away with this."

I can hardly believe my ears. "Really? I mean, thank you, Ma'am. I . . . I appreciate it."

"Me too, Ma'am," Yvette says enthusiastically.

"Well, we can't let a few bad apples bring down the morale of the whole company, can we?" the lieutenant says brightly. She stands up, comes around to the front of her desk and shakes our hands. "All right, you can both go now. And Specialist Brady, I know this wasn't easy for you, so I commend your courage and persistence here."

"Thank you, Ma'am." I'm even more amazed.

"You'll be hearing from me. Meanwhile, I suggest you keep this to yourselves."

"Yes, Ma'am." We thank her once more, salute and leave.

"Wow!" I say as soon as we're out of earshot. "She's incredible!"

"Yeah, didn't I tell you? Why didn't you go to her before?"

"'Cause I didn't believe it'd do any good. You know how most females are around here. I thought she'd just tell me I'm a skank and send me away."

"Not everybody's out to get you, you know," Yvette says with a chuckle. "You need to relax, babe."

I look at her sideways, then I smile too. "Thanks for doing this, Yvette. It was real good of you."

"Hey, no problemo. We females gotta stick together, right?"

"Yeah." I pause. "Yvette?" I say then, kind of shy. "I've been thinking. When—if—we get home safe, you want to room together? Like, find a house somewhere and share the rent?"

She turns and looks at me, her face tiny under her helmet. "You for real? I thought you were gonna go home to your family and fiancé and shit."

"No, I'm not doing that anymore. I want to move somewhere I've never been and share a house with you."

A huge smile spreads across her skinny face. "Yeah. Okay. That'd be cool."

After our visit to Lieutenant Hopkins, nothing much happens for a couple of weeks. Yvette goes out on her night convoys and comes back too pooped to talk. Third Eye lies on her rack, staring at the ceiling, her face blank as a concrete block. Macktruck keeps up his usual filth. I hear nothing from Hopkins or anyone else about my report. And Naema's dad never shows up again in my compound. But the thing that really hurts, hurts so much it overwhelms everything else, is that Jimmy won't go running with me or visit me in my tower anymore. He's polite in the Humvee to and from our shifts, but he acts like he doesn't know me or even like me much now. And maybe he doesn't.

I wait for him anyway. Can't help it. Every morning and all the way through lunchtime, when he always used to visit, I hold my breath in the hope he'll come. Every afternoon too. I spend more hours scanning the edge of the compound to see if he's going to appear around the corner than I do watching the frickin' prisoners. And I keep thinking I do see him, because on windy days, when the sand and moondust are swirling around in great billowing clouds, it's easy to see the shape of a human being even when there isn't one. It's like the air is full of ghosts, only it's daytime and you're wide-awake.

July ends and August rolls in, the days grinding along one exactly like the other. Without Jimmy's visits to look forward to, I've got nothing to wake up to but dread, and nothing to do all day but sit alone in my tower, wondering why I never see Naema's dad and how the hell I can find out what happened to him. Meanwhile, inside of me, a black ooze of hopelessness is spreading through my organs like a poison. And nothing I do or think can stop it.

At the end of one of those long, empty days, I find Yvette in our tent, covered in dust and sand as usual, but jiggling with excitement. "Freckles!" she says when I walk in. "Come here." She lowers her voice so no one can hear us. "I just got word from Lieutenant Hopkins. You and me need to report to NCO quarters right now. I think we got some action at last, girl!"

"Right now?"

"Yeah." She puts her hands on her tiny hips and cocks her head sideways. "What's wrong? Ain't you glad? Isn't this the thing you been waiting for?"

"I guess." But I can't make myself care anymore. It'll all be a lot of hassle for nothing, I'm sure of it.

"Come on, babe. They said it's an order, so we better move our asses."

"All right. It's not going to do any good though."

On our way, Yvette gives me a pep talk. "Listen, I know things get pretty damn discouraging around here. I know it's hard to believe in Army values or anything they taught us when this company and this war are being run by a bunch of know-nothing mofos and pervs. But you gotta have faith, y'know? You gotta keep trying. Otherwise you sink, baby. You sink clear down to hell. So I want to see that fightin' spirit I know you got in there, okay, Freckles? You promise me?"

I have to smile at that. "You're too much, you know that, Yvette?"

When we reach the NCO quarters and report our business to the grunt standing guard, we get a surprise. Instead of being sent over to report to Hopkins, like we expect, we're ordered inside to see suckass Henley.

"Shit," Yvette whispers on the way. "I don't like the smell of this at all."

Once we're inside, we get an even bigger surprise. Lieutenant Hopkins is there after all, sitting next to Henley behind his plywood desk and looking as polished and perfect as ever. She gives us each a formal nod. Relieved, we salute her and stand at attention.

"At ease," Henley says, his Daddy Bush lips white and tight. I bet the dickwad's been practicing that phrase since he was eight years old. I can just see him as a pudgy little brat barking it at his army of toy soldiers while his mommy feeds him cookies. "I have orders here that pertain to the both of you," he goes on. "Specialist Brady and Private First Class Sanchez, you are both ordered to move out at oh six hundred hours tomorrow on a convoy up to Baquba. As outstanding soldiers, you have been selected for the honor of being assigned to a shooter mission. There will probably be a promotion for both of you at the end of it."

We stare at him. A shooter mission? That's what they do to soldiers to punish them! It means you pull security for convoys. Not like Yvette's been doing, riding in a middle truck somewhere, but right in the front or at the very rear of the whole convoy, sitting in the passenger seat with your weapon sticking out the window. It means you're the first line of defense, the first to take fire and the first to get a body part blown off if you hit an IED. It means, in our case, that Henley's trying to get rid of us.

"Sergeant, is this meant to be punitive?" Yvette blurts.

"I'm surprised to hear you ask such a thing, Private," he answers coolly. "As said, it's a vote of confidence in both of you. You should take it as an honor."

I glare at his sun-dried face, and then at Hopkins, whose own face is as smooth and hard as the shellacked hair on her head. Is this the best she can do with all her sympathy and understanding? She's a lieutenant; she outranks Henley— what the fuck happened here? Did she believe Kormick's bullshit about me trying to seduce him? Did she buy that graffiti about me being a Sand Queen? Or is she just another Army bitch looking out for herself by keeping other females down, like I feared all along?

"Ma'am," I say desperately, "permission to speak frankly?"

"Denied," she replies, avoiding my eyes. "We've heard quite enough of your frank talk, Specialist. Both of you, dismissed."

We've got no choice but to salute and leave.

As soon as we're out of the tent, Yvette explodes. "Motherfuckers! I can't believe it! No wonder she told us not to tell anybody else! I bet Henley has something on her. Fucking bitch!"

I let her fume for a while without saying anything. I'm too overwhelmed. These bastards are sending me and Yvette on a suicide mission. And it's my fault.

"NURSE? WHAT DAY is it?"

The nurse puts the breakfast tray down by the bed. "It's Monday, honey-pie. Says so right there on that newspaper."

The nurse has to know by now that her patient can't look at newspapers. Any more than she can watch TV.

"What's the date, though?"

"October twenty-two. Know what that means, honey? Means you kept your bed dry a whole week now. Means you getting better. Now move your little butt. Therapy starts in twenty minutes."

If it's October 22nd already, the soldier realizes, she's been rotting in this place for five whole weeks.

The soldier waits while the nurse bustles about, then as soon as she's left, climbs gingerly out of bed to dress. Jeans, sneakers and a faded blue T-shirt from home. She chooses the shirt because nothing is printed on it at all. No corporate logo, no asinine jokes. No U.S. Army. Over that she puts on a denim jacket. Time to execute her plan.

She brushes what's left of her hair, still thin and limp from Iraq, stuffs her toilet articles in her backpack with the rest of the things she packed the previous night, and adds the cash she sneaked from the ATM in the hospital lobby. Then she swallows a bunch of painkillers so she can walk, packs them too, and pokes her head out the door. Nobody in sight.

Moving quickly, she heads down the empty white corridor and into the back elevator. Sinks to the ground floor . . . and she's free. Easy as that.

Parking lot. Sun. Dazzle. She puts on her shades and

works on remembering that she's not in the desert anymore. The October air helps, cold, with a cheek-slapping wind. She walks out of the hospital grounds as fast as she can with her wrecked-up back and neck.

*Bye Dr. Pokerass. Bye Betty Boop and the rest of you loser ladies who think you've got it so tough. Bye the whole sorry-ass bunch of you.*

She heads for a bus stop, concentrating on making it down the road without flipping out. A plastic bag flaps in the wind, caught underneath a fence, and she flinches, eyeing it uneasily. She's already breathing too hard and her back's cramping. So she starts a prayer in her head, a prayer she's been saying to nobody for weeks now, since Jesus and the rest of His clan seem to have stopped listening: *Let me forget, please let me forget.*

The only person at the bus stop is an old woman in a baggy tan raincoat who pays the soldier no attention. There isn't a shelter or even a bench, so the soldier has to wait out in the open. The back pain is shooting through her worse than ever, in spite of the painkillers, and the cold's penetrating her flimsy jacket. She puts her pack on the ground and sits on it stiffly, watching a coffee-stained Styrofoam cup roll down the road in the wind.

At least she knows where she's going. What she doesn't know is what's going to happen when she gets there.

The bus doesn't come for half an hour, and by the time it does her head is light and woozy, she's shuddering with cold and her nerves are zinging like breaking guitar strings. It's the first time she's been out on her own since she got back from Iraq, and every time a car drives by she cringes. When a garbage truck bangs somewhere behind her, she barely manages to stop herself from dropping to the ground. She goes back to praying. *Please don't let me hear any cars backfiring. Please don't let me hear a shout or a scream. Please don't let me see a soldier.*

Inside the bus, she does the same thing: prays to nobody. She prays looking out the window while the bus chugs and creaks through the streets. Prays staring down at her hands, which are still shaking. Prays when a young guy with short hair and an angry face gets on. Prays that she can keep herself together, not lose where she is, not piss her pants. Not hurt anybody.

The bus rattles through the back streets of Albany. Redbrick blocks and half-empty strip malls, dollar stores and gated liquor-shop windows. Overflowing garbage cans. Fat people struggling in and out of cars.

Finally, the bus moves into the suburbs. It's better here, peaceful. She leans her forehead on the window and looks out with relief, letting the fall colors wash over her. Red sugar maples. Yellow bushes. Heaps of orange leaves in the gutters. It looks so good after the brown desert and relentless white of the hospital that it makes her eyes sting.

The bus stops on a corner and two passengers climb on: a teenage girl in skintight jeans and a baggy gold sweater, and a middle-aged woman wearing a short black skirt and highheeled white boots. The soldier has no idea if what they're wearing is cool or slutty, fashionable or cheap. She's been in a time warp and come back to the future.

The teenager flings herself into the seat in front of the soldier, sticks wires in her ears and starts nodding her head to the tinny music seeping out from her earphones. Her long ponytail, brown and wavy, dangles over the seat back, swinging from side to side as she nods. The soldier stares at it, mesmerized. Back and forth, back and forth. She feels a powerful urge to take out the penknife in her pack and cut the fucking thing off.

She sits on her hands to stop herself, shuts her eyes and starts praying again. *Please don't let me do something dumb. Please don't let me screw up.* But most of all she prays this will work out. Because if it doesn't, she has no idea what she'll do.

[ PART THREE ]

# CONVOY

## [ KATE ]

"YOU CLEANED UP your rifle real good last night, I hope?" Yvette says the day of our new mission. We're standing outside our tent in the morning twilight, shivering with sleep deprivation and nerves. "It better work smooth girl, 'cause out on that convoy it's all you're gonna have between you and Hajji."

"Don't worry, I got it." I pat myself over to make sure I'm complete: Kevlar, night-vision goggles, dog tags, flak jacket, utility vest, canteen, knife, ammo clips, grenades, M-16 cleaning kit, gas mask, gloves, JSLIST (compressed suit to protect me from being melted alive by a chemical attack), casualty card, medevac card, rules of engagement card, code of conduct card, rifle . . . and most important of all, a packet of Skittles I can suck on so I won't have to drink or piss.

Yvette watches me a moment, then pulls the crucifix I gave her over her head and hands it to me. "Here, take this back. It'll do you more good than all that shit."

"No, I want you to keep it," I say, still shivering like a cornered mouse. "It's yours now."

"But this is your first time outside the wire, babe. You need all the Jesus you can get."

I push it firmly back into her hand. "No, you deserve it more than I do. You shouldn't even be doing this mission. It's all my fault."

Yvette clucks her tongue, hangs the crucifix back around her neck and straps her Kevlar over her bony little head. "Nothing's your fault, Freckles. Come on, let's go." She flings her arms around me, gives me a squeeze, then scoots off to the motor pool quick as a sparrow, as if the eighty pounds of gear strapped to her body weigh nothing at all. I lumber after her, my neck and back already throbbing.

The way it turns out is this: Yvette gets put in the Humvee that guards the head of the convoy, right in the line of fucking fire, while I'm put in the one that brings up the rear—the convoy's asshole. Between us are twenty tractor-trailers and a middle gun truck, but nobody's in as much danger as Yvette. *Please*, I pray to Mom's crucifix, *please look after my friend.*

Our mission, as turdface Henley explained, is to escort those trucks, most of which are driven by untrained, under-fed, non-English-speaking civilians, nearly three hundred miles up the Highway of Death to Baquba, a city just north of Baghdad. There, we're supposed to unload whatever the hell is inside them, spend the night at a base called Camp Warhorse, then drive back again. That's how most of us so-called soldiers spend our time in this war: as a frigging delivery service.

When I reach my assigned Humvee, I climb into the front seat, still jumpy as hell. This is a whole different kettle of crap than what I've been used to. The jerk-offs and scorpion-tossing detainees are nothing compared to what's out there beyond the wire: Mortar shells filled with shrapnel designed to tear a human to shreds. Rocket-propelled grenades capable of blowing off your hand in a blink. Homemade bombs strong enough to blast a Humvee and all the suckers inside it into itty-bitty pieces. People with AK-47s who hate me. And the only armor I can see is the Vietnam-era flak jacket I'm wearing myself, which is useless against those same AK-47s or anything else Hajji might send my way.

My driver turns out to be this gigantic sergeant called Nielsen, with a huge slab of a face the color of salami. His eyes are pink with moondust irritation and he saw the backside of forty a long time ago, but at least his body looks strong. He grunts in surprise when I climb in. "What the fuck did they send me a girl for?"

"'Morning to you, too, Sergeant." I pull the condom off the end of my M-16 (condom courtesy of Jimmy, back when we were still talking) and drape it over the rearview mirror, just for the hell of it.

Nielsen chuckles. "Better than a rabbit's foot, huh, Specialist?" he says. Then he snatches the condom and kisses it.

Wonderful. Another frickin' nutball.

I settle in and try to get comfortable. Not that comfortable is something anybody can be in a Humvee. Whoever designed those things couldn't possibly have had a human body in mind. For one, the shocks are so bad that driving in the desert feels like being dragged over rocks on a cafeteria tray. For another, like I said, the Humvees are always stuffed with so much crap you have to sit with your knees folded up around your ears like a frigging grasshopper.

Just as I've found myself a half-bearable position, the convoy shakes awake with a roar of engines and begins to rumble slowly out of the motor pool in a long, snaking line.

The sun rises as we approach the camp entrance, turning up the heat like an oven dial, and through the dust I can see a clump of thirty or so civilians standing outside the wire, same as when I worked there. I look for Naema—Third Eye told me she's still turning up every day—but I can't see her. Again I feel her dad's head under my foot, see the blood clotting on his smashed face, hear him struggling to breathe . . .

No point thinking about that now. No point in thinking about anything, for that matter.

Once we're out on the highway, the noise is ear-numbing, all those sand-clogged engines and broken shock absorbers grinding and clanking and shrieking. The stink is powerful too, the trucks farting their fumes right into my face, and being in the rear, I have the pleasure of breathing it all in. I pull my scarf over my nose but I can still smell and even taste the oil and diesel and soot. Within minutes I'm covered in a greasy black crust, like an overcooked pizza.

I stick my weapon out the side window, tell my zinging nerves to shut the fuck up and hunker down to my job.

For a long time the dust is so thick I can't see anything at all. I know it's better than being in the front like Yvette, jumping at the sight of every damn plastic bag or dead dog on the road, but this blindness is its own kind of scary. I'm supposed to be looking out for those wacko suicide car bombers we've just begun hearing about, and for insurgents who might zoom out of nowhere and throw a grenade or shoot at us. But all I can see are those daytime ghosts, human-shaped dust swirls that loom up in front of me then fall into nothing, leaving my heart hammering, my rifle on lock and load and my head buzzing like a swarm of panicked bees.

"I feel like I'm friggin' blindfolded," I shout to Nielsen over the racket. "Can't see a fucking thing."

"Maybe you should climb in the back and keep watch out the rear," he yells in reply.

I glance over my shoulder at him. Is he serious? There's nothing back there, not even a shield.

"Yeah," he goes on, like he's talking to himself. "Good idea. Get in the back."

So I have to. He is a sergeant, after all.

This is what I should have to do my job right: A tank, or at least an up-armored gun truck. A real bulletproof vest. A long-range scope. A belt-fed machine gun. And a gun turret.

This is what I actually have: A soft-top Humvee with an open back and canvas doors. A useless flak jacket. And a rifle rapidly clogging up with sand. I might as well be riding into war in a go-cart, wearing a bikini and waving a parasol.

The drive goes on so long it turns hypnotic. The rumble and clank of our Humvee bumping along the tarmac. The deafening roar of all those engines in front of us. The wind whistling and whooshing.

I stare over my rifle through the dust. The desert stretches out in a haze on either side of us, littered with garbage and tire shreds and blocks of squat yellow houses, same color as the sand. Pieces of abandoned military equipment are poking out of the desert, too: shards of rusting metal, shells of old tanks and bombs, bits of airplane left over from the last war.

We pass a dead goat lying on its side, so bloated with rot its legs stick out like toothpicks in a sausage.

We pass the husk of a charred car, the people inside it contorted black skeletons.

We pass a body run over so often it's flat as a puddle.

We pass a vulture pulling at what looks like a pile of clothes but turns out to be a little boy.

After that I stop looking.

More hours crawl by. Rumble, stink, rumble. *Don't look. Don't see.* Back aching. Head aching. Arms burning from holding up the rifle.

Apaches fly past, giant black hornets against the sun—*whomp, whomp, whomp*—the air batting around my ears. Sand and more sand. Rumble, stink, rumble.

What's Jimmy doing? Has he come looking for me? Does he know where I am? Is he worried? Will he ever know how much I love him?

Is Yvette okay? Is Third Eye okay? Are Naema and her dad okay?

I need water. I need a piss. I need Jimmy. I need, I need . . .

*BOOM!*

The blast is so loud it's like a kick to my chest. The Humvee slams to a halt and I'm flying onto my back. Black smoke blinding me, choking me, radio shrieking—*eye-ee-dee, eye-ee-dee*—but I don't know what it means or where my breath's gone or if I'm hurt or if I'm even alive.

Then I hear: "Fuck!"

I lie there helpless and winded, trying to make my lungs work and running my mind over my body: No pain, no wounds, no missing limbs that I can tell. I struggle to breathe a moment longer, then soon as I can, heave myself upright and turn around. Nielsen's face is running with blood.

"Shit! You hurt?" I scramble into the front.

"Gimme something," he groans. I pull off my scarf and hand it to him, grease and all. He wipes his face, smearing blood. "Damn. I'm always getting these friggin' nosebleeds."

I stare.

"What the fuck's your problem?" He thrusts my blood-and-snot-covered scarf back at me. "Radio says a truck up front got hit by an IED. Now we got to sit tight as a nun's cunt till ordnance gives the all clear."

"Sit? Why can't we pull out? Aren't we supposed to keep moving no matter what?" Then I remember Yvette. I throw open the door to jump out.

Nielsen clutches my utility vest and hauls me back in. "Where the hell are you going?"

"My friend's up front! I've got to find her!" I try again to leave but Nielsen won't let go of me.

"You ain't going nowhere. I know it's rough, kid, but you gotta sit here, you know that. Now shut that door quick."

"I can't! I have to find out if she's okay, I have to!"

"What you have to do is stay here. Shut the door!"

I do. But when I turn back to him, I'm surprised to see his meaty face looking sympathetic. "Pray, that's all we can do right now," he says gently. "Come on, let's join hands and pray to the Lord to help us." He reaches out, but I pull back. The last fucking thing I want to do at this moment is pray, and the second last thing is hold his sweaty paw.

"Thanks, but I'm returning to guard position," I say firmly and clamber into the rear again, rifle in my hands.

We sit and sit. I don't hear Nielsen doing any more praying than I am. He's just staring at the radio like it holds the secret of the frickin' universe. But the radio isn't talking, and nor, for a while, are we.

We sit for another ten minutes or so, while I worry about Yvette. *Please let her be alive*, I chant in my head over and over, so I guess I am praying after all.

"Brady?" Nielsen calls back to me after a while. "That is your name, right?"

"Yup."

"You ever think we might die any moment?"

What a mulchbrain. "Sar'nt, all I'm thinking about right now is my friend."

"I know, I know." His voice shakes a little. "But you ever think how sad it would be to die without, you know, having experienced the whole of life?"

I don't answer. Just keep my mind on Yvette. If I keep thinking about her real hard, maybe I can keep her safe. Maybe my thoughts will flow over her like a shell, like armor, like a cushion from harm.

"Brady? You listening to me?"

I hear a noise and glance back at him. Nielsen is climbing over the seat toward me with this scared, needy look on his face. I don't know what he wants. And I certainly don't intend to find out.

"Oncoming vehicle!" I shout, although there's nothing in sight but dust. "Oncoming fast, Sar'nt! Isn't slowing down!"

"Fuck!" He flings himself back into the front and ducks below the windshield. "Fire!" he screams.

I do. Right up into the harmless air.

"You hit 'em?" he calls, his voice squeaking. I take a peek at him—he's still lying facedown across the front seats. How a condom-kissing wimp like him ever got to be sergeant, I've no idea.

"Just a warning shot, Sar'nt. They're driving away now. No weapons visible."

"Good. Keep an eye out there, Brady." Shakily, he heaves himself up. "Don't take your eyes off that road for one minute." He sticks his own weapon out the driver's window and fixes his eyes on the desert.

Now that I've shut the wimp up for the time being, all I can hear is the wind and the blood in my ears thudding and whomping like a chopper flying around inside my head. I wait and wait, muscles taut, trigger finger trembling. Who knows what might come at us while we sit here like toddlers on a toilet? Another homemade bomb? An ambush?

We sit like this for almost an hour, no movement, no news, while, presumably, ordnance clears the road ahead of us of more hidden bombs. I listen for medevac Black Hawks, trying not to imagine the worst for Yvette. Nothing. I listen for another attack. More nothing. Just tension and dread crackling around us like electric wires.

Finally, after what feels like three fucking days, the radio wakes up with a screech, making us both jump. "All clear," it squawks. The convoy rumbles awake, like a dragon shaking itself out of a nap, and one vehicle at a time, it at last begins to roll.

In a few minutes we pass two of our trucks in the middle of the road, burning. One is tipped over on its side, the other still upright, but both are billowing so much flame and smoke they're barely visible. I don't know if it was the IED that did that, or if we set the trucks on fire ourselves so the locals can't salvage anything from them—we do that to our own vehicles all the time, even if there's nothing wrong but a flat tire. *Please don't let Yvette have been in one of those trucks. Please.*

At first Nielsen has to drive excruciatingly slow, being right at the end of the dragon's tail like we are, which frustrates me so much I want to shoot him in the face. But gradually the convoy picks up speed, even more than before—the dragon's scared now—and soon we're barreling along at sixty, swinging into the oncoming lane whenever there's a block ahead, regardless of who might be there. Cars career off the shoulder to get out of our way. Families stand stranded by the side of the road, blown by our dust and fumes and wind, looking frightened to death. Some idiot with a pickup full of kids tries to squeeze between us and the truck in front, so we wave our rifles at him and scream at him to get the fuck out of the way. But there's still no news of casualties from the radio, and still no news of Yvette.

"Yvette," I swear in my head, "if you're in one piece and we get back from this shithole alive, I'm going to share everything I have and everything I ever get with you. We'll help each other get through it, okay? Just be alive and whole, *please*."

[ N A E M A ]


FOR NEARLY THREE hours, Mama, Granny and I sit
in the traffic jam in Umm Qasr, and still nobody can move.
Rather, it grows worse, for more people keep arriving, pressing frantically toward the hospital. Everywhere, panicked
faces. Everywhere, wounds and illness. Everywhere, cars
and people pushing and shoving. Yet we remain trapped.

An old man hobbles up and thrusts an anguished face
into our car window. "Water? Sisters, please, do you have
water?" he begs in a tremulous voice. "I need water for my
wounded grandson, please!"

"I have no water, grandfather, I'm sorry," I say, kicking
our extra bottle under my seat with one foot. My callousness
shames me, but I have to keep Granny alive.

Groaning, the man moves on to the next car while I look
in horror at the scenes around me. How have my people
been driven to this? What has become of my country?

"Naema, look! Something's wrong!" Mama cries at that
moment. "We must leave the car now!"

I turn around quickly. Granny's emaciated face is stretched
in new pain, her toothless mouth gasping. Clearly, her vital
signs are failing—she needs oxygen and rehydration, and

she needs them both now. I jump out of the car and Mama and I lift her up. Making a chair with our arms, we rush into the crowd with her. The car we abandon to its fate.

Granny moans as we move her, her breath rattling, her murky eyes rolling in fear and confusion. We press ever harder through the mass of people around us, ruthlessly pushing the small and old out of our way while we pass more and more wounded and sick. A baby with her leg dangling in oozing shreds. A man with a flayed face, flies buzzing hungrily over the wounds. And when we have finally struggled all the way to the hospital entrance, we force ourselves desperately through the door, surrounded by others equally forceful, equally desperate.

But here it is no better. The hospital corridors are swarming with people! A few blood-splattered nurses are trying to restore order, but the place is more like an overcrowded refugee camp than a house of rest and healing. And it is filthy! Beside us stands a sink full of bloody test tubes waiting to be washed. A tiny child lies alone and screaming on a urine-stained gurney, its face and body so blistered with burns I cannot tell its sex. A boy is carried past with a metal shard impaled in his skull, his eyes rolling in agony. In one corner a cluster of people is drinking out of an oil drum, but when I draw near I see that the water is covered with slimy, gray scum.

"What's going on here?" I call to a woman beside me.

"The hospital's had no water for three days," she replies, raising her voice above the din. "There is only one doctor! Thousands of people have come for help. But there isn't any help!"

"Where are the British doctors?"

"What British doctors? There's nobody here, I tell you!"

"O Allah!" Mama wails when she hears this. "What's to become of my mother?"

I look about me, wondering if they have put together a triage team in this hellish place. It is hard to admit, but were I in charge, I would tend to these wounded children first, not to an old woman so near her time.

"Granny," I whisper in her ear, "forgive me, but I must do this." To Mama I say, "Let's carry her over to that corner. You wait with her there. I'm going to help. My medical training is too precious to waste here."

Mama agrees and I see in her eyes the same knowledge I have. We have gone to all this effort only to bring Granny Maryam to her death.

For the rest of the day I do not see Mama or Granny once. As soon as I explain myself to the nearest aid worker, she commandeers me. "We have twelve beds, no electricity, and no water," she tells me dully. "I have no gloves, no equipment to offer you. Stem what bleeding you can. A woman over there is giving birth—help her. Separate the dying; we can't save them. Make everyone who can walk leave."

I work and work, using what few skills I have. Time becomes one long stream of agonized faces, heartbroken parents, of blood and burns and mutilations. I seal over my mind, clench my teeth and simply do what I must. The baby is born alive—I tie and cut the umbilical cord and force the mother to get up and go. The boy with the shrapnel in his head dies the minute I touch him. I send him home with his parents, who stagger away, their faces stricken. The burnt child on the urine-soaked gurney, who stopped screaming some time ago, turns out to be dead. Those who are merely sick or diseased I order to leave in cold command. I pull out shrapnel with no anesthetic, waving away swarms of blood-thirsty flies. Bind up legs with shreds of material torn from my own dusty skirt, legs that are little more than a mush of flesh and bone. And soon I, too, am drenched in blood, the deepening red of it seeping through my clothes and chilling my flesh.

I work and work through the rest of the daylight and into the night, until I lose all awareness of my body, and all sense of time.

## [ KATE ]

**WE DON'T REACH** Camp Warhorse until six that evening. Twelve fucking hours on the road just to go three hundred miles. The convoy parks in a huge circle and the civilian drivers stumble out, shocked and sweaty. I jump out too, the second Nielsen lets me, and run to the lead truck to find Yvette. *Please please please.*

That's when I see the stretchers. Medics are lifting the wounded from a truck and carrying them to a waiting ambulance. Blood and torn flesh everywhere. I run from stretcher to stretcher in a panic, looking for her, getting in people's way. A civilian driver with his leg a mass of gore, a white knob of exposed bone where his knee should be. A boy soldier with his arm a ragged stump of blood and skin. A girl soldier with half her face seared off, oozing pink-blood-black.

The bile rises to my mouth.

But still no Yvette.

"Either move your ass or help," a medic shouts at me, and the next thing I know I'm holding one end of a stretcher and hurrying across the sand with it, trying not to puke. The soldier I'm carrying is the boy whose arm has been blown off and he's shuddering with shock, his face a stretch of gray agony under the blood and soot. I feel his shock entering me till I'm shuddering too. *God, don't let me find Yvette like this.*

I help the medic load the poor kid onto the ambulance and turn around to run back for more. Then I hear behind me, "You still here?"

I whirl around. And there she is, all five-foot-one of her standing in the sand looking at me. I throw my arms around her and break into sobs.

"Hey, take it easy, babe. We're both okay, thank the Lord, huh?" She pushes me away gently and stares at the stretchers. "Look at those poor boys and girls. God, what I'd give to be able to fix those kids."

"Move!" a medic yells and shoves us aside so he can jump into the back of the open ambulance as it drives off. We watch it go. Then, since there's nothing left for us to do, we turn and trudge toward the tents.

"Why didn't medevac come?" I ask when I've pushed down the nausea enough to speak.

"It was that piece-of-crap radio. It didn't work! Fucking cheap-shit war." And there's nothing else to say.

I follow Yvette through the base—she's been here a bunch of times, so knows the way. Rows of dusty tan tents crammed up close together, a few limp sandbags piled around their entrances. Dirty gray sand blotched with pools of motor oil. The usual racket of choppers and trucks.

After I take my long-awaited piss, she walks me over to the chow hall, a huge KBR tent she says is filled with row after row of canteen tables and chairs, just like the ones back at Fort Dix. We can't go in right away, though, because a humungous line of sand-covered, worn-out soldiers is standing out front, waiting. So we have to stand there with them. It takes almost an hour.

Still, we make it inside at last, load up on beef stew, salad, OJ and lime Jell-O, and look around for somewhere to sit. After six months of tasteless MREs and T-Rat mush, I should be pretty excited about getting real food at last. But I feel too sick after what I've seen to have any kind of an appetite.

We weave our way through the hundreds of men around us, their eyes stripping and mind-fucking us, same as at Bucca, to some empty seats at the end of a table. I pick at my food and Yvette eats fast, both of us too uncomfortable with those thousands of eyes on us even to talk. Then we split for the MWR building. MWR stands for Morale, Welfare and Recreation, which is military bullcrap for a big metal barn full of Ping-Pong tables and treadmills. But it also has a whole bank of computers that Yvette says actually work at a decent speed, not like those slow-ass machines we have at Bucca.

After another long wait in line, Yvette finally gets a computer at the end of the row while I get one in the middle, and within a few minutes I'm connected. I open my mailbox, stomach fluttering. I need so bad to hear from my old friends right now, Robin or any of the other people I've lost track of since becoming a soldier. Anyone, really, so long as it isn't Tyler. I need to forget what I saw on the road. The squashed bodies, the vulture eating a kid. That poor boy with his arm in shreds. I need to be reminded that there's a world out there apart from this one, a world where people have normal, nonviolent lives.

Thirty messages! I run my eyes down them eagerly.

Five ads for Viagra. Three for porn. One offering to extend my penis. And a whole bunch for diets and dating services—pretty ironic under the circumstances. And there, tucked away right at the bottom, the only four real messages on the whole screen. Four.

I open them, trying not to let the disappointment get to me. A sweet one from April full of misspellings. A couple friends from high school telling me they hope I stay safe. And yes, one from Robin. I lean forward to gulp it down.

She's found a modeling agency. She's posing for clothes catalogs. She loves the city. She has a new boyfriend. All is happiness and light. But at the bottom she's written: "Did you hear Bush lied about the WMDs? Why are you guys still there?"

I've heard this kind of thing from her before. She was always against the war, and no matter how often I told her that soldiers can't choose their wars and aren't free to quit whenever they feel like it anyhow, she never believed I couldn't just walk away. We fought about it a lot till Tyler persuaded her to lay off of me, since I was going whatever she said. "Don't preach to me about my choices," I remember telling her. "You want to be a model. What good is that going to do for the world?"

"You've got no right to talk," she snapped in return. "You just signed up to be a baby killer."

This is getting depressing. Fucking e-mail.

I close my eyes a moment, the gray face and bloody stump of that soldier searing across my vision. The bile rises again.

A shriek—a shriek so piercing my eardrums press into my skull and snap. I slap my hands over my ears and stare into the eyes of the guy next to me. "Get down!" he screams.

There's a blinding flash and the air sucks right out of my lungs. Then the whole building lifts and explodes.

I fling myself to the ground face-first and grope for my helmet, but it's pitch black now and I can't see it. Dense, gritty smoke is clogging my throat, and pieces of window and machinery and wall are crashing down all around me. I pull myself to my feet and run bent over, coughing and gagging, trying to find my way out, stumbling over things I can't see in the dark, hard things, soft things. "Where's the way out?" I scream.

"Here!" Somebody grabs my hand and drags me out of the exit. A second mortar explodes. "Down!" he yells and I hit the ground again.

Flat on my stomach, arms over my head, I wait to feel it: Metal spearing my back. Leg ripping off. Head caving in, a weight pressing me down and down . . .

Nothing.

I sit up, hacking and spitting, amazed that I'm still alive. And that's when I hear the cries from inside the building: "God help me!" "Jesus! Mommy! Jesus!"

I jump up and run back in.

Pulling off the miniature flashlight pinned to my lapel, I shine it around in the dark. Six bodies in the rubble on the ground, soaked in blood and soot. Three have people crouched over them already, so I run to one of the others—an Iraqi worker, a long piece of shrapnel jutting from his throat. Blood is pulsing out of his neck and his black eyes are staring at me, terrified and pleading. I crouch down to find a way to help him, but just as I touch him something makes me look over at the other two bodies to see if they're soldiers. They are. And right away, even in the dark, even in the smoke, I know.

"Yvette!" I abandon the Iraqi and stumble over to her. She's lying twisted and broken, her head thrown back, neck arched, her limbs in all the wrong places—she looks like a giant hand has crumpled her up and tossed her to the ground. I sweep my flashlight over her to see what's wrong. She's covered in so much blood I can't even tell where it's coming from. "Yvette! Talk to me!"

She doesn't. I lean over to stare into her eyes. She looks right back at me. She even has a little smile.

I grasp her wrist, slippery with blood, and feel for her pulse. It's there—thank God! Running my hands all over her quickly, I try to wipe away the ooze to see where she's wounded. She's full of shrapnel—like a pincushion, there's so much in her.

"Moan, damn you!" I call to her in a sob. "Moan! Make a noise!"

And then she does. Just a sigh, like you sigh when you lie down at the end of a long day.

I pick her up—she's such a little stick of a thing—heave her over my back and stagger outside. Through the smoke I can see other soldiers loading the wounded into the rear of a Humvee, so I head over to them. One lifts Yvette off of me and helps me lay her down with the others. I jump up there, too, sitting with her among the wounded, listening to them groan and cry, holding her wet, bony little hand and staring into the flames and smoke and screams.

We drive fast as we can in the dark with no headlights. A third mortar comes shrieking in, falling fifty meters away from us with such a powerful explosion it rips open the ground like an earthquake, sending our Humvee careening out of control. I throw myself over the wounded and grab

Yvette, my face pressed so tightly against her chest I can taste her blood seeping into my mouth. I hug her and hug her with all my strength, trying to keep the life inside of her.

As soon as we reach the field hospital, medics come running out of the dark with stretchers. "Be careful, she's hurt real bad!" I yell to one. He helps me slide Yvette onto a stretcher. I take one end and we run inside.

A nurse rushes up to me. "You hurt?"

"No it's my friend! Do something!"

The nurse keeps staring at me. "You sure?" Her eyes won't stop running over me, so I glance down at myself. Every part of me—from my hands to my boots—is slick with blood.

"It's not mine, it's hers!" I shout, pointing to Yvette, whose stretcher is lying on the ground. I look around . . . where the fuck is the medic? Why isn't anyone helping her? "Do something!" I yell again.

The nurse steps forward, takes me firmly by the arm and leads me away. Somehow I'm in a chair then and time has slowed down and everybody is moving in slow motion and doing everything they can not to help Yvette. I want to scream and scream till they move.

"Soldier," the nurse says, bending to look into my eyes. "You need to get some rest."

THE BUS RATTLES through the outskirts of Albany for forty minutes before it finally reaches the soldier's stop. But now that she's here, she's not so sure she wants to be. She'd rather spend the rest of her life on this bus, cozy and enclosed, at neither one place nor another, all decisions and destinations suspended.

That being impossible, though, she forces herself to stand up, heaves her backpack over her shoulders with a wince and makes her way carefully down the aisle, trying not to jar her back. The passengers eye her. She knows her walk looks weird—half a swagger like a man, half a hobble like an old lady. She forgot how to walk normally in the Army because if you look at all feminine when you walk, the guys won't leave you alone. That, and the injuries.

She clambers off the bus and watches it drive away, wishing she could call it back. Her hands are shaking more than ever and her stomach's churning acid. But it's too late to turn back now, as the song says. So she hitches up her backpack a little higher and forces herself down the hill, every swing of her leg sending a spasm through her messed-up spine.

There's no sidewalk here, just leaf-strewn grass, which she doesn't like walking on because she knows each step is murdering something. A ladybug or an ant. An earthworm or a flower.

She walks past rows of houses, snug and smug behind their fences, their lawns heaped with autumn leaves: ocher and copper and bronze. But she passes no people. People don't walk in this part of the world, they only drive. So even though she sees kids' tricycles, pumpkin-colored garbage bags, swing sets, early Halloween decorations, it feels as if the world's ended and everyone's been vaporized but her.

She tramps on, her sneakers rustling through the dying leaves. Bright red berries signal from bushes. The trees shimmer burnished gold. The air snaps. A bare ginkgo stands in a pool of tiny yellow fans, like a woman who's just dropped her dress. A skeletal face pokes out of a window, leering at her, eyes bleeding. She falls to a crouch, back shooting pain, groping for her rifle . . .

*Stand up, stupid. It's only a mask.*

Back on her feet, embarrassed. One foot in front of the other. *Keep going, just keep going.*

Birds are carrying on all around her—cardinals, robins, jays—although she can't hear their songs as well as she used to because her eardrums are fucked. A dog barks, making her jump—she can hear that just fine. A woodpecker hammers on a telephone pole beside her, *rat-tat-tat*. She clenches her teeth and keeps walking.

The further down the hill she gets, the more the houses are spaced apart, a lot of them with yards as big as fields. Some are messy with junked cars and lawnmowers. Some are decorated with deer statues, bear cutouts, skiing witches plastered face-first against trees. Some are so manicured their lawns look like Velcro. She thinks of the yellow mud houses in Iraq, the lean-tos made of cardboard stuffed with rags. The little kids begging.

A strange awareness seizes her, as if her body has shrunk inside her clothes and now they're flapping around her like the sides of a tent. She's a Halloween skeleton dangling off a porch, only wrapped in a sack. Separated from her skin. Bones and flesh but no soul.

*Stop this. Keep going.*

The walk feels a hundred miles long. She doesn't care. She's so scared of what might happen that she half never wants to get there at all. But she does get there, of course— long before she's ready to—because what you don't want is what always comes easiest.

So here she is, standing in front of this house she's dreamed of for months, her heart stuck halfway up her throat and her knees quivering so badly she's afraid she'll fall down.

What if she's making a terrible mistake?

## [ KATE ]

**THEY WON'T LET** me out of the Warhorse field hospital till the morning after the mortar attack, and only then once they've doped me up with tranquilizers, washed the worst of the blood off of me and given me some dead soldier's helmet, since I lost mine. I walk out of there feeling like air jets are shooting from the soles of my boots. People's voices are echoing strangely, too, like I'm in an indoor pool and my ears are filled with water.

They order me to take the return convoy to Bucca right away, so the next thing I know I'm back in my go-cart with salami-faced Nielsen.

"I see you and me are still here," he says when I clamber in. "That was a bastard of a night, huh?"

I don't react.

"Your buddy turned out to be okay, though, I hope?"

"How long till we move?" is all I say.

"Ten minutes."

Breaking down my rifle, I wipe it clean of moondust, give the magazine spring a light lube and snap it back together, making sure the action is good and smooth. Then I slide on another condom to keep out the sand. This baby can shoot seven hundred rounds a minute if I want. I stick it out the window and turn my back to Nielsen. Even that lamebrain knows not to say another word.

Off we go again, although with fewer trucks this time. I wonder what the hell we delivered. They never tell us. Could be weapons. Could be toilet paper. Could be nothing at all. Some of those trucks really are empty—I've seen them. We suckers are dying out here, getting our legs and faces sheared off, just to deliver trucks full of air.

The convoy rumbles out of the base, back the way it came, predictable as a fucking pendulum. What a good idea. Let's send those camel jockeys a time-table, telling them exactly where and when to kill us. We might as well hang signs around our necks: Shoot Me Here.

I clean off my sun goggles, fit my rifle on my shoulder and look through its sights. I'm still floating on Ativan and Valium, or whatever the hell those medics pumped into me, but I'm wound tight as a hair trigger anyway. There are way too many people on the road for my liking, and there's way too much garbage too. Anything can hold an IED. Cardboard box. Mound of rags. Plastic bag. Anything.

Soon we're out of Camp Mortarhorse (as I've found out too late Warhorse is called) and back on the same highway we took to get to this dump. The same shit is all around us, too: the desert, the tire shreds, the bits of artillery sticking like weird sculptures out of the sand. The stranded families, confused civilians, the camels and carts and crumpled old cars getting in our way. I practice aiming at all of them. Just in case.

"Hey, Brady, pull your fuckin' weapon inside. No need to go crazy here," Nielsen barks. I ignore him.

Then I spot this skinny little boy, about seven or so, walking beside the road. He's leading a donkey harnessed to a rickety two-wheel cart. I stare at him, hard. You can hide a cannon in a cart. You can hide the biggest damn IED you ever saw in a cart. You can hide enough RPGs and ammo in a cart to blow up a whole frickin' convoy and every sorry sucker inside of it.

I train my sights on him. *One swerve, you fucking miniature towelhead, and I'm taking you out.* I was always a good shot on the firing range in basic training—a lot of us females were. We used to brag that we could shoot the hairy left ball off of our drill sergeant at thirty meters away, easy.

The boy looks over at our trucks roaring past him and pulls at the donkey's harness, like he's trying to position it somehow. I don't like the look of that at all. I flip the safety off my rifle and squint down its barrel.

"What the fuck are you doin' now?" Nielsen snaps.

"Just my job, Sar'nt."

"Don't go shootin' nothing unless I tell you. You know that, right?"

The donkey tosses its head and tries to move further off the road, but the boy yanks it back toward us for some reason. Then the donkey jerks its head again, and I don't know why, but it makes me real nervous.

I aim at its left temple. And I watch.

The donkey's even more jittery now, edging closer and closer to us. I could swear the boy's pushing it our way. On purpose.

So I shoot.

Bull's-eye.

"Jesus!" Nielsen screeches. "Gimme that weapon!"

The donkey falls to its knees, hesitates for a moment like it's praying, then collapses onto its side, pulling the cart over with it. Oranges and lemons tumble out, spinning all over the road. *Orange, yellow, orange, yellow.*

Next I train my sights on the boy. He's clutching his head, his mouth wide open. The donkey thrashes on the ground a second, legs jerking wildly. Then it shudders and falls still. Blood oozes from its ears and mouth, and from the hole in its temple where I shot it.

"Are you nuts?" Nielsen yells again. "Give me that fucking rifle!"

I lean out so I have the boy's ear right in my crosshairs. He's lying on top of the donkey now, crying and stroking it. The oranges and lemons are still spinning over the road.

*Orange.*

*Yellow.*

*Orange.*

*Yellow.*

The boy's clinging to the donkey hard as he can, his mouth open and wailing, his face streaming with tears. His arms are around the donkey's neck and he's hugging and hugging it. Just like I hugged Yvette.

I pull my rifle inside, put it down on my lap, and stare.

The rest of the trip back to Camp Bucca goes by "without incident," as we say in the Army. Nothing but rumble, rumble, wind, soot and dust. I don't even notice the time. Only sit with my rifle across my lap, eyes straight ahead, seeing nothing.

Nielsen doesn't say a word. Too scared I'll shoot him, probably. But soon as we pull into Camp Bucca, he snatches my weapon right out of my hands and says, "You better come with me, Brady. You need help."

I follow him in a daze. My ears are ringing real loud all of a sudden and I can't hear much of anything else. I keep shaking my head because it sounds like a bunch of cicadas have nested in my ear canal. I'm still shaking it when we arrive at the aid station.

People's mouths are moving, eyes looking, but I'm too bothered by my private noise to notice what anybody's doing to me till I'm swallowing a bunch more pills and being made to lie down. Next thing I know it's dark and someone's leading me somewhere. And I'm back in my tent.

When I walk in, DJ and Rickman and everybody else rushes up to me. "You okay? We heard it sucked real bad up there."

I push through them and make my way over to Yvette. She's the only one I want to talk to right now. She'll understand—she goes out on convoys all the time. I get to her rack and look down at it, staring at its emptiness in my fog. Then I turn to Third Eye, who's standing beside me with her mouth all twisted up. "Why isn't she back yet?" I say.

Third Eye puts her hand on my arm. "You better get some sleep."

Then I remember.

I lie face down on Yvette's rack. I can smell her in the pillow—only faintly, but she's there. Reaching out my arms, I wrap them around the edges of her cot. And I hold on, clutching it tight as I can for the rest of the night.

THE HOUSE IS big and white and old, much grander than the soldier imagined it. It's like a New England inn, with a deep front porch and a green door that matches the window shutters. Carved pillars hold up the porch roof and latticework frames its edges like a row of lace. The door even has stained-glass panels in it, red and blue and amber. No gory Halloween decorations, though, thank God.

The windows are dark. All the soldier can see in them is the reflection of the trees behind her. Maybe that means nobody's home.

She steps up to the porch and looks for a bell. There isn't one. So she knocks on the wood of the door, careful not to touch the colored glass in case she cracks it.

She waits a long time, hearing nothing. Maybe she didn't knock loudly enough, but she doesn't want to look like a fool and knock again. What she really wants to do is run back to the bus and ride on forever.

She gazes around as she waits, examining the house more closely. On second glance, it's not in such great shape. The paint on the porch, the same rich green as the door and shutters, is lifting off the wood in long, cracking blisters. An abandoned wasp's nest is bulging from behind one of the shutters, its pitted comb gray and crumbling. Spiders have spun tightropes between the pillars, and the white clapboard walls are dusted with faint blue mildew.

Whoever once cared about this house is clearly long gone.

The soldier waits, but still no movement within. So she forces herself to knock again, louder this time. A dog barks inside. A biting dog, by the sound of it. She steps back and reaches again for her M-16, groping at her shoulder a second before she remembers.

Then she hears footsteps. The door rattles while somebody fidgets with its lock. Suddenly, the soldier needs to run.

Backing up, she turns to flee. But just as she's reached the bottom of the porch steps, the door opens and a voice catches her.

"Yes?"

The soldier turns slowly and stares up at the face looking down at her.

It's a woman. A young woman with long black hair and bangs. A big-eyed woman. A woman any idiot can see is pretty as hell.

*Fuck.*

## [ KATE ]

"KATE! HEY, KATE!" Somebody's shaking me by the shoulders. "Wake up!"

"Uhn?"

"Come *on!*"

I turn over slowly on Yvette's cot and peel open my eyes. Third Eye's leaning over me in the grayish gloom. She looks blurred and shimmery, like she's covered in plastic wrap.

"Get up! There's an E4 outside says he has orders to bring you to SFC Henley. You need to move ass!"

"What?" My head's throbbing and my ears are still stuffed with cicadas.

"Jesus, come on! He's outside the tent right now!"

I stare at her, blinking, my brain still clogged from the drugs they stuffed into me last night. I wish they'd given me even more because I'm remembering everything now.

"Oh for fuck's sake!" Third Eye yanks my arm. "You'll be in deep shit if you don't get moving!"

I shake her off. "Leave me alone." Sitting up with an effort, I gulp down a bottle of water and grope for my rifle and helmet. I'm still in my uniform, stiff and brown with

Yvette's blood. Pushing myself to my feet, I stagger out, the cicadas screaming.

The E4 is some guy I don't know, although I've seen him running errands for Henley before. He's Mexican, short and stocky, with a round flat face like a penny. He nods at me and escorts me through the grayness to the NCO tent. It feels like I'm under arrest, although he doesn't say so. When I ask him to wait while I run into a reeking latrine, he doesn't say anything either. I've no idea if this means I'm in trouble or if he just doesn't like to talk.

At the NCO tent, he leaves me, still without a word. I go into Henley's section and stand staring at him, my jaw clenched, waiting till the cocksucker bothers to look up.

"So," he says finally, without looking at me. "Specialist Brady. Take a seat." I do, sitting up stiff. He folds his hands on his desk and fixes his eyes on my hairline, his Daddy Bush mouth clamped tight as an asshole.

"First, my condolences about your friend Private Sanchez. It's always a sad day for the Army when we lose a fine soldier like her. We'll be having the MFH for her and the other casualties tomorrow. You will, of course, be excused from duty to attend."

He pauses, expecting me to say something. But I hate him too much.

"I know it's hard when we lose our comrades, but remember, she's not the only fine soldier to lose his life yesterday. Three others died as well, and two were severely wounded. We must honor the noble sacrifices of them all."

"*Her* life, Sergeant."

"What?"

"She lost *her* life. Not his."

Henley narrows his pinpoint eyes. "Well anyway, I called you in to say that, under the circumstances, and due to a disturbing report from your convoy sergeant, we think it best to remove you from the shooter mission and return you to guard duty. This means, Brady, that you will not be getting that promotion I mentioned. You understand?"

"Yes, Sergeant." Like I give a shit.

"You should also know that, if we see any more of this erratic behavior you insist on, we can put you back on shooter mission at any time. You understand me?"

"Yes, Sergeant."

"All right, you can go."

I stand up to leave, but before I do, I glare at Henley in silence a long time. *It's because of you Yvette died*, my glare says. *Because of me, too, but mostly because of you. You and Kormick together. You're no better than murderers. And if you think you can shut me up with your dumbass threats, you can think again!*

He glances at me uneasily. "I said you can go. And Brady? Change your uniform, for Christ's sake."

I do. Thirty minutes later, I'm back in my tower.


Jimmy comes to see me at lunchtime, his first visit in weeks. He finds me hunched in my chair, rifle pointed at the prison compound, head twitching to get the cicadas out. Hands trembling more than ever.

"Hey," he says cautiously, stepping off the ladder. "Feel like a visit?"

I don't answer. I don't look at him either. I don't want him to see how grateful I am that he's come.

He walks over and crouches beside me anyway. "I heard what happened to your convoy. Jesus."

I glance behind him. "You alone?"

"Yeah, why?"

"I keep hearing things." I shake my head again. "You hear anything weird?"

He listens. "Just the wind."

"It's like these cicadas are stuck in my head. I think the mortars did something to my eardrums." I bang the side of my head with my wrist. It doesn't help.

Jimmy's quiet a moment. But then he touches my hand. "I heard about Yvette, too," he says softly. "I know she was a good friend to you. I know you really cared for her. I'm so sorry, Kate."

I nod, swallowing. "Yeah." I pause till I can talk again. "She was only on that suicide mission 'cause of me."

"That can't be true."

"It is. It was me they wanted to get rid of, Jimmy. Not her. She only got caught up in it because she was helping me report Kormick."

He puts his arms around me then, as easy as if nothing's ever gone wrong between us. I lean against him, so relieved—to hell with the prisoners, already jeering and pumping their hips below us. His salty warmth, familiar, comforting smell. I close my eyes and just breathe.

"We were going to be roomies when we got home," I tell him eventually, my voice muffled in his shoulder. "We were going to find a house together and help each other through."

"I'm so sorry," he whispers again, and keeps on holding me. It's the best thing anyone could do. Much better than pills.

I don't cry, though. I still haven't been able to cry.

. . .

The service for Yvette and the other three soldiers who died is held in the chapel, which is only another saggy-ass tent, except super big and light tan. More than a hundred of us show up for it and sit in rows, just like at church, only with fold-up metal chairs instead of wooden pews. I look around. We've all made some kind of effort to clean ourselves up, even Third Eye. Yvette would've liked that.

The altar is nothing but an unpainted plywood platform, with another unpainted plywood panel propped up behind it to make a fake wall. On either side is an American flag stuck into a sand-filled garbage can, like a potted plant. And hanging on the fake wall is a giant black heart, with our company's insignia stamped in the middle of it.

None of that does much for me. But what does get to me is what they've put on the platform itself: the dead soldiers' empty boots. Four pairs of them sitting in a row, dusty and battered, as if the soldiers stepped out of them only a moment ago. And between each pair of boots is the dead soldier's rifle, propped up like a body; the dead soldier's dog tags dangling from it like necklaces around a neck; and the dead soldier's helmet and goggles balanced on top like a head and a pair of eyes.

Soldier ghosts. Or, like Jimmy said, robots.

The company commander starts off the service. He's this huge, thuggish-looking colonel with a polished bald head and a voice like a bass drum. He steps up to the podium and leads us in the national anthem. Rows and rows of us robots, standing to attention, hands over our robot hearts, growling and squeaking out our national pride. Rows and rows of bare robot heads, the men's fuzzy with crew cuts, the women's shiny and flat with hair grease. Rows and rows of robots wondering the same thing: *When's it going to be my boots up there?*

Then the commander tells us to sit, and with his voice booming through a crackly microphone, calls the company chaplain to come up and read a few tear-jerky verses from the Bible. Doesn't jerk my tears, though. Only makes me think about Mom and Dad and Father Slattery, and all their naïve crap about lifting the downtrodden and being protected by Jesus. Jesus clearly didn't give a fuck about protecting Yvette, even after she made her tenderhearted deal with His dad. We soldiers are nothing more than work and killing machines, and neither Jesus nor God has anything to do with it. Or I hope they don't.

Then the commander takes over again, and in a flat, expressionless voice, spouts a bunch of empty phrases calling the four dead robots heroes who sacrificed their robot lives for our country and freedom. Telling us how the dead robots personified bravery and valor, and how dying for your country is the biggest honor a robot could ask for.

Fuck valor and honor. Yvette was killed in the middle of writing a frigging e-mail, for Christ's sake, because the Army was too damn cheap and disorganized to have installed a siren system in the MWR, let alone a mortar-proof bunker for us to shelter in. She was killed because that shithead Henley is buddies with Kormick, and Kormick wanted revenge on me for reporting his sick, perverted ass. Valor and honor? Shit.

The commander finally shuts up, not a moment too soon, and somebody plays a recording of Taps, which always chokes me up, so we all stand and salute again. I glance over at Third Eye to see how she's taking this crap—after all, she was close to Yvette too. Her face is like rock.

After Taps is over, we sit back down and a few robots clomp up to the podium to speak about their dead robot friends. One talks about how brave and funny nineteen-year-old Private First Class Robot Molsen was, and how the poor sucker wanted to be a firefighter when he grew up. Another says Sergeant Robot Miller was a devoted husband and dad to his three kids, and how proud they'll be that their robot daddy died for his country. (Yeah, right.) A third tells us that Specialist Robot Gomez was the toughest and most loyal robot he ever met, and real great on the guitar, even though he was only eighteen.

I can't stand it. I can't stand the waste of human lives.

Then it's DJ's turn to talk about Yvette. He asked me if I wanted to do it, but I told him no way. If I got up there, I know what I'd say: *You fuckers murdered her. Every one of you. Don't talk to me about honor.*

"Private First Class Sanchez was everything a soldier should be," DJ begins, reading from the piece of paper where I watched him scribble his speech last night. "She went on convoys nearly every night for three months, enduring many attacks without complaint. She was a fine soldier, a good friend . . ."

I stop listening. I know DJ means well, but he's making her sound like all the other robots. Easy to sacrifice, easy to forget.

DJ leaves the podium at last, and one by one, he and the other three robots who spoke lay Purple Hearts in front of each of the four soldier ghosts. Then we all stand to sing

"Amazing Grace" and bow our heads to pray. But the whole time that I'm standing there—staring first at my toes, then at the toes of Yvette's empty boots—all I can think about is why I let this happen to her. Why didn't I stop her from going to Hopkins and making waves when I knew perfectly well that making waves only gets you fucked in the Army? Why did I think Mom's stupid little plastic crucifix would protect her? Why was I so careless with her life?

The speeches and hymns are finally over. The prayers ended. The metal chairs folded and stacked. Yvette's nothing but a body in a box now, while an American flag, folded into a perfect triangle, is supposedly on its way home to her family.

But Yvette hasn't got a family. All she's ever had in her twenty short years of life is loneliness. She was always saying that we robots were her family, the only family she's ever loved. And we're the ones who killed her.

# [ NAEMA ]

"NAEMA?" I FEEL a tug on my sleeve. "Naema, my love, listen!"

Blearily, I look up from the child I am tending, the hundredth or so I have seen in this filthy hospital fatally wounded by shrapnel, bombs or fire. Mama's face is swimming before my exhausted eyes. "I can't talk now," I tell her. "What's the time? Is it morning yet?"

She grasps my arm. "Naema, pay attention. Your grandmother, she . . ." She breaks down in tears.

"Where is she? What have you done with her?" I say slowly, casting my eyes over the bedlam of the hospital. I have been working nonstop for some eighteen hours now and am so deeply fatigued I feel as if I am at the bottom of a river.

Mama pulls at me. "Come see for yourself."

"But I . . ."

"Come!"

"Wait, let me finish here." I look down at the child I am tending, a little boy of about five. He is lying on the floor, which is splattered with blood, vomit and urine, but he lacks even a sheet to protect him. The hospital has no more sheets, let alone gurneys or beds. His face is charred black, as is much of his body, one arm is burnt off and he is crawling with flies and rotting alive with infection. I have nothing to give him but words, but he is in too much pain to hear them, thus I have nothing to give him at all. He stares at me, his eyes huge with agony, too far gone even to cry.

"Go to sleep, little one," I tell him. "It'll stop hurting soon." As it will.

Turning away, I leave his side and follow Mama, weaving through the other patients laid out on the floor and the wailing relatives gathered around them. If I have ever seen hell on earth, I am seeing it now.

Mama leads me back to the corner where I left her and Granny Maryam so many hours ago. Granny resembles a heap of rags more than a human being, lying curled up in her black abaya, her body oddly crumpled and still. I take one look and know she is dead.

"To Allah we belong and to Allah we return," I mutter automatically. But I have seen too much this past night to feel anything.

"We must carry her home right now!" Mama says. "We have to prepare her for burial. We can't leave her poor body like this, Allah have mercy on her."

"Yes, all right," I say numbly. "How long since she died?"

"I don't know! I fell asleep and when I awoke she was gone, may Allah forgive me. How could I—"

"Mama, shush. You aren't to blame. Let me tell a nurse I have to leave."

The nurse I find is unhappy to let me go, but of course she cannot stop me. "I'll come back as soon as I can to keep helping," I tell her, but she is already too caught up in the next emergency to answer.

So I return to my mother. Together, we lift Granny's little body, twisted and stiff, and carry her out of the hospital and through the crowd to our car, which we find exactly as we left it. Mama climbs into the back, trying tearfully to keep Granny's rigid body and head decently wrapped in her dusty shawl. I sit alone in the front, hunched over the steering wheel, drenched in other people's blood and nearly blind with exhaustion. And once again, I drive excruciatingly slowly for hours through turmoil and danger.

Why must we go through these things? Why can't we and all those other suffering people in the hospital be left alone to lead peaceful, ordinary lives? Granny Maryam should have died in her own house, saying her last prayers to Allah, not abandoned in a filthy corner like a poisoned dog. She should have been able to lie in her own bed while Mama and I washed her tenderly with lotus leaves and camphor. She should have been able to die with dignity, not amidst blood and ruin. Is it so much to ask that a good-hearted old woman be allowed to die in peace—or that those poor children I saw tonight be allowed to live?

[ KATE ]

NOTHING'S THE SAME now that Yvette's dead. I
can't eat without feeling her blood in my mouth. Can't sleep
without seeing her body pincushioned with shrapnel. Can't
get through the day without thinking that I'm seeing her
over and over. She comes walking out of a dust cloud, only
to dissolve into air. She turns to grin at me when I enter
the tent, only to change into somebody else. Her voice is
everywhere, too, telling me to look after myself, telling me
to trust her. And when I try to cry, she says, "Be a soldier,
baby," and the tears turn to sand.

Jimmy comes to see me as often as he can. We're almost
a real couple now, although we still haven't done any more
than kiss. He's waiting for me to recover from Yvette and
the attacks, if such a thing's possible. I'm waiting to feel clean
enough in my conscience to deserve him. But he comes every
morning to pick me up for our shift (I can't get it together
to run anymore), he comes at lunchtime to my tower and he
comes over to my tent at night when he can, too, so we can
sneak outside for a cuddle. "I love you, I've always loved
you," he tells me, and it's so good to hear. The only moments
I feel even near to normal are when I'm with him.

If only I could get over the sense that everything I am and everything I say is a lie.

One day in mid-August, a couple weeks after Yvette's funeral, he climbs up to my tower as usual, only this time he seems uneasy. We sit together quietly a while, watching the prisoners milling around in the dust—I hate them so much, the bile churns around inside of me all the time now. Then he heaves a sigh.

"Kate, I got something to tell you."

"That sounds bad." I try to sound jokey, but already my stomach's in a knot. I'm always expecting him to see the light after all and dump me.

"I spoke to Ortiz last night. He asked me to give you this. It's not good."

I forgot all about Ortiz. Yvette's driven everything else from my head.

Jimmy pulls something out of his utility vest and hands it to me. It's the torn-in-half photo of Naema's little brother I gave to Ortiz all those weeks ago, only crinkled and faded. The kid's still grinning out at me from his goofy long face, but three jagged creases run across his head now, and I notice more writing on the back than was there before. I turn the photo over. His name is still there in Naema's handwriting, *Zaki Jassim.* But next to it, in different writing, is scrawled:

*July 9, 2003, shot in attempted escape. Deceased July 10.*

I stare at it a second. July 10th. That was around the time Naema's dad freaked out in the compound. The time I stamped on him and ground his face in the sand.

I crumple the photo up and throw it off the tower.

"What are you doing?" Jimmy says.

"I don't give a fuck," I answer. "Those people killed Yvette. They tried to kill all of us. They're stinking animals and I don't give a damn what happens to any of them."

Jimmy stares at me. "It doesn't bother you that we shot a thirteen-year-old kid?"

"I wanted to shoot a kid myself out there on the convoy. A little kid, about seven, same as April. Shot his donkey instead."

Jimmy's looking shocked now, but I can't stop. "I wanted to kill him. *Really* wanted to." I glare into Jimmy's face. "That's who I am now. See?"

"Don't talk like that!"

"It's true. I've hurt so many people, you don't even know. I'm bad news." I begin to laugh. "And this is just the beginning because there's other people I'm going to kill too! Starting with fuckface Henley."

Jimmy takes me by the shoulders. "Snap out of it, Kate! You're talking wild. You're just messed up 'cause of all the bad shit that's happened. You'll be all right, sweetie, you will." And he hugs me.

But I see it in his eye, I hear it in his voice: doubt.

"I need to go back to my post now," he says gently. "But I'll come see you tonight so we can talk about it more, okay? Just hold on till then. You'll feel different soon."

But when I walk back into the tent tonight, I don't feel different at all. I feel hard and tough and cold inside. I feel like a soldier now. A real robot soldier. I know who I hate and I know who I want to kill. All the rest is bullshit.

"Third Eye?" I poke her in the arm. She's lying on her cot, staring into space like a dead woman, as usual. She's been a robot for a long time now. I just didn't see it before.

"What?"

"I got a message for that Naema girl. She is still coming to the checkpoint, right?"

Third Eye turns her head in her slow-motion way and looks at me. "Yeah, she's still coming. Or was till the last couple of days, at least. She's a pain in the ass. Always insisting that we tell her this, tell her that. I think she wants to blow the crap out of us."

"Well, this'll shut her up. Tell her that her little brother's dead. And probably her dad, too."

Third Eye looks startled. "Where'd you hear that?"

I unsnap the fasteners on my utility vest. "From this guy who guards the boys' compound. He says the kid was shot trying to escape, but who knows? He probably thumbed his nose at an MP who got pissed off and blew him away. Whatever. But the dad flipped out when he heard, got himself beaten up, and I haven't seen him since. Naema told me he has a heart condition, so my guess is, kaput."

Third Eye swings her legs off her rack and sits up. "Why the hell should I tell her all that? I'm not the one around here who likes to cozy up with those fucking hajjis."

"Don't tell her then, I don't give a shit." I pull off my vest.

Third Eye frowns at me. "I thought you cared about her."

"That's over." And I walk out of the tent to meet Jimmy.

Whenever I meet Jimmy at night, we hide in this shadowy patch between my tent and its neighbor. Most couples sneak off to the motor pool to find an empty two-and-a-half ton truck with a cover on it, where they can have sex in private. But, like I said, we haven't gotten to that point yet.

He's already there when I duck out of the tent, and once we've turned the corner to get out of sight, he gives me a hug. "Feeling any better?"

"Not really."

He lets go of me and steps back to look into my face. His own is so sad. I can see that even in the moon shadows.

"I know you feel bad now," he says quietly. "But you're a good person, Kate. Don't let this place make you forget that." He put his arms around me again. "Don't push me away, okay? We need each other. I know things are fucked-up here, of course they are. But I love you, and I want us to help each other when we get home."

I pull out of his arms. His words make my whole body ache. But I know, I really know that he's wrong.

"Jimmy." My voice comes out detached and icy, a real robot voice. "This isn't going to work. I've decided."

"What do you mean? Decided what?"

"I'm going back to Tyler."

"*Tyler*? Why?" Jimmy's voice holds so much pain it makes my whole body ache.

"Because he's the best side of me. Because if I don't find that side of me again, I don't know how I'm going to live the rest of my life."

"So what's that make me?" Jimmy says bitterly. "The evil side?"

"No, I don't mean that. You're the real thing. You're kind and brave and honest. You're the best person I've ever met."

He pulls a wry face. "But?"

"But we're in a nightmare here. I mean it's real but it's not real. It's got nothing to do with life at home. And if we're together, we'll be stuck in the nightmare forever."

"That's not true! We'll help each other cope, don't you see?"

"But I don't want to be the person I am with you, Jimmy. I hate who I am here. I hate who I am even with you."

He steps away again, and now he looks angry. "Well, don't come crying to me when you hate who you are with everybody else, too. You are who you are, Kate. You can't change that."

We stand silent a moment, both of us staring at the shadowy ground. "Jimmy, please try to understand. I'm just so tired of screwing up people's lives."

"Then why did you just do it again? Fuck." He turns away from me and leaves.

Back in my tent, I can't sleep even for a second. My conversation with Jimmy keeps playing over and over in my head, coming out the way I want it to instead of the way it did: *Don't worry, Kate, I'll wait for you, no matter what you say.* But Jimmy never said anything like that, and I know he never will. So I lie here writhing and twisting like a fly with its wings torn off. Sit up, lie down. Kick off my sheet, pull it back on. Shake my head to get out the words and cicadas. Makes no difference. One minute crawls after another like the slow drips of sweat running down my ribs. Soon, all I can focus on is Macktruck snoring in my ear, and it irritates me so bad I want to shoot him in the fucking neck.

I peer around the edge of my poncho to check on him. He's flat on his back, stomach bulging like a pillow. He seems to be asleep, although how he can sleep at the same time as making all that racket is a mystery to me.

"Mack!" I pick up my rifle and poke him in the ribs with it.

He wakes up with a start. "Uh, what?" He sounds pretty shocked to hear me speak to him at all.

"You think you could shut the fuck up? You sound like a dying pig."

"Uh, okay, I'll try." He heaves himself over on his side.

"And Mack?"

"Yeah?"

"If you come anywhere near me ever again, snore one more snore, or bother me in any of your fucking pervert ways at all, I'm blowing a hole in you so big a friggin' convoy could drive through it."

A pause while he thinks this over.

"You're losing it, Brady, you know that?" he says then.

"Yeah, I know. That's the point."

After that, he doesn't say another word.

I still can't sleep, though. Each time somebody sighs in his rack, a critter runs across our plywood floor with its scratchy little feet, or a prisoner cries out in the distance, adrenaline jolts through me, bringing back Naema's mourning dad and what I did to him, that Iraqi worker's pleading eyes in the mortar attack, the boy and his donkey, Yvette's last little sigh. Her blood all over my body.

All the rest of that night, I lie on my back, eyes wide open, rifle clasped to my chest. Head exploding with despair.

The second the sky begins to lighten, I get up with relief and yank on my uniform. I try taking a couple bites of T-Rats for energy, but each time I bring the food near my lips I think of Yvette, and my mouth fills again with the taste of her blood.

Giving Macktruck a warning glare—he steps out of my way pretty fast—I head out to the latrines with Third Eye, who's back to her rock-faced self. The lack of sleep and food is making me lightheaded, and black spots keep skittering across my vision like bees, but since that's how I feel most of the time anyway, I pay no attention. When I climb into the Humvee with Jimmy and the rest of my team, he doesn't look at me once.

It's extra hot up in my tower today—hundred and forty, I'm sure, at least in the sun. I sit sweating till I've soaked through my underwear, my uniform, even my flak jacket. I have water with me but it tastes of blood too, so I push the bottles into the tiny square of shade under my roof and leave them there to cook.

One hour. Two.

Another hour. Four.

Heat. Sweat. Flies. Black bees swirling. Yellow sand, blaring sky, white dust. Unshaven men in shabby clothes wandering around, staring at the ground, staring at the wire, staring at me.

My Kevlar feels hot and heavy, much more than usual, its four pounds of weight more like forty. A hot cauldron bearing down on my spine. I yank it off and toss it behind me. Let the mortars whistle into my brain. Who the fuck cares.

But I forgot what the sight of female hair does to those prisoners, 'specially red hair like mine. They've been yelling at me to take off my helmet for months already, so the minute they catch sight of my bare head—mayhem. They cluster around, yelling and hooting. I might as well be treating them to a striptease. The starer comes up close, leering and licking his lips. So does the jerk-off, of course. He walks right up to the wire under my tower, calls out something, pulls out his dick yet again and sets to.

I raise my rifle and squint down the sights at him. Black bees buzzing.

He laughs, staring right at me, and keeps going. His dick brown and wormy.

I flip off the safety.

He laughs again, pumping away.

"Last chance, fuckhead," I whisper. "I've been waiting for this." And I begin to count.

*One.*

He won't stop, even though I'm pointing my rifle right at his wormy dick.

*Two.*

He still won't stop.

*Three.*

The asshole still isn't getting the message.

*Four.*

*Okay, baby. You asked for it.*

Fire!

Red blooms from his groin. He stares down at it. Nobody moves. Not me, not the prisoners. Not even the wind.

Then he throws back his head and screams.

I jump up and rush to the edge of the platform, ready to shoot him again, or any other sand jockey who tries anything. They don't know who they're messing with—I'm a real robot now. I'd be happy to shoot every one of those fuckers in the prick or the heart—their choice. *Who wants to be next, gentlemen?*

But just as I take aim, a wave of dizziness slams into my head like a fist. I sway. Stagger. The bees buzz louder.

Everything goes blinding white.

Then everything goes black.

"CAN I HELP you?" The pretty woman stands in the doorway, sweeping suspicious eyes over the soldier. Her dog, a brown, square-headed mutt, pokes its head around her legs and takes a look too, its long tongue dripping. It isn't barking anymore but the soldier backs up anyway.

"Well?" the woman says.

"Uh, no, it's okay. I got the wrong house. Sorry to disturb you." The soldier turns, ready to run.

"Kate?"

It's Jimmy's voice but she keeps going. She should have left him alone. What a fool.

"Kate!"

She walks a few more paces. Then stops. She doesn't want to but she can't resist his voice, her need for it. Helplessly, she turns around.

He's peering over the woman's shoulder. Then he pushes past her and comes out on the porch. He looks beautiful. And terrible.

"You should come in," he says. "Now that you're here."

His hair is longer now, black and wavy, and he's wearing a stained gray T-shirt, worn-out jeans and sneakers with no socks, in spite of the cold. He has glasses on, normal ones with thin brown frames. But his eyes are circled with shadows.

He turns to the woman. "Lock Daisy up, will you?"

The woman's face flickers annoyance, but she grabs the dog by its collar and hauls it away.

Jimmy turns back. "Come in," he says. "It's okay. Really." But his voice doesn't sound okay. It doesn't sound soft and welcoming the way it used to. It sounds hard and wary.

Kate follows him in anyhow. She doesn't know what else to do.

The house is a dump inside. Much worse than she expected, even from the flaking paint and mildew. Maybe it's just that she's not used to people's houses anymore, having spent no more than a couple weeks in her own between hospitals, but it looks dark and gloomy, and it's littered with garbage. Magazines and beer bottles. Overflowing ashtrays. Cartons of leftover Chinese food. And, propped against a dead fireplace, a rifle.

She drops her pack to the ground and walks over to it. She's not sure exactly what she's doing, but she seems to be picking it up and holding it to her chest.

Jimmy watches her, nodding.

The pretty woman comes back in, dogless, and looks at her. "Shit," she says under her breath. Then, more loudly, "You want a beer or something?"

Kate takes a better look at her. Long bangs falling into sticky black eyes. Big lippy mouth. Low-cut pink T-shirt, tight jeans, high-heeled boots. The woman might be pretty, but she's a skank.

Kate nods. "Yeah. Please." The skank walks out of the room.

"Sit," Jimmy says, and hands Kate a pack of smokes. Ignoring the chairs, she settles on the floor with her sore back pressed up against the wall by the fireplace, the rifle across her lap. He leans over to light her cigarette for her. She draws it in deep, the first smoke she's been allowed for weeks.

The skank returns with three open bottles of beer and hands them around. "I'm Mandy," she says.

"I'm Kate. Thanks." Kate takes a long swallow. The beer and the cigarette make her dizzy and colder than ever.

"We were in the war together," Jimmy says then. And he laughs.

"Who would've thought?" Mandy mutters, dropping onto the newspaper-strewn couch. "You people keep coming around here. It's like Jimmy's a magnet for broken-down soldiers. We might as well open a fucking halfway house."

"Shut up," he snaps, and Kate is startled. She's never heard him talk to anybody like that.

"Don't worry," Kate says quickly, almost sorry for Mandy now. "I'm harmless."

Mandy's eyes drop to the rifle on Kate's lap, but she doesn't reply.

Kate takes a second long swig of beer and stares at the dusty floor in front of her. Now what will she do? She never expected Jimmy to have a woman. She expected him to not want her, to send her away, to be angry and hurt like before. And she hoped she would talk him out of it. But for some dumb reason she never expected this.

They sit still a while—Kate on the floor, Jimmy nearby in a ratty blue armchair, Mandy on the cluttered orange couch—drinking their beers and smoking in the dim brown light. It's sunny outside but you'd never know it in there, except for the leaf-shaped shadows on the floor. They don't say much. They can't, not with Mandy there. She's like a blast wall dividing the room and Kate's on the wrong side. Kate wonders if Jimmy loves Mandy, and where she'll go if he does.

SAND QUEEN

292

"When did you all get back?" she asks him finally. "I haven't heard from anybody." It hurts her, that. She thought at least DJ would call to see how she's doing.

"Beginning of last month. Rumor is we'll be redeployed soon."

She's silent, this unwelcome news crowding into her head. But then she asks, "You heard anything about anyone?" even though she's not sure she wants to know.

"Some. That fucker Kormick reenlisted." Jimmy sends her a knowing look. "Boner, too."

Kate doesn't answer. It's been a long time since she heard those names spoken aloud and it sends her hands trembling worse than ever. Jimmy glances at them and frowns. "You okay?" he murmurs. For a moment he sounds like his old self.

She picks up the rifle, grips it to steady her hands, and examines it. It's a mess, all rusted-up. Probably wouldn't shoot at all.

"I hope that thing's not loaded," Mandy says. "Would you mind putting it down?"

"Leave her alone," Jimmy snaps again, then turns back to Kate. "DJ came around the other day. He's doing good. He and his lady are working on having a third baby."

"Oh yeah? That's nice." Kate swallows. She's afraid to ask the next question, but she needs to know. So she squeezes out the words. "What about Third Eye? You heard anything from her?"

Jimmy gives her a quick look. Then he gets up and crosses over to Mandy. He leans down, kisses her—it's like a knife in Kate when he does that—and whispers something. Kate stares at the floor.

Mandy mumbles a reply, sounding irritated. But then she stands up, tossing back her skanky hair. "I'm going to the store. Either of you want anything?"

Kate shakes her head.

"More beer," Jimmy says. Mandy nods and walks out of the room, her butt swaying. Kate watches her. That's the walk she can't do anymore.

They wait in silence till they hear Mandy drive off. Then Jimmy gets out of his chair, comes over to Kate and sits cross-legged on the floor facing her. He takes off his glasses. She wants so badly to hug him her arms ache.

"So?" he says, his wonderful blue eyes searching her face. "What's going on?"

"Where are your little brothers?" is all she answers. "I wanted to meet them."

His gaze skitters. "They're still with our aunt. I couldn't . . . I can't . . ." He looks away, his thin face sad.

"You don't want me here, do you?" Kate says then. "I didn't know . . ." She nods at the door. "I'll leave."

"No. Stay, it's okay, really." He runs his eyes over her face. "It's been bad for you, hasn't it?" he murmurs.

She shrugs and looks again at the floor.

"Does your family know where you are?"

"Fuck my family."

"I take it that means no. What about Tyler?"

"Same."

He pauses.

"And the hospital—anyone there know where you are?"

"Nope."

"Stay here with me, then. I want you to. I'll explain it to Mandy. She'll come around."

"You sure?" She looks back up at him.

"Yeah." His eyes hold hers. "I'm sure."

"Thanks." She wants to say more, but nothing will come. "You got any other broken soldiers here?" She tries to smile.

Jimmy leans back on his hands. "One left yesterday. You know him. Creeley."

"Button Nose? What's wrong with him?"

"He lost a hand. Couple weeks after you left. We were out on the road and a grenade came flying into our Humvee. He was trying to throw it back out when it went off."

"Shit. Poor kid."

"Yeah, but it could've been worse. Got him out of a second tour, at least." Jimmy rocks forward again and looks at her a moment, his brow creased. "What about you? Can they make you go again?"

She shakes her head. "Medical."

"Thank God."

"And you?" Kate says then. "Do you really have to go back?"

He shrugs, turns his eyes away. "Of course."

The words slice into her. She can't bear it, the thought of him going back there without her, the thought of him getting hurt. But all she can do is nod and stay silent.

"Come," Jimmy says then, getting up off the floor. "I'll show you where you can sleep."

He picks up her backpack and climbs the stairs, Kate following him. They walk up to a landing and down a hallway, past a bedroom with its door open. Inside, she glimpses a double bed, its sheets rumpled. She looks away quickly.

"Here," he says, pushing open a door and ushering her inside. He turns to her. "It's good to see you again, Kate." And, for the first time, he smiles.

[ KATE ]

I HAVE NO idea where I am. A tan tent, that much I can tell. A softer bed than usual. Daytime, because the light filtering through the canvas is hot and pale. I try to look around but the minute I move an unbelievable pain shoots through my neck and I hear a shriek. I have an idea it's mine.

A man's face leans into my vision. Sweaty and red and topped by tiny sprigs of wiry ginger hair. "You awake?" it says.

Is this one of my nightmares? I try to lift my arm to see if there's any blood but that sends another spasm of pain searing through me. "Shit!" I yelp. "What the fuck's going on?"

"How you feeling?" the man asks brightly. "Talk to me, soldier. Come on."

I blink at him a few moments, trying to figure out if he's real. "What happened? Where the hell am I?"

"You had an accident. You're in the aid station. I'm a medic. Now tell me your name, rank and what year it is."

"Why?" I genuinely want to know.

He looks annoyed. "I don't have all day, just do what I said."

"Where's Jimmy?"

"Will you answer me?"

I try to move, but another unbelievable pain pierces my back. Now I'm scared.

"Come on," the medic says wearily. "Name?"

"Kate Brady. What the fuck's wrong with my back? Ow! And my arm? What happened to me?"

"Rank, age, year."

"E4. Shit, ow! Twenty. Two thousand three. Christ! I need to see Jimmy."

"Well, your brain seems all right. Your right arm's broken and you wrenched your back, far as we can tell. Nothing too serious, don't worry. But we're shipping you to Kuwait for tests."

"Kuwait? When?"

"Today. Medevac's taking you with a couple other wounded."

"But I have to see Jimmy!"

"Ain't no Jimmy here. Now quiet down so I can give you a shot."

"Jimmy didn't visit me?"

"Not yet, soldier. Not yet." And the man sticks a needle into my thigh.

Jimmy never does come. Never. But to my surprise Third Eye shows up, just before they carry me out.

"Hey Freckles, aren't you the lucky camper?" she says.

"I am?"

"Yeah. You're getting out of this craphole, aren't you? Listen, I'll look you up when I get home, okay? We'll get a couple beers together."

"Okay," I say unsteadily. "What the hell happened to me, do you know?"

"You fell off your tower, you stupid bitch. Blacked out or something and, plop, off you went."

"Did I shoot somebody? I think I shot somebody."

"Yeah. You'd be in big trouble if you hadn't got hurt. You didn't fall off that tower on purpose, did you?"

I just look at her when she says that.

"Listen," she adds after a second. "Teach said to give you this." She puts a piece of paper in my left hand, the hand that isn't wrapped in a cast. It's only an address and phone number, no message, but I read it over and over, like it's the Bible, a prayer, like it contains the only hope I have left.

"Why didn't he come see me?" I say to Third Eye.

Two medics walk in just then, lift me onto a stretcher, which hurts like fuck, and strap me down while Third Eye stands back, watching. Then they carry me out and lever me into the back of a Black Hawk, along with a couple other soldiers who look much worse off than me.

"Happy travels," Third Eye calls just before they close the hatch. "Lucky cunt!"

After that, it's a blur of hospitals and drugs and doctors. Kuwait for a few days, X-rays and needles. Germany for a week, more X-rays and needles. Interviews with doctors, interviews with shrinks. Diagnosis: Two cracked vertebrae and a bunch of wrenched muscles from the fall. Spine compressed from the weight I had to carry day and night. Neck fucked from jolting around in the Humvee, banging my head on its goddamn roof. Brain injury from the mortars. Dehydration, malnourishment, hearing loss, depression . . .

At least my spine isn't broken. As for my arm, it's a clean break, so it mends pretty fast. I'm lucky, they say, that

I didn't fall on my rifle and shoot myself just as I hit the ground. That's what lucky means in the Army.

Then they send me home at the end of August with muscle relaxants and painkillers and antidepressants and sleeping pills to medicate myself back into a robot, numb enough to redeploy when they want me. Meanwhile, the medical board gets busy and decides that no, they don't want me after all. Too trigger-happy, I guess, even for the Army. Either that, or Henley and Kormick made sure to end my career.

The first day I get back home, I hobble around my parents' house, desperate for any drop of booze I can find. They aren't big drinkers, but stuffed in the back of a kitchen cupboard I find the dusty bottles of whiskey and wine that Mom's been given over the years by drug companies trying to bribe her doctor boss.

I lock my bedroom door to keep everyone out and spend the next two weeks or so in bed drinking my contraband hooch, taking my pills and longing for Jimmy. Every step I take hurts my back, every thought hurts my heart. I can't stand the sight of Tyler. Can't stand Mom or Dad. Can't stand our house or Willowglen or anyone in it, except April. Can't sleep or eat either. Can't even pray or think about God. Blood is in my eyes and my soul. Yvette's blood, Zaki's blood, the jerk-off's blood, the blood of the Iraqi worker I let die in the mortar attack. The blood of that little boy's donkey. Naema's dad covered in it as I ground his face into the sand.

I look in the mirror. Pale skin, empty eyes. Half robot, half fucked-up human being, the two sides fighting to the death. I have no idea which one will win.

[ PART FOUR ]

# WAR

[ KATE ]

THE ROOM JIMMY'S giving me is perfect. Old-fash-
ioned and cozy, with four tall windows and butter-yellow
walls. After he shows me in, I stand in the middle of it for
a second, just to soak it up. Cream curtains. An old quilt on
the bed, embroidered with yellow flowers and pale leaves.
The wide floorboards painted dark green, like moss. It
makes me feel safer than I've felt in months. Or maybe it's
only knowing he's so close.

"Is this the house you grew up in?" I ask him after a
moment.

"Yeah, but it's all mine now. Least till my brothers come
back."

I don't want to make him explain why his mom isn't here.
Back in the loony bin, probably. Poor Jimmy.

He puts my backpack on the bed and turns to me. It's still
overwhelming to see him here, right next to me, alive and
solid. He's the only person I've seen since I got back who
feels real. It makes me need him so bad I can hardly breathe.

"You think you'll be okay here?" he says.

"Oh, yes. I . . . I never expected to land anywhere nice as
this." I try to smile, but I can't.

"Well, let me know if you need anything. You can stay as long as you want. I mean it." He smiles at me again. "I'm glad you came."

My throat aches at that. I wish I could just walk over and hug him. We hover in silence a minute.

"Jimmy?" I finally screw up the courage to say. "Can I ask you something?"

"Sure." He looks at me gently. Those eyes again.

"How long have you and Mandy. Um. Been together?"

He pauses. "Month or so. Since I got back." Then, still looking at me, he adds quietly, "She doesn't live here, you know."

"Oh." I gaze back at him, a flicker of hope jumping up inside of me like a pilot light. I'm longing to ask more, but instead other words push out, words I don't even want to say. "Will you tell me about Third Eye now? I can handle it."

"You sure?"

I nod. But I'm not sure at all.

Jimmy takes my hand and leads me to the bed, where we sit side by side on its edge. He picks up my other hand and folds them both between his. His touch sends a warmth through me like nothing has for months.

"Kate." He looks into my eyes.

I wait.

"Third Eye's dead."

I take a deep breath. "When?"

"About a week after we got back. DJ told me. He said she called him once, drunk, talking wild. She was at her dad's place, you know, in Coxsackie? The next day she shot herself in his garage."

I nod. "I knew she'd do something like that." My voice is calm.

But then I'm crumpling forward, falling and falling till my head rests on our joined hands.

"I didn't protect her, Jimmy," I whisper as the tears come. "I didn't protect Yvette either, or Naema's dad or her little brother. I've killed so many of them. Oh God, when will it stop?"

[ NAEMA ]

BY THE TIME we have returned from Umm Qasr to
Granny Maryam's house, having braved the traffic and convoys and checkpoints once again, we are in the heat of mid-
day and Granny's body has been lying in the backseat for
hours. Mama and I hurriedly climb out of the car, shuddering with shock and fatigue, and carry our sad burden inside
to lay her down on her bed. There, we quickly undress
and prepare her for burial, so as not to further violate the
Qur'an's prohibition against allowing the dead to linger
above ground.

We bathe her three times, according to custom, and
wash and braid her long gray hair into three parts. At least
the rigor mortis is passing by now, so we are able to move
her limbs, may Allah have mercy on her. Then we bind up
her jaw with a strip of cloth and drape her in a clean white
sheet. Only two days ago I would have struggled against
my revulsion at these duties, for her body is full of foul flu-
ids we have to expel by leaning gently on her stomach. I
would have been mortified at the sight of her sparse, gray
pubic hair and the dangling pudenda my mother has to
wash and stop up with cotton. But after the suffering I saw

at the hospital, I am beyond revulsion or pity. I am beyond any feeling at all.

"Naema, look in that trunk over in the corner," Mama says quietly. "See that bundle of white sheets? Those are the *kafan* my mother prepared. Bring them here."

I obey, unfolding the burial sheets to spread out beside her: a sleeveless tunic and four pieces of varying sizes. "Now," Mama says, "watch what I do so you can bury me properly when my time comes."

First she reaches for the gourd of perfume beside the bed and dabs a little on Granny's forehead, nose, hands, knees and feet: the parts Granny used to rest upon when in prayer. Then Mama winds a narrow strip of sheet around Granny's thighs and pelvis as a loincloth, after which she wraps a longer, wider piece around and around Granny's frail waist. Together, we then lift Granny up so Mama can slip the tunic over her head and down her body; it looks like the dress of a little girl. We lay her back down and, finally, Mama arranges a small, square sheet into a veil around my poor grandmother's head.

Mama performs all this in silence, although I can hear the cries and prayers sealed up inside her so loudly they deafen me to everything else. I know she is crying inside not only for Granny but also for Papa and Zaki. And as I watch her prepare her own mother so tenderly for the grave, my shock and numbness give way at last and I feel a great love for her swell within me. Mama is newly precious to me now, for seeing her lose her own mother makes me desperately fear losing mine.

"Say your last good-bye now," she finally whispers. "My mother is going away forever." And quietly, she quotes the traditional words of mourning as she places Granny's left hand on her chest, puts her right hand over it in the sign of prayer and folds the last and largest sheet around her until we can see no more of the Granny Maryam we knew, only a cold white shroud.

All that life in Granny, all her suffering and joy, mischief and love—gone. I turn to tell Zaki this thought, to share with my little brother my sorrow. But, of course, Zaki is not here either.

In the afternoon, many more people come to Granny Maryam's funeral than I would think possible in this time of fear and danger. Kind Abu Mustafa and his wife and sister come from next door, of course (I think Abu Mustafa has always been a little in love with Granny), but so do their grown sons, who live nearby. Friends and cousins come from the village with their children, and even Granny's in-laws arrive, although she has been widowed these many years. All these people flock to honor this woman they loved, bearing food and condolences, despite the marauding soldiers and their tanks and roadblocks. It is such a comfort to poor Mama, this generosity, especially after our ordeal at the hospital.

Because Papa and Zaki are absent, two of Abu Mustafa's sons perform the duties of the family men. They lift the platform on which Granny's shrouded body lies and carry her to the burial grounds, the other men following, where they will place Granny in the earth, laying her on her right side to ready her for the Day of Judgment, while the imam leads their prayers. We women stay behind in the house to pray, for women are not allowed at burials in this conservative village of my mother's youth.

Finally, the men return to offer us their last condolences

and more prayers before gathering their families to leave for their homes, in a hurry to get back before dark and all its dangers.

And so it is over—much too quickly, it seems—and now Mama and I are left in Granny's small house alone, our once boisterous family reduced to two saddened scarecrow women with no control over our fates and no knowledge of our futures. We wander through the empty rooms, gazing at the leftovers of what was once a family life: Zaki's guitar. Papa's books and poems and letters. Granny's bright pillows, embroidered by her own hand, already dimming with dust. We spin in our quiet loneliness, missing their voices, missing their love, missing all that we once took so naturally for granted.

Still, I refuse to allow even this to stop my quest. In fact, Granny's death makes me all the more determined to find my brother and father, to bring our family back to what it once was. So, as soon as the funeral and our three days of mourning have passed, I arise eagerly at dawn, embrace my poor mother and once again join stout little Zahra and widow Fatima on our trek to the prison, keeping an eye out for al-Sadr's thugs and the American soldiers and their merciless guns.

Yet, as determined as I am, it is different this time. For all the way to the prison, as I walk along the highway and across the desert with my two steadfast companions, my usual yearnings and outrage are silenced. I cannot think of Khalil and whether he is safe, of my future or of home. I cannot even whip up my habitual anger against the Americans and their senseless war. For all I can hear, echoing relentlessly in my head, are the words of mourning Mama spoke over

Granny Maryam's body as she wrapped her in that shroud. Words that seem determined to extinguish, one by one, each tender flame of my hope.

> *I am the house of remoteness.*
> *I am the house of loneliness.*
> *I am the house of soil.*
> *I am the house of worms.*

# [ AUTHOR'S NOTE ]

THIS NOVEL IS set in 2003, at the beginning of the war in Iraq, known in the military as OIF, Operation Iraqi Freedom. As I write these final notes, it is seven years later and the United States is withdrawing the bulk—although not all—of its troops. Yet everyday conditions for Iraqis are not much better than they were in the time Naema describes. The United Nations reports that hundreds of thousands of Iraqi civilians have been killed, two million have fled the country and two million more have been internally displaced. The water and sewage systems, electricity and hospitals continue to be barely operational and much worse than they were before the war. Daily violence continues and corruption is rife, while disease and birth defects are on the rise from depleted uranium and other pollutants of war. The 1959 Family Code that protected Iraqi women and gave them more autonomy than Muslim women anywhere in the Middle East outside of Turkey has been dismantled, pushing back women's rights fifty years.

"Our armies do not come into your cities and lands as conquerors or enemies, but as liberators."
—General Stanley Maude on invading Iraq, March 1917

"We are coming not to occupy their country, not to oppress them, but to liberate their country."
—Secretary of Defense Donald Rumsfeld
on invading Iraq, March 2004

"When I see an American tank on the street, I feel it rolling over my own heart."
—Muhammad al-Naji, Iraqi hotel manager
in *About Baghdad* by Sinan Antoon, 2003

# [ ACKNOWLEDGMENTS ]

MUCH OF THE material for this novel was culled from the research I did for my nonfiction book, *The Lonely Soldier: The Private War of Women Serving in Iraq*. Although this is fiction, I have been helped and inspired by my interviews with more than forty veterans of the Iraq War, several of whom served at Camp Bucca and many of whom survived combat and mortar attacks. My special thanks go to veterans Rolanda Freeman-Ard, Mkesha Clayton, Eli Painted-Crow, Chantelle Henneberry, Mickiela Montoya, Laura Naylor, Abbie Pickett, Marti Ribeiro and Jennifer Spranger. Without their courage and honesty, and their willingness to tell me their stories, I could never have written about Kate Brady's experiences at war.

I also want to thank Elizabeth O'Herrin, who served in Iraq with the Air Force, for her support and careful reading of the manuscript; Leila al-Arian for sending me to Nour al-Khal; and Nour al-Khal herself, who helped me invaluably with Naema Jassim and did her best, with patience and grace, to correct my mistakes. Any errors I have made are entirely my own.

HELEN BENEDICT

Hala Alazzawi and her daughter Hiba Alsaffar also generously gave of their time and hearts to help me with Naema's story, as did Mohanad Alobaide. To these and other Iraqi refugees I send my gratitude and heartfelt wish that life in America were not so unwelcoming. We should do better by you.

Once again, huge thanks to my faithful and brilliant reader and friend, Rebecca Stowe; to my children, Simon and Emma Benedict O'Connor, whose talents and compassion never fail to move and impress me; and, above all, to Stephen O'Connor, my partner in life and art, for his encouragement and help, his belief in what we do and for his faith in this story.

For their enthusiasm, time and suggestions, my deepest thanks also to Bishop Regina Nicolosi, feminist Catholic and rebel extraordinaire; and to Zainab Chaudhry and Susan Davies, both of whom work tirelessly to help Iraqi refugees and yet found time to talk to me for hours. I regard you all with awe.

My gratitude also to the Virginia Center for the Creative Arts for peaceful and fruitful residencies in both Virginia and Auvillar, France. I wrote much of this novel in these exquisite places, with a concentration impossible to achieve elsewhere.

I consulted many sources for *Sand Queen*, but the following were of particular help: *The Taguba Report* on Abu Ghraib and Camp Bucca (*news.findlaw.com/hdocs/docs/iraq/tagubarpt.html*); BBC, CBC and other news outlets for accounts of conditions at the Umm Qasr hospital in 2003; reports on Iraq, Iraqi refugees and violence against Iraqi women by Amnesty International and Human Rights

Watch; the brilliant blog, *Baghdad Burning* by Riverbend; the documentary *About Baghdad* and the novel *I'jaam*, both by Sinan Antoon; *Two Grandmothers from Baghdad* by Rebecca Joubin; *Contemporary Iraqi Fiction*, edited and translated by Shakir Mustafa; *Cell Block Five* by Fadhil al-Azzawi; *Literature from the "Axis of Evil,"* a Words Without Borders anthology; *The Occupation: War and Resistance in Iraq* by Patrick Cockburn; and *Nobody Told Us We Are Defeated: Stories from the New Iraq* by Rory McCarthy.